reckoning

LAURY FALTER

First Edition: December 2011

The characters and events portrayed in this book are fictitious. Any
similarity to real persons, living or dead, is coincidental and not
intended by the author.

Falter, Laury, 1972-
Fallen: a novel / by Laury Falter – 1st ed.

Summary: Maggie and Eran create the spark that ignites the final battle
between Fallen Ones and Alterums.

ISBN: 0-615-58386-5
ISBN-13: 978-0615583860

For Babs – of course. Without you, this trilogy would still be rattling around in my head. Thank you for your unlimited support and confidence as Maggie and Eran's saga was written.

I love you.

∞

CONTENTS

∞

1. PABLO ALEDA

Juarez, Mexico

I was being watched.

I knew this for the last fifteen minutes as I bought a soda from a grungy storefront, a sausage roll from a street vendor with broken teeth, and then entered a dark alleyway.

Here, clusters of men lined both sides, lingering beside the exits of various nightclubs, whispering within their respective circles.

None of these men were the one following me. He hadn't shown himself yet but he was there. The skin prickling at the back of my neck gave me undeniable proof.

As I stepped around a pile of trash collected at the alley's entrance, thunder rumbled overhead announcing a storm's arrival. In response, I pulled the hood of my sweatshirt over my head, as much for protection from the rain as from the prying eyes of the men lining the narrow passageway.

My hood, a modern day cloak, was my greatest defense right now. I didn't want any trouble with these men. I came to start trouble with just one and he wasn't human.

That didn't seem to matter much to them though.

I'd made it halfway down the alley before one of them stepped in to my path, grinning. He was shorter than the rest but with arms twice their size. This was a man who had seen the inside of a jail cell more than once.

He squinted and ducked down to peer in to the darkness of my hood before his grin deepened.

"Step aside and you won't be injured," I said not bothering to speak in his native tongue. I'd seen and evaluated him the moment I came around the corner, noting that the names of his tattoos were spelled in English.

He twisted slightly at the waist and chuckled back at the other two men lining each side of the door they'd been hovering by. In an accent, thickened to project authority, he said, "Little girl's got some nerve." He turned back to me and said, "What? You can't be more than fifteen."

I didn't bother responding. My senses were already heightened and because of them I knew what was coming.

The heart of the man directly in front of me was already beating louder. The sweat from the other two men had begun to seep faster in anticipation of their friend's next move. From behind me, I heard the scuff of feet as bodies closed in on me, their shadows creeping higher along the brick walls on each side of the alley.

"I don't want to hurt you," I stated again, more firmly.

This announcement caused the release of several hissed chuckles and judging by their location I knew that I was now completely surrounded.

Any eighteen-year-old girl, my true age, would probably have panicked at this point, eyes darting for the nearest exit, muscles contracting as her subconscious decided between a fight or flight response. And her reaction would have been completely understandable.

With me, however, fleeing is never an option.

I spun around with such speed that the ex-con didn't have time to react. The heel of my steel-toed boot connected nicely with his jaw where I felt the resounding pop of it dislocating from its joint. My feet landed firmly on the ground again, my eyes already meeting his friends'.

They advanced, with a slight hint of shock and fear that was quickly replaced with vengeance.

Knowing I had little time, I propelled myself through the air and allowed my body to pivot, my legs loosening to form the same rotation as helicopter blades. From several feet above, the edges of my boots slammed in to the heads of the men at near simultaneous contact and they collapsed in a pile alongside their friend.

I landed; my feet planting on the ground again, and drew a sigh.

Staring back at the remaining five men crowded together, watching me, I asked resignedly, "So, who's next?"

They didn't move immediately, and I could sense in them an uncomfortable patience as they waited to see whether anyone would speak up. Each one had seen what I was capable of and despite the impossibility of it they couldn't deny it. My slight five foot tall frame had just taken down three ominous men in less than a minute and without so much as a quickened breath, and I was ready for more.

Finally, one released a scoff but turned on his heel anyways and headed back for the street. He said something in Spanish that started with "crazy" and ended in a curse word which the rest of the men agreed with as they followed him out. Apparently, I wasn't worth the effort and that was fine with me.

They weren't the ones I had come to engage.

I knew that I was intentionally picking a fight by showing up in this city alone and that my follower, the one I was after, would be showing himself soon enough.

No sooner had I acknowledged this to myself did I hear his voice.

"Me…" he said, his heavy Spanish accent echoing off the walls just over the nightclub's thumping, muffled beat. "I'm next."

I turned, narrowing in on his location the moment he spoke.

At the end of the alley stood a man nearly the same height as me. He was shifted to one hip, relaxed and ready for what was to come. Muscles protruded from his dark leather vest and pressed against the thighs of his loosened jeans telling me that I was in for a good fight. The boots he wore had tips, glinting off the broken lamp head above as if they intended to tease me. His cowboy hat, titled low over his forehead, hid all but his sneer. All together, I had to admit, he looked imposing.

"Pablo Aleda?" I asked cordially, though I already knew the answer. The hair at the back of my neck was prickling furiously, a clear sign this was the man I had come to find.

His head tilted to the side in a mock gesture. He knew as well as I did that my question was needless. He felt me as strongly as I felt him.

"Radar's a funny thing, ain't it," he said more as an observation than a question. "Knew you was in town before you crossed the city limit. Knew it when you stopped in at Roberta's fer directions."

I nodded my understanding. "Good burrito," I replied offhandedly.

He didn't respond right away, taking a moment to judge me. "You're more pleasant than they said you were."

Now it was me who tilted my head. "And what do they say about me?"

"Feisty. Impatient. Good with the sword."

He'd left out one other trait, I noticed. I was also direct. "And you, Pablo, are a murderer."

His chin lifted, the dim light exposing his face and the grin he wore. "I am." He paused and then prodded me, "Guess I figured you'd know more than that about me."

"You've lived on earth for two hundred years, staying mostly to the Latin American countries. You've never held a job. You have no companions. Your choice drink is tequila. You prefer papaya for breakfast. You are excellent in hand to hand combat and lean towards this discipline when engaging in conflict. You returned to earth with the ability to sense danger from great distances. This, I believe, is how you knew I was here."

He chuckled lightly. "That's good...but you did forget one thing." Before I could respond thick grey wings stretching the length of the alleyway snapped out from behind him. The feathers were long and thick and the muscles beneath them were strong. "I'm very fast."

He suddenly leaned forward and soared towards me, his wings pumping forcefully to increase his speed.

He hadn't exaggerated.

Instantly, I felt my sweatshirt tighten around me, making room for the extension of my own appendages. Moving through slits cut along the back of my clothes, my own wings sprang out just as Pablo reached me, the tips of them brushing the brick walls on both sides.

I squatted and pushed myself in to the air, my feet grazing Pablo's shoulders as he moved by me, beneath me, narrowly missing a full collision. My wings propelled me upward until I had room to circle back around and attack from behind.

Then the rain came, hard and relentless.

My wings, exposed to its onslaught, thickened. My feathers became individual weights holding me down as I struggled to stay aloft.

It only took me a moment to realize I was in trouble or to notice Pablo was standing again, facing me, watching with a sneer.

My landing was haphazard which humored Pablo, judging from his expression.

Knowing I had only moments before his next attack came I retracted my wings and ripped the sweatshirt from my body. Hidden beneath was a black leather suit layered with small straps, and from those straps hung weapons of all types.

In those brief moments, as the rain poured down around us, I became beaded with raindrops, something I was thankful for. It would make me slick and difficult to grasp and it was an advantage I would need if I was going to fight Pablo in hand to hand combat.

When his assault came it was merciless. His hands moved in a blinding array, blending from one movement to the next. He had boasted speed and this was when he truly showed it off. I was just able to keep up, looking for an opportunity, an opening. Several minutes passed before it came. I took it and delivered a jab to the chin, with force beyond what even I was expecting.

Pablo stumbled back, a look of surprise on his face, and then fell to the ground, his eyes rolling up before closing entirely.

I didn't hesitate, moving in for the final blow.

Stepping over him, my gaze swept across the buildings, ensuring I wouldn't be caught off guard in case someone intended on coming to Pablo's defense.

That was when I saw him, catching a glimpse from the corner of my eye. Still moving swiftly, I had already returned to Pablo before I registered who it was I'd seen.

He was someone unmistakable to me. Someone I had dreamt about, ached for over the past weeks. He had lived in every one of my thoughts since I'd last seen him, an ever present memory teasing me and magnifying the void I felt without him.

Standing on the corner edge of a rooftop overlooking the alley, facing me, was Eran.

My head swiveled back.

Less than a second had passed but there, high above where he had been standing, the space was now empty. Only the pounding rain could be seen.

It was him, wasn't it? I questioned myself.

The figure's shoulders were broad, his legs were long and his stance was reassured, confident. It had to be Eran.

Time stood still in that moment, the only movement being the rain streaming down my face and down the hand at my waist that still held the handle of my sword. A deep, blunt pain throbbed in my chest, which I only vaguely realized was the exact location of my heart. The world around me fell away, my focus held entirely to that spot where I had seen my eternal love and was now willing him to return.

A movement below me stirred my awareness then and without much thought at all I pulled my sword from its sheath, swiped it through the air, and felt Pablo's head severe from his body. I did this emotionless, without any notion of victory or relief.

Stepping aside, I allowed the rain to clean the steal, my face still turned up and locked on the rooftop. I didn't move immediately, unable to will my body away from the spot where I had seen Eran. It had been too long and I wasn't willing to let go of the memory just yet. Torn somewhere between shock, a deep yearning, and frustration, I debated whether it had been him or whether my longing for him had conjured his image in my mind. He wouldn't make himself known if he had found me, I

reasoned. He knew I had left him with a purpose that needed fulfilling before I could return. It was then I realized that Eran couldn't have been here. I was a good hunter but, having had years of experience, I was an even better hider. I was impossible to find.

"Shake it off," I demanded quietly, though my eyes still remained on the spot where I'd glimpsed the figure.

It was only after female voices drifted over the pounding rain did I recall where I was and that I was standing over a dead body. I glanced down to ensure Pablo's wings had sunk back in just as the girls stepped in to view. With heads turned, they didn't see my wings slip smoothly from between my shoulder blades, extend to their full length, and pump forcefully twice. I lifted in to the air, rising above the rooftop where Eran had been, and flew over the city towards the New Mexico border.

A few minutes later, I was standing outside a gas station on I-25 paying an old man twenty dollars for watching my Harley Davidson. The unnerving feeling of seeing Eran was beginning to lift but I was still half-concentrating on the memory of him...or at least the figment of my imagination I had thought was him.

The old man cleared his throat to get my attention. "Ground's dry here, sky's clear and the temperature's agreeable."

"Yes, it is," I replied avoiding a direct look at him.

He took the twenty, slipped it in his pocket, and settled back in his seat, one that looked well worn and familiar with his shape.

"Yet your hair and clothes are wet..." he continued. "Whachya do? Pick a fight with a car wash?"

I chuckled softly to myself. "Something like that."

He watched quietly as I stepped on to my bike and it was then I got the sense he wanted to tell me something.

"I don't mind watchin' your bike for you."

"Thank you for that."

"Easy money. But makes me wonder when you leave it parked here, walk around the station," he waved towards the corner farthest from the road, "and disappear."

I glanced in his direction. "You've followed me?"

"I have."

Unsure if I felt unnerved by it or not, I asked, "And what have you seen?"

"That's the problem…I don't see nothing. Nothing at all. You're gone." He made a whistling sound from between is lips, insinuating speed.

I wasn't sure how many weeks I'd been on the road, flatly refusing to pay attention since all it did was reinforce how much time I'd spent away from Eran. But the last two of them had been in the southwestern states and I'd used this man and his gas station as my base of operations, leaving my beloved Harley Davidson bike in his care a number of times. He'd been amiable but reserved; a perfect babysitter for my bike. He wasn't foolish and from his perch on the front porch of his rundown gas station he didn't miss much of anything.

He was telling me in not so many words that while he hadn't seen anything at all he still understood what he had seen.

Very slowly I felt a smile spread across my face while still wondering about his intentions.

Then, very slowly a smile spread across his face.

"What do you do out there?" he asked, sincerely interested.

"Me?" I said thoughtfully. "I just clean the streets."

His smile returned. "I wondered if you might."

I enjoyed the old man's approach to life, relaxed and nonjudgmental, but what I liked most about him is that he never messed with my bike or anything on it…including the most important item I owned. I unlocked this item from my seat compartment and flipped it open, the black leather binding creaking as I flipped to the page I'd last

read. I took the pen from its binding and marked a red X from each corner to the next before turning to the following page.

This one, as with all the rest, read like a police file. Each spread was a dossier filled with information and images of those who had been expelled from the afterlife for committing inhumane crimes. It was now up to me to eradicate them from the face of the earth. Among other facts, this book told me who they were, their strengths and weaknesses, what they feared, what they excelled at and, most importantly, where they lived.

As the book fell shut, the old man asked, "Where you off to now?"

"Well," I said, replacing the book in its compartment. "Looks like I'm headed for San Francisco."

"Got some street cleaning to do there, ha?"

"It seems I do," I replied as I strapped on my helmet. "See you around."

"Doubt it…" said the old man.

Though I didn't mention it, I agreed with him completely.

I'd already found each of the Fallen Ones within this territory. They had been simple to hunt and even easier to kill. But, I was now headed to the West Coast where I would find more dangerous enemies. Whether I survived them or not, I wouldn't be returning to New Mexico any time soon.

* * *

San Francisco, California

Claden Markett was one of the wealthiest and most corrupt arms dealers on the West Coast, using the San Francisco docks as his preferred place to conduct business. He had

once dominated New York City using the same tactics of murder, thievery, and intimidation but that was back in the mid-1800s. No one would remember him now, especially with his new, fictitious name.

More importantly, he was good with handguns, wielding them as effortless as an old western gangster, and he maintained a small group of bodyguards equally as dangerous.

This was just a small summary what his dossier told me and it would come in handy this evening.

I'd watched him throughout the day, careful to duck from cover each time he looked up in search of me. He knew I was nearby but he couldn't pinpoint me. His radar was less precise than Pablo's had been.

Every once in a while he spun quickly around only to find behind him an elderly lady struggling with grocery bags or snapped his head in the direction of a stray dog approaching. Knowing that none of these were me, he grew tenser, more agitated throughout the day, a clear advantage to me.

Finally night fell and he withdrew to an office on the docks, where all but two of his cohorts filtered in behind him. The windows, grimy with years of buildup, obscured any possibility of a view but my senses were up and I could hear them clearly.

Claden was issuing orders for the evening and they involved me.

"We have company," he told them. "Keep your eyes open."

By the time he'd finished his warning, the two men outside his office were already unconscious and dragged around back. When the next two emerged from the small building, they too were rendered useless and piled with their friends.

Humans had never been a challenge for me, my strength and skill far exceeding any level a man could reach. Claden's men, in particular, were merely inconvenient and annoying obstructions to the one I had come for.

When the last two had fallen, I waited just outside the door, leaning against a stack of crates with arms crossed, and whistled.

Claden opened the door slowly, a handgun at his side.

"Magdalene," he stated almost jadedly.

"So we meet again," I replied.

His head ducked to the side and he smiled in memory of our last reunion, which hadn't been pleasant other than the fact he'd survived it. He lifted his eyes and looked directly at me then.

"Heard you were comin'," he said wistfully.

"Oh yeah? From who?"

"Word's spread. You can take out two of us, even three, and we won't notice." He paused to suck in a deep breath from between his teeth. "But fifty of us…well that makes us a little uneasy."

"Sixty three," I corrected him, surprised at the arrogance in my tone.

Claden didn't seem to notice. "You do understand that the attempt to decimate us has been done before and failed."

My eyes narrowed. "I won't fail."

"Be honest with yourself, Magdalene. There is only one of you and there are hundreds of us."

The insinuation was clear yet I chose to ignore it. "I like those odds," I said with calm confidence. "I will prevail, you will die, and the humans will live in peace."

He paused to stare at me before asking, "Why do you love them so much?"

"Why do you hate them so much?" I asked.

"I don't hate them. They serve a purpose. They provide for me, whether they like it or not."

"They are not here to provide for you."

He grinned lightly. "Oh yes they are…" His face fell slightly then. "Everyone serves a purpose, Magdalene. Take Eran, for example." My muscles tensed at the sound of his name and Claden found he'd sparked in me the reaction he'd intended, which only emboldened him. "Eran is your guardian, dedicated to protecting you at all costs. That is his purpose and yet…" He swept his hand across the dock. "Yet, he isn't here to defend you."

"I don't need his help, Claden," I replied, stepping forward.

The gun in his hand shifted and I realized Claden had strengthened his grip as I closed the distance between us. He was still frightened of me, I realized, but tried to hide it by continuing.

"You will find yourself regretting those words," he threatened.

"I don't believe so," I said, taking another step. With a rapid snap of my shoulders, my appendages released, stretching wide and imposing.

Claden raised his arm, the gun barrel pointing directly at my chest, even as his own appendages extended. They looked a sickeningly dull grey color in the dim light of the dock.

His expression grew dark a moment later and his finger cautiously squeezed the trigger. I was ready for it.

My wings pumped once and I sprang several stories high, the bullets riddling from the end of his gun and each aimed in my direction. With heightened senses, I knew where each bullet would pass well before it reached me and my body swerved effortlessly to avoid them.

When the cartridge was empty, Claden threw it aside and reached inside the door. He faced me again with two more guns, these ones being .50 caliber Desert Eagle's.

These sounded like small canons launching, echoing down the lengthy San Francisco dock.

Still, these too missed.

When he had exhausted his supply of ammunition, I hovered above him, waiting to catch his eye.

Then I grinned with arrogance, swiftly moving to a position of attack and launching myself towards him.

Our bodies collided with such force that we tumbled along the hard, rutted dock, peeling back shards of wood the size of lamp posts.

It was now a test of speed and strength, both in which we seemed equally matched.

Our fight took us over the water and back again, landing us against the wall of his small office.

Then something happened that I least expected…Claden got the upper hand. He slammed me against the wall and held me there with one arm to my neck, his free hand hastily digging inside his jeans.

That brief distraction turned the fight in my favor, or so I thought. As I drew a dagger from my suit and thrust it up through his heart I found a second later that Claden had a gun to my head with his finger on the trigger. He only needed to squeeze.

But he never got the chance.

Claden's body was suddenly thrown back, his limbs flailing weakly. He landed with a thud and tumbled until his body rolled over the edge of the dock and into the water.

In his place, standing before me, was Eran.

2. HOME

Eran's eyes were wild, even madly delirious for a moment before reasoning could work its way back in.

"Damnit, Magdalene," he seethed. "That was too close. No more. I draw the line here. No more!"

He stepped back and turned away, his hands running through his dark, wavy hair. He was breathing hard but not from exertion, from nervous frustration.

Still in a surreal state and trying to grasp that he was here, not safely back in New Orleans and not a figment of my imagination, I struggled to respond appropriately and failed.

"How did you find me, Eran?" I heard myself say quietly.

His head snapped in my direction and his charming English accent took on an ever firmer tone. "Do you understand me, Magdalene? I'm serious. No more hunting Fallen Ones. No more."

I blinked a few times trying to clear my thoughts, which were running as fragments through my hurried mind. "I don't understand. How are you here? How did you find me? I was so careful…"

What I really wanted to tell him was: I want you here, need you here, desperately ache to have you here beside me, but I want you to leave. Now. I came alone with a purpose and that was to keep you safe, well away from the Fallen Ones I'm now hunting. If you are here, you are not safe.

He was still for the moment, staring blindly at me. It was almost as if he was confused by my question. So I repeated it.

"How did you find me?"

He sighed and dipped his head. His hands were now on his hips and he leaned to the side slightly as if he were taking time to debate whether to answer me.

I opened my mouth to repeat my question but he beat me to it.

"I never found you," he said, glancing in my direction for a reaction. My brow creased in confusion so he lifted his head and clarified, "I never needed to find you because I never lost you. I was here with you the entire time."

His words slowly sunk in and when they did my surreal state was replaced with anger.

"You followed me?" I demanded.

He nodded, not wanting to admit the truth in so many words.

"Florida?"

He nodded.

"Texas?"

He nodded again.

"Colorado? Oklahoma? Kansas? Arizona? Mexico?"

"The entire time, Magdalene."

"Then you were there in Juarez. I did see you in the rain…"

"I was there," he admitted. "I-I thought you might need my help so I stayed close." He shrugged lightly. "Closer than usual."

My shoulders dropped in annoyance.

In response, he approached me and placed his hands on them and dipped his head to catch my eyes, which I was certain reflected a burning fury.

In a soft, placating tone, he explained, "If I hadn't followed you, I wouldn't have been here tonight. And if I hadn't been here tonight..." He paused to swallow back uncomfortable thoughts. "You wouldn't be here either. Not anymore. Because of that, I'll accept my fate...that you're angry with me...but I do not regret my decision. You are too important."

The anger I held quickly dissipated. What welled up were all the emotions that I'd subdued, denied over the last few weeks: misery, loneliness, grief...

"I-I've missed you so much," I whispered and then collapsed inside the safety and comfort of his encircling arms.

His embrace was strong, reassuring me that everything would be fine now; and again I battled internally over clinging to the consolation Eran offered or to shun him for his own safety. He shouldn't be here. He didn't deserve this horrid life of hunting on the road. He deserved better.

In the end, the choice, however, was not left up to me.

When I stirred against him, he drew in a breath and spoke again, this time more hesitantly. "I'm bringing you back to New Orleans."

My jaw dropped and I instantly stepped out of his grasp. "That is not up to you to decide."

"I am your guardian. I decide what is best to keep you out of trouble."

This was our argument, an unending debate, on who had authority over my fate. Of course, as my guardian, it wasn't likely that he'd ever see that there was only one person with the power over my destiny and that was me.

He continued explaining his point which only aggravated me more. "I've let you take on the last sixty four Fallen Ones on your own. You've eliminated the least dangerous of our enemies and you've done a fine job of it but you are now in new territory. You're beginning to encounter more perilous Fallen Ones and I won't allow you to continue as you have been. Tonight was only a hint of what awaits out there. The ones remaining are far more treacherous and they know you are coming. More important, you – as skilled a fighter as you are - are not prepared to handle them."

My ego took an enormous hit at his assertion but that was just my emotions speaking to me. The truth was, as much as I wanted to disagree with him, I knew he had a point. I was not a guardian. I was a messenger and had only trained myself in defense in the case I should run across one of our enemies. Hunting and attacking Fallen Ones was an offensive strategy and required a different set of skills, ones that I had never honed.

In a last ditch effort to make me go quietly, he added, "Magdalene, you need a break. Come back to New Orleans with me." His voice had a hint of pleading behind it; whether it was manufactured to influence me or was sincere I couldn't be sure. "You can always sneak out again," he finished with a half-smile, attempting to cajole me.

I ignored it. "And then you'll follow me again."

His expression turned to a frown. "Yes, Magdalene. I will. You know I will."

"Eran," I stated firmly. "The reason I left before was because I am tired of putting those I love in harm's way. I will not…cannot allow you to follow me."

"And I won't allow you to enter harm's way, most certainly not without me." He crossed his muscular arms across his broad chest to emphasize his stubbornness.

I released a groan in amazement.

His lips pinched together then as he debated on whether to say what was on his mind, finally deciding to simply acknowledge it openly. "I-I miss you."

I wanted to oppose him, disagree with him, tell him that he was only using those words as a ploy to get me back to New Orleans. The truth was I believed him, I felt it in him, and any remaining anger over his approach to convincing me to break from hunting disappeared completely then. More so, in that brief moment I realized that his absence had done more to me than I had realized.

Inside, I had been slowly dying.

Eran, far stronger than me, had broken through the wall I'd created to prevent the loneliness from penetrating. And here I stood, staring at the one person who I desperately needed, admitting that he needed me too, and it was something no wall could shut out. I'd gotten a taste of what my world was like without him and it was nothing but buildings and faceless people. It was a tasteless, colorless world void of emotion. It was death on earth.

"Eran…" I mouthed, though no sound came out.

Again, his arms came around me, warm, caring, and firm.

"I'm-I'm torn…I'm so torn…"

"I know," he whispered against my hair. "I know…"

One of his arms fell to the middle of my back while his other slipped behind my knees, and the next thing I knew I was being lifted.

My head fell against his chest, his stimulating scent collecting around my face. I breathed deeply, enjoying a part of Eran I'd missed so much. Only vaguely was I aware of where he was taking me. If I were honest with myself, it really didn't matter.

We passed over the city and seconds later landed in the vacant driveway of a brownstone duplex in a more upscale neighborhood. I recognized it as the place I'd stashed my bike so that it would remain untouched.

Gently, he encouraged me on to the bike and collected the helmets from a small storage compartment.

As I watched him, I wondered aloud, "How do you think everyone is back home?"

I hadn't allowed myself to think about them during my travels. It hurt too much.

"Worried about you, would be my guess."

Eran watched me, a slight frown still tainting his beautiful face. His eyes, always a clear aqua-blue, lingered on me, waiting to see what my next move might be.

When he handed me a helmet and I took it, his frown changed to a slight, hesitant smile.

Still torn, I didn't want him to get his hopes up. "I ca-I can't stay long," I warned quietly, hating the way I sounded weak in my determination.

He nodded, breaking in to a pinched grin. He didn't want to appear too excited. Without another word, we strapped on our helmets, mounted my bike, and set out for New Orleans.

Ironically, I realized that we looked like a typical couple out for a late night bike ride. Those we crossed paths with had no idea that the worst black arms dealer on the West Coast had just tried to kill me or that his body now lay at the bottom of San Francisco bay.

Gradually, the population dwindled until we reached a stretch of unoccupied land, where Eran's wings extended and carried us through the air.

I ignored the pestering feeling that I was leaving my mission to eradicate Fallen Ones from existence – the same feeling that had urged me on over the last weeks despite my exhaustion and utter sorrow at being separated from Eran. I brushed away those thoughts completely so I could concentrate on something more encouraging. I focused on enjoying every inch of Eran's body pressed next to mine, the heat that penetrated his clothes, and the flexing of muscles as he maneuvered the bike on the ground and then as he carried us through the air. I was deeply disappointed as we came up to the New Orleans city lights.

Eran had taken the 'quick' route by using his appendages to lift us through the air and curtail the delay of the roadways. Up here, it was a straight shot so we made it to New Orleans just as dawn broke.

Landing my bike at the back door of our old Victorian-style home on Magazine Street seemed surreal to me. It was only a few weeks ago that I had snuck out of this very same door. Since then, my focus, my instincts, my habits had changed. Hunting Fallen Ones was not easy and it required a different way of thinking, of being, in order to survive. I had changed to accommodate it and yet I still recalled what it felt like to be me when I'd lived here. I could relate it best to feeling like someone returning home from college for the first time, still the same person but with a widened perspective on life.

"The lights are on," I noted, taking off my helmet.

Eran had already stowed his in the compartment and took mine to do the same.

"And I smell coffee," I added, which didn't surprise me. Each house has a distinct aroma to it. Ours could be likened to the sweet, nutty smell of a Starbucks coffee shop.

As I waited for Eran, a large, swarthy woman passed by the back window, which looked directly in to the kitchen. She was carrying a large mug with her, which again did not surprise me.

"She'll be happy to see you," Eran said, coming up behind me.

"Me too," I murmured, taking the door knob and opening it to a screaming gaggle.

In an instant, chairs were tossed aside, the kitchen table skidded two feet, and arms were wrapped around me and Eran, some thick and brawny and some long and wiry.

Rufus and Felix, our other two housemates, took their time ending their impassioned embrace, shaking us from side to side in their excitement. When they released us, Ezra, who stood behind them holding a coffee mug and smiling warmly, approached us. Her hug was briefer but just as welcoming.

She evaluated me. "You've lost weight."

"I've been…active."

My slight five foot frame didn't have much weight to lose but somehow I'd managed it. The black leather pants I wore had started to slip over my hips at times which didn't help during skirmishes with Fallen Ones. I'd need to have another combat suit made or start eating again.

"Your hair is longer, Mags," said Felix, taking a strand from my shoulder and holding it up as if that would prove it. He leaned in and whispered, "I can help you with that."

"Ehh…" Rufus grunted. "She looks fine to me," he said in his deep Irish brogue, waving off any contention of it with a meaty, tattooed hand.

"Thank you," I said, proudly. He was always supportive of me, something I would never stop appreciating.

Glancing at Ezra, I noticed that she and Eran were silently communicating. Her expression told me that she disapproved of me leaving but was thankful he'd brought me home. "And you…" she said, looking Eran up and down. She placed her hands on his shoulders, pulling him in for a tight embrace. "You could use a good meal too. Rufus…Felix," she released Eran and clapped her hands. "Breakfast!"

The kitchen broke in to chaos then. Another pot of coffee was brewed; Rufus dropped more Cajun sausages on an already sizzling pan; and Felix added batter to his succotash and pumpkin beignets.

Breakfast conversation started with me recounting where I'd been and what I'd been doing, but when I saw their disapproving expressions begin to manifest after telling of my encounters with Fallen Ones I quickly changed the topic. The people sitting around me were the closest I had to a family and I didn't want to disturb them any more than I already had.

"Do you think Mr. Warden will let Eran and me back in to classes?" I asked before biting through a sausage and savoring the taste of it. For the most part, meals on the road had consisted of artificial, pre-packaged food nuked at small, obscure convenience stores.

Ezra was shaking her head, deep in thought. "You're over halfway through the semester now. It'll be a tough sell."

"I'll make him take ya back," Rufus declared gruffly.

Eran and I met each other's glance from the corner of our eyes as both of us attempted to hold back a smile. Eran may be my guardian but Rufus would always be our biggest defender.

"There might be an easier way in..." I proposed, hoping to avoid a direct confrontation with our school principal. "Is Ms. Beedinwigg still teaching there?"

Slowly, Ezra began to smile. "Why yes she is...And she'd love to see you back."

"Excellent, what day is it?" I asked, hoping it was a school day and I could visit her on campus.

My housemates exchanged looks telling me that they were concerned that I hadn't kept up with the societal standards of a calendar.

I sighed. "A calendar wasn't needed for the job I was doing."

The abrupt reminder of my life over the last few weeks made them each flinch but Eran stepped in and smoothed over the conversation.

"I believe it is Saturday," he said, his hand sliding beneath the table to find my knee and give it a soft squeeze. It was a wonderful feeling but one that surprised me because he left it there.

Weeks ago, before we'd run off, he would have withdrawn his hand out of respect for Ezra. She had distinct household rules which Eran abided to an extreme level. He had barely touched me before and never in the presence of anyone else. This was a nice change, especially the comforting warmth left by his hand as it penetrated my jeans.

I allowed myself to enjoy the excitement of it while also focusing on the conversation at hand. "I'll see if I can visit her sometime this weekend…maybe after The Square."

Felix clapped his hands giddily. "You'll be coming to The Square? That's great!"

I smiled at him in thanks for his excitement at having me back. "Well…I figured I might as well deliver messages for as long as I'm here."

I realized what I'd said only after the words were spoken but by then it was too late.

"You're leaving again?" Ezra inquired disappointed and concerned. Rufus's head tilted to an odd, confused angle and Felix's fork dropped to his plate in distress.

I swallowed, not having wanted to let them in on my plans. It was easier to sneak out than it was to say goodbye.

"I-I…" Trying to find the words was like pulling a piece of glass from the bottom of my foot, slow and painful.

Again, Eran stepped in to comfort them. "Magdalene is here to recuperate. Once she's recovered from her travels, she'll be heading out again. But…" he let the word hang in the air, hesitant to make his next announcement. "When she does leave, I'm going with her and it will only be for one night at a time."

My brow creased as I heard myself say, "What?" I hadn't agreed to that.

"She's an intelligent, rational woman," Eran went on, a clear attempt to butter me up. "She knows that she can't keep the same level of endurance that is needed to do what she's intent on doing. So, she will return to hunting but it will be one night at a time and I'll be accompanying her."

"Accompanying?" I asked, perturbed.

"Who's the better fighter here?" he asked.

I didn't answer, knowing it was him.

Everyone sat in stunned silence with all eyes on Eran. Then Rufus spoke and it seemed to relax the mood.

"Sounds like a bloody good idea to me," he said with a carefree shrug. "Betta' than sleepin' in strange beds…"

"Or eating processed foods…" added Felix with a nod.

"Or wearing yourself down until you can no longer fight," Eran supplemented with a lift of his eyebrow towards me.

Ezra leaned back in her chair, reserved. "While I can't share everyone else's enthusiasm, I suppose if you need to continue this…mission of yours…" she said trying to identify exactly how to characterize what I was doing without acknowledging the insanity of it. "I suppose that is the best approach."

I was now the only one who had not agreed to this arrangement and my inclination was still to argue against it. Agreeing would mean that Eran would be coming with me and therefore endangering himself.

Knowing what I was thinking, he leaned towards me and explained in a lowered voice, "With the type of Fallen Ones you'll begin to engage, you will need eyes in the back of your head. Since you don't have them, I will be yours and yours will be mine. You want to do this alone…I understand. But that is at the risk of failing in your objective. The goal far outweighs the means in achieving it." He let me ponder this for a moment and then

25

a smile crept up. "Besides, knowing how well you handle yourself in defense, I have a feeling you'd actually be interested in learning a good offense."

"I've been doing well on my own...offensively," I reminded him.

"You have," he said, "and that's how I know you would do well sweeping a room or clearing a house, planning an offensive strategy, divide and distraction techniques-"

"All right," I cut him off. "All right. We both know you are a better fighter."

In fact, Eran was a brilliant fighter. Being an expert in warfare of all kinds, having led his army through large-scale battles with Fallen Ones, and having personally hunted our enemies, I couldn't have asked for anyone better.

He was still waiting for my answer so I gave him the best one I could agree to. "I'll think about it."

Immediately, the tension in the room dropped, shoulders relaxed, they began to smile. Ezra took another beignet and joyfully bit in to it, despite the odd taste of succotash embedded in the pastry.

I was happy to make them feel better with my acknowledgement but I meant what I said. When the time came again to hunt, I would make the decision at that moment; I would try to invite him. If I decided against it, he would need to abide by my choice. On the flip side, if he were to come with me and his life were in direct risk at any time, I would end the hunt and return to the life of a solo hunter.

Eran knew this, based on his expression and the fact he was still analyzing my feelings. Yet, he'd won a small victory today and decided against pushing anything further.

After breakfast, Felix and Rufus left for The Square, knowing that Eran and I would follow shortly. As Ezra disappeared in to her office and behind a mountain of paperwork, Eran and I went about getting showered and dressed for the day.

Standing just inside my room, I did a cursory overview of the things I had acquired during the months I'd lived here. Prior to my life in New Orleans, I'd traveled with my aunt so often that our lifestyle didn't allow for anything more than a few pieces of clothing and, only recently, a bed. Since I'd landed here the articles I'd collected that had been so important before now seemed borderline frivolous.

A full-length standing mirror was set just to my left and I realized I hadn't seen my reflection since I'd last stood in front of it. I'd never been someone to stare at a mirror for too long but weeks had gone by without a single glance at myself. With my focus so entirely on hunting and destroying I couldn't have cared less about my appearance. I could have hair growing out of my ears and I wouldn't have realized it. A dresser stood off to the left, just beyond the closet door, cluttered with magazines, knick knacks, lotions, pens and pencils, jewelry – which rarely found its way on to my body. An old wingback chair sat in the corner with a throw blanket draped over one side. Next to my bed were two nightstands each with matching lamps. A clock, a vase, a ceramic sculpture were all items that still sat next to the lamp bases as if I was never gone.

I had left behind a life of normalcy...forgone to find and execute those who made the world unsafe...who endangered my loved ones. And now I was back, a changed person, and nothing seemed to fit right in this surreal, parallel world.

I shook my head just as Eran came up behind me.

"We can live on so much less," I mused.

"And we have," he replied. "But since it's all here now, we might as well use it."

"It just seems so odd," I said not bothering to turn from my room and face him. "I really thought I wouldn't come back here until…"

"Until you'd annihilated the Fallen Ones?" His hands slipped over my shoulders, rubbing gently.

I nodded. "Until I knew you were all safe again."

"That time will come, Magdalene. Until then, take it from someone with a little experience in this area…" He was understating himself and I knew it so I listened. "You'll recuperate faster if you fall in to your old routine."

That sounded like excellent advice. The faster I recuperated, the faster I could get back to hunting. "Then I'll see you downstairs in twenty," I replied, heading for my closet.

"Well…all right then…" Eran replied with the same amount of surprise and relief.

His footsteps told me that he was heading back to his room directly across the hall as I pulled jeans and a t-shirt from my closet. Placing the t-shirt on my bed, I stood back.

Having slept on just about every surface over the last few weeks made me exulted in knowing this bed awaited me at the end of today, and it would be far more comfortable than a discarded, sunken mattress or the rocky dirt surface of the Arizona desert or a pile of leaves behind a vacant warehouse. Tomorrow might be the first time in weeks that I wake up without any muscle aches.

Slowly, I felt my face soften. Eran had been right. I did need a little time to revive myself…but just a little.

I showered slowly, enjoying the feeling of cleanliness as the hot water rushed over my body. Bruises still showed along my limbs and torso but they were turning yellow and would soon heal. A few scrapes down my waist told me that Claden had done a good job at defending himself and it only reinforced Eran's message to me that the Fallen

Ones I was beginning to encounter were stronger, faster, and more skilled.

That thought hovered in the back of my mind like a pesky fly as I headed back to my room.

I stopped at the edge of my bed and realized that something was off, not quite right. Then it occurred to me what it was and what I needed to do. I took the scissors from a drawer in my dresser and cut two long holes in the back of my t-shirt, directly between the shoulder blades. After I dressed, I did the same to every other shirt I owned. There was no way I would allow a need for my wings only to have them extend and rip my shirt off.

Feeling more at home with this small modification, I headed downstairs where I found Eran waiting in the kitchen. He gave me a half-smile and said, "You look more rested already."

"I'm finding ways to mold my current life alongside my old one…"

"Speaking of, are you ready to get back to delivering messages?" His eyes were eager, almost seeming to sparkle.

"Eager for it, actually," I admitted.

"Good…" Eran breathed, thankful.

I think he had a sense that delivering messages would help me recall what it felt like to be my more innocent, remedial self.

I followed him to my bike already parked outside the shed and just a few minutes later we were weaving our way through tourists to reach Rufus and Felix. They each had customers but they'd gone the extra effort to set up my area for me beforehand.

Two folding chairs and a sign announcing that I could deliver messages to those who had passed on to the afterlife were already waiting for me.

Mardi Gras had just ended so I was surprised to find so many people filling The Square. Typically, tourists returned to their normal life but this time a few appeared to straggle behind. It didn't take longer than ten minutes before my first customer approached me. By the time I was through taking down her message a small line had formed. By the end of the day, I had memorized almost thirty messages. Tonight I would deliver them and they would keep me busy until morning.

Eran, who had mingled around The Square, keeping an eye on me throughout the day, came through the dissipating crowd as the sun set. He strolled like the confident walk of someone who had seen everything and through innate abilities had survived it. Glancing up at him, his eyes locked on me and my heart skipped a beat. This was the image of Eran - the conceited, calm, alert man that captivated me - I'd intentionally tried to ignore those weeks on the road. This time, I allowed myself the time to enjoy it.

The t-shirt he wore was tight enough to cast shadows across his chest, distinguishing his protruding muscles, and the jeans seemed to be custom made to his body, moving easily in some places and fitting snugly in others. As always, he looked casually stylish. I openly appraised him and when I found him smirking at me I knew he'd seen.

He bent down so that our faces were inches apart before whispering, "You're nice to look at too." His gorgeous aqua-blue eyes smoldered with his announcement, taking my breath away.

"Tease," I whispered softly in return.

"Yes, I am," he admitted brazenly.

"And you aren't sorry for it, are you?"

"If it keeps you interested, not in the least."

Before I could respond, he stood and started collapsing my sign.

"Was it a good day for you too?" he asked Felix and Rufus. While receiving a brief shrug from Rufus, Felix launched in to story after story about his most interesting customers' futures. As both a tarot card and palm reader, Felix took his work very seriously.

At home, dinner was much easier than breakfast had been because we avoided the topic of me and further hunting. Rufus flatly refused to allow Felix to cook, declaring that my first dinner back should be something familiar. Instead, Rufus grilled steak and vegetables, which was incredibly appetizing. Felix, not allowing Rufus to take away his fun, defied him with dessert – good old fashioned bread pudding. It actually smelled perfect…before he poured creamed carrots over it. I didn't care much, though. It was nice simply to be surrounded by those I love.

As was my duty, I washed and dried the dishes, with Eran's help. Unfortunately, he kept his distance, skirting me at times when we may have bumped against each other. That, I found, was extremely irritating. Other than innocent rides on my motorcycle in which there was no way for our bodies to avoid touching, he had not made one move to come in contact with me. Typically, I could read his emotions and identify when he was interested or not. Not this time. He had mastered the ability to hide his feelings when needed, a trait required for someone in warfare, and he was using this ability now.

By the time we were upstairs and preparing for bed, I was thoroughly annoyed. Having been away from him for so long – at least while I thought I had been – had caused my emotions to bubble to the surface. I wanted to know he had missed me as much as I had missed him, but I simply did not get that feeling. Opening my balcony doors and taking a seat in one of the plastic chairs along the railing, I tried to calm myself down.

A few minutes passed when the creaking of floorboards told me that Eran was going to sit with me on the balcony. My stomach tightened with nerves at the thought of it. For the first time in a very long time, I was allowing myself to feel some emotion and they seemed to be amplified.

"Nice night," he muttered.

"Uh huh," I replied.

He sat in the plastic chair next to me, which was positioned cattycorner so although we faced each other we weren't looking directly at each other.

"There was a night like this in Texas...clear, fresh air, countless shooting stars. You were headed to El Paso..."

"Johnny Marringer," I stated, noting the name of the Fallen One I had gone to find.

"That's right. You had pulled off the highway and there wasn't a single light...generated by electricity...for miles. There was only the full moon and the stars to brighten the desert floor. When you stopped, you walked out in the brush and looked up at the sky. And you stood there...looking up...for a long time." His eyes were on me now, waiting for my response. "There was a cool breeze but other than that nothing moved. No snakes, no desert mice, no bats or owls. It felt as if we were completely alone."

"I did feel completely alone out there," I reflected.

He sighed, allowing his head to dip slightly. "I can't tell you how often I wanted to show myself, Magdalene. It took every bit of my will power to stop. Because I knew the moment I had, you would find some way to try and lose me. It was just...better to stay hidden."

"I understand," I said and he looked at me skeptically. "I do. I know guarding me isn't the easiest job in the world."

His jaw slackened in shock. "You admit it? Do you know...you have never once admitted that to me? Not in all the centuries I've known you have you ever spoken those words."

"Well don't expect me to repeat it."

"Oh," he laughed to himself. "I wouldn't dare get my hopes up."

His feet swung down and landed with a thump on the balcony's wooden floorboards. Then, to my surprise, he leaned forward and took my hands. The heat radiating from his skin was both comforting and thrilling, coaxing my stomach in to flip flops.

"Do you know what I've missed most about you?"

I shook my head, unable to speak. After all these years I was still exhilarated at the very touch of his skin.

"This...this right now. Being able to sit with you and know that you see me and I see you. It is such a precious gift..." His hands tightened around mine before he dropped his head and laughed to himself. "Before I fell, before I came here in human form, I would sit this close to you."

My eyes widened. "You did? When? I never saw you."

"And you wouldn't have. But I was there with you...always. Here on the balcony, beside you in classes at your new school, next to you at The Square. I was always with you. But I could never touch you." He rubbed his thumb along the contours of my hand. "That was the most difficult part and that was what I went through again these last weeks."

"So you do want to touch me?" I asked innocently.

He tilted his head back and released a bellow of laughter. "You think I don't?"

"Well, you haven't...not since I left you..." My head tilted to the side briefly. "I mean, not since I thought I left you."

"I was giving you time, Magdalene, to readjust." He said this while trying to hold back a smile.

Instantly, I felt foolish. "Ah..."

He released one of my hands and I worried he might be pulling away, despite what he'd just mentioned. To my relief, he cupped my chin in his hand and said, "Your health and safety is my first priority. As your guardian it needs to be this way. My need to feel you comes second."

I swallowed, excitement growing in me the longer he stared. "I'm healthy...and I'm safe."

His face tightened then as a wave of passion coursed through him. I could almost see the intensity of it feverishly boiling in him.

He leaned closer, his breath quickening, and placed his lips on mine. They were soft at first but our passion took over and before I knew it, we were standing, our hips pressed against one another. My fingers were in his shaggy, curly hair; his were gripping my waist, pulling me closer.

In the heat of it, he picked me up, his arms wrapping iron-clad around my waist, and carried me in to my bedroom. A few steps across the room and the door was kicked closed. I was on my back then, his warm, firm body on top of me. His hands were in my hair now, entwining with my curls. My lips crushed his and he responded with equal enthusiasm. The bed gave way to our weight, creaking slightly, as we moved towards the headboard. His thumbs were in my jeans, pulling them down. Our bodies moved in a rhythm, following each other as they lifted and fell, twisting together until the bedcovers were tangled around us. He groaned and roughly yanked the covers aside and then he paused.

"What?" I asked. "What's wrong?"

He drew in a ragged breath. "Not like this..." he muttered and rolled to the side, his arms coming off me and lifting above his head. He was still breathing heavily when I laid my cheek on his shoulder. "Not like this..." He reached down and brushed the hair from my face. "You deserve better."

"Eran, I'm already your wife," I reminded him.

"No...I mean yes. You are my wife spiritually." He shook his head, still trying to catch his breath. He groaned then and slapped a hand over his eyes, brushing the hair from his forehead in aggravation. Then he explained, "Magdalene, when was the last time we made love?"

"I don't remember." Now I was thoroughly confused.

"I do and it was on our wedding night." He said this with such declaration I couldn't have misunderstood his meaning.

My breath caught in my chest. "We've only made love once…"

"Only once and over a hundred years ago," he confirmed. "And…" he sat up, lifting himself off the bed, "…I'd like it to be more special than a quick roll in the covers before our housemates find us."

"You're going to leave me like this?" I asked, dumbfounded.

He laughed mockingly at himself. "No, Magdalene. I'm leaving myself like this…at least until I can find a way for us to be together without any inhibition, without housemates, without time constraints." He started for the door, almost as if he was fearful of second guessing his decision.

When he had nearly reached it, I said softly, "I'm sorry watching over me is such a challenge."

He stopped, sensing the concern in my voice. "You're worth every frustrating moment," he replied with a smirk, trying to turn my statement to a more lighthearted one.

I started to ask, "Do you ever…"

He paused and turned back to me. "Ever?" he prompted.

"Do you ever regret the decision to be my guardian?" The words came out with a struggle, half of me needing to hear the answer and half of me abhorring the truth.

He marched across the room, took my hands, and then waited for me to look at him. When I did, I found his expression softened, almost sympathetic. He knew how hard it was for me to ask that question.

"Never," he declared, which allowed me to breath easily again. His signature smirk rose up then. "If I weren't your guardian, if you weren't my ward, and we were in the very same situation as we are now I would be behaving the same way. I want you, all of you, and I want you tonight and every night for the rest of our existence. This has nothing to do with being your guardian, Magdalene. This has to do with ensuring we can make love without getting caught."

I couldn't help myself then. I laughed and soon he was laughing with me. Despite being hundreds of years old, he suffered from the same classic dilemma as any other teenage boy, and that we found humorous.

As his laughter settled down, he said tenderly to me, "I do love you. I will find a way for us to be together."

"Good," I said firmly.

"Now," he released me and stepped across the room, placing his hand on the light switch, "go to sleep. The afterlife is waiting."

He turned off my lights and closed the door.

I sighed heavily and then spent the next several minutes before sleep overtook me trying to quiet my craving to slip across the hall and into his bedroom.

The last thing I thought before I awoke in the Hall of Records was very reassuring: Thankfully, Eran always kept his word. I just hoped he would fulfill his promise soon.

3. WELCOME BACK

Ms. Beedinwigg had been a teacher at the private high school that Eran and I attended for exactly three months and already she had built herself a reputation.

Mr. Warden, our principal, liked her even less than he disliked me.

And that was saying something.

I discovered this important fact at breakfast the following morning, the very same morning that I planned to ask Ms. Beedinwigg to help convince Mr. Warden to allow Eran and me back to school.

Ezra, true to her nature, was awake for hours before me. Because of her early risings, she had already been on the phone with Ms. Beedinwigg by then. When I entered the kitchen she was leaning against the counter nearest the phone, grasping her steaming coffee mug, and staring at the tiled floor. When my movement caught her attention she looked up.

"I'm not sure how she did it but Ms. Beedinwigg got you back in…"

"Really? How?" I implored more surprised than excited. After all, we were talking about school.

Ezra shook her head. "She is one resourceful woman," she added glancing at me. "Do you know Mr. Warden placed her at the top of his so-to-speak hit list after you failed to show up on campus again?"

"No," I said, stunned. Ms. Beedinwigg was my favorite teacher so I would gladly have taken her place. My heart softened even more for her in that moment, knowing personally how malicious The Warden could be. Then something occurred to me. "How could she possibly have gotten me and Eran back in then?"

Ezra shrugged. "You'll have to ask her...tomorrow morning at 8 o'clock sharp." That was a clear hint not to be late to my first scheduled class.

"What happens tomorrow morning?" asked Felix as he entered the kitchen.

Eran was directly behind him, his eyes already on me, a sly grin showing that he was remembering last night.

In response, I actually felt my cheeks heat up.

He grinned deeper and, while passing by, leaned towards me allowing his lips to graze my cheek before whispering in my ear. "You're blushing, my love."

That, of course, intensified it.

Thankfully, Ezra showed no signs of noticing, although experience told me that she had. Instead, she recounted the phone conversations between her and Ms. Beedinwigg this morning as they plotted our return to school. I took a seat at the kitchen table and allowed most of my attention to follow Eran around the room.

Inside, my stomach was doing somersaults each time he glanced in my direction.

Just as Ezra finished, Rufus entered the kitchen.

"The Warden," he muttered with unmasked contempt. "Sharp as a beach ball, that one..."

Eran chuckled lightly as he pulled two bowls and a box of cereal from the cabinet.

"Tut tut tut!" Felix stopped him, physically taking the bowls and cereal to replace them in the cabinets. "This calls for a celebratory breakfast!"

Those very words whisked away any hunger pangs about to rise up. Eran lifted his eyebrows at me, showing he was just as hesitant.

To our surprise, Felix came through for us this meal. He prepared a traditional New Orleans breakfast of Eggs Nouvelle Orleans or specifically poached eggs served on a bed of lump crabmeat and topped with a brandy-cream sauce. It left me full while still wanting more, something that had never happened with any of Felix's culinary treats. Unfortunately, he was back to himself by the end of the meal, suggesting he make oysters in raspberry sauce for dinner.

We each simultaneously declined his offer.

Breakfast had taken a while so by the time we reached The Square that morning I had customers already waiting for me. I delivered their messages from those loved ones in the afterlife who they'd asked me to visit the night before as efficiently as I could. But, my main distraction kept moving in to my view and reminding me of the night before. Whether by design or accident, he was teasing me and I'm sure it showed. Stumbling over my words, taking deep breaths to clear my thoughts, blinking back the memory of him on top of me were all attempts to give my customers their due attention…and none of it worked.

It was a very long day.

He approached me at sunset wearing his signature smirk. He knew he'd gotten to me.

Without saying a word, he simply went about collecting my chairs and sign to place in the trunk of Felix's car.

On the bike as we drove home he was no different, leaning back against me, laying his cheek on the side of my helmet.

"Careful," he warned more than once as my concentration remained on him and I nearly hit a curb or took out a construction cone.

Dinner was no different. He kept one eye on me as we each moved around the kitchen, me setting the table and him helping Felix with snail jambalaya.

At the table, he pressed his leg against mine, tenderly so that I wasn't sure if he meant to or was simply stretching. My heart fluttered more than once throughout dinner.

By the end of the night, I was thoroughly annoyed with him and with myself for being unable to control his impact on me.

Apparently, I wasn't the only one who noticed either.

"Would ya two stop that now?" Rufus muttered, shaking his head at us. "Makin' me sicker than Felix's jambalaya…"

"What?" Felix's head snapped up. "You don't like my dinner?"

"Is that any surprise?" Ezra asked, though she said it delicately so that Felix wasn't too offended. She didn't give him time to answer, instead turned to chastise us. "You two do need to end it. You've been at it every time I see you."

"At what? Been at what?" Felix implored, confused.

"Eat your jambalaya, Felix," Ezra coaxed softly.

Felix's head swung between the rest of us trying to pick up any hint of what he'd missed, but he found nothing. Rufus was back to challenging himself to finish what was in his bowl and Ezra had preoccupied herself with a gnat that was circling her head, although I thought that might be a fake diversion.

When I glanced at Eran, he was already looking at me, watching my reaction. Despite the fact that I had every right to behave stoically romantic with my husband and that I wasn't even the one making the gestures, I felt my cheeks burning.

Being reprimanded by Ezra was what I figured was equivalent to being scolded by a mother.

Eran, for his part, was not blushing. He was confident and mischievous, and to make matters worse, his leg leaned further in to mine.

The rest of dinner was short and then I helped with the dishes. Eran allowed Rufus to dry and instead kept his eyes on me from the table. I knew this because I felt it and then confirmed it with quick glances in the reflection of the window above the sink.

He held a conversation with Felix about the virtues of southern cuisine until I'd finished my chore. Then he smoothly transitioned out of the conversation to follow me upstairs.

The silence coming from the kitchen after we left told me that my housemates were not fooled, Ezra least of all. I expected to hear her footsteps approaching the second floor in ten minutes.

She knew very well that I was married to Eran in my past life and yet while he was the guardian of my life she was the protector of my virtue.

I felt like I should be wearing a chastity belt.

As I entered my room, Eran surprised me by not coming up behind me. Instead, he stayed leaning against the door jam, his arms crossed so that his muscles rolled up over his chest. I was already at the French doors of my balcony, flinging them open when he spoke.

"Do you have any idea what you've done to me today?" he asked in a hushed tone.

"You?" I spun around. "What I've done to you?"

"Yes." He nodded, innocently.

My head shook in amazement.

41

"Why do you think I'm not coming in?" he asked, tipping his head towards my room. "I don't trust myself. Not after what you've been doing."

My mouth fell open but no words came out.

"You've done this a few times before," he reflected. "Paris…the cabin…"

"Do what?" I asked my voice just below a shout. How could he be accusing me of anything when it was his motions that had driven me mad the entire day?

"Keep me…impassioned," he thought better of what he was trying to tell me and then added, "Tantalized."

Part of me was in shock and part of me was undeniably proud. The fact that I could tease this man who kept me on my sexual edge whenever I knew he was in the room, made me feel like I'd succeeded in something.

Not knowing what else to say, I replied, "Well I can tell you that you've been doing the same to me."

"I have?" he asked, astonished. His eyebrows lifted and his head tilted forward telling me that his surprise was genuine. He had no idea.

"Yes," I stated firmly.

We stared at each other, the distance a palpable thing between us but neither one of us knowing how to shake our muscles in to moving towards one another. In him, I could – for the first time - see that he fought the same circumstance as me. Neither of us had any hint of an idea how completely inflamed with passion we each were with the other. Apparently, we'd just discovered a limitation in our ability to feel each other's emotions. Unfortunately, it stopped at the sexual level.

"So what did you do about it? Back then in Paris…at the cabin," I asked quietly, demurely though I wasn't trying to be.

His eyes took on a gleam. "I'll show you."

He strode in the room, took my face in his hands, and guided me to him. Our lips met and then our arms were around each other and our thighs were pressing against one another and I could feel his lips move along my jaw and down my neck and then…I heard Ezra's footsteps.

Eran pulled away at exactly that same moment, his muscles strained, his breathing coming in short gasps.

"I'm leaving now," he called out, defeated and yet irritated at the same time.

The footsteps stopped.

"Excellent," said Ezra from around the corner. "I'll see you both in the morning."

He frowned down at me.

"School tomorrow," she reminded, her voice already fading as she descended the stairs.

Eran laughed through his nose. "School tomorrow," he repeated in a tender whisper. "Sleep well."

"You too," I said watching him leave my room.

He winked at me before closing the door, which gave me something enjoyable to think about as I lay in bed waiting for sleep to take over. Because of it, that night, I rested fully and woke up refreshed the next morning.

The smell of bacon and eggs greeted me then. Rufus was in the kitchen, parked at his usual place at the stove. Felix was rushing from cupboard to cabinet to refrigerator and back to the cupboard. Ezra was seated at the table, mug in one hand, newspaper in the other.

For the first time, I felt like things were back to normal.

A few minutes later, as Rufus slid bacon and eggs on to our plates, Eran entered the kitchen. In a fitted black sweater, jeans that seemed to be tailored to accentuate his physique, and a black leather jacket thrown over his shoulder, he reminded me more of a model than a high school student.

We ate quickly since being late to the first day after we were allowed back from an extended absence would definitely not sit well with Mr. Warden.

Saying our goodbyes, we headed out the door and rode my bike to school. Students were still milling around the parking lot and expansive lawn leading to the Main Hall so we knew first bell hadn't rung.

My eyes swept the grounds and I realized instantly what I was doing. Out of habit, I was looking for danger, any risk posed by Fallen Ones or any hazards they may have left behind. It occurred to me then this was the first time I'd set foot on campus without the hair rising at the back of my neck, without my radar screaming at me that a Fallen One was nearby and I was in danger. Right now, I felt…nothing. It felt…abnormal, I realized. It was a reminder that Fallen Ones still existed, living in obscurity somewhere out there until they were ready to emerge and again hurt a human or, their moral counterparts, the Alterums.

After parking my bike, we walked through the throng of students until we had almost reached the main entrance. At that point, Eran leaned towards me to whisper, "We have quite an audience."

"No…You have an audience," I told him.

His eyebrows lifted but he didn't ask for further clarification. Not that he would need to. The whisperings in the hallway were enough to help him fill in the blanks.

"…prison…"

"Germany."

"…gone for weeks."

As was the case with most rumors, the one about Eran that had spread through our school just weeks ago was only half-true. Eran had spent time in a German prison. But, unknown to anyone except Eran, me, and Ms. Beedinwigg, it wasn't one designed for humans.

The stares didn't end when we reached Biochemistry. In fact, the moment we entered, it seemed as if everyone's head turned in our direction simultaneously, including Ms. Beedinwigg.

She grinned subtly and called out from her desk, "Welcome back."

We dropped our book bags at our seats and met her at the front of the class.

Oddly, I couldn't seem to contain my smile.

"So…is it good to be back?" she asked, doing her best to judge my expression.

"Yes…," I said and then admitted, "and no."

"More are out there, I take it?" she asked, tensely.

I confirmed with a nod.

"So you'll be leaving again?" she inquired glancing at both Eran and me while keeping her voice low so students in the front row didn't overhear.

Eran waited for me to answer, his silence reaffirming that the decision was up to me.

My chin lifted slightly before answering. I wasn't sure if I would hear the same level of opposition from her as I had from Eran but I readied myself for it. "Yes, I'll be leaving again soon. Thank you though…for convincing The Warden-"

"Mr. Warden," she corrected.

Again, I rolled my eyes. "For convincing him to take us back."

"You're welcome," she said, warmly.

"How did you get him to take us back?" Eran asked, gleaming at the thought of her having any measure of authority over The Warden.

Ms. Beedinwigg cleared her throat and dipped her head slightly to hide her grin. "You won't be too happy with me after you hear this…" she said, looking up from beneath her lashes at us. "I promised him that you would both behave."

My jaw dropped then. No one said it but we all knew that was impossible. Then she added the icing to that sweet news.

45

"Any punishment you are handed down will result in one that is twofold for me."

I sucked in my breath.

She leaned forward slightly to whisper, "I have full confidence in you."

I started shaking my head, unable to conjure the words to tell her that she'd made a foolish mistake. Mr. Warden hated us both. He'd be looking for reasons to expel us.

Appearing as if she wanted to change the subject, she openly assessed me. "You look tired, Maggie."

Already irritated by her agreement with The Warden, I rolled my eyes. I was more tired of hearing it.

"It was smart of you to bring her back," she told Eran.

He nodded in agreement. "Yes it was."

Before I was able to insist I was almost back to my regular energy level, the first bell rang and we had to head to our seats.

Just before she began to start her lecture, Ms. Beedinwigg gave me a hard look. It was one that I knew intuitively. The demure woman standing before me, hair in a bun, glasses hanging from her neck, wearing a shapeless printed dress, once again reminded me of the aggressive warrior hidden behind her camouflaged outfit.

Her look was telling me that when I was ready to return to training I knew where to go.

The hour-long class felt short on time but it wasn't long enough to make me forget that a few days ago, I was drowning a Fallen One.

The next few hours were easier. Although Eran wasn't with me, I was distracted in other ways. The rumor about Eran was traveling again across school grounds and, surprisingly, a few students had the courage to approach me about it.

In my third period class, Mark Mitchell leaned towards me and asked, "So's it true what I heard about Eran Talor?"

I shrugged. "What'd you hear?" I avoided him by focusing on pulling out my books before class started.

"That he was in prison…" he said excitedly. "In Germany."

I turned to stare at him, expressionless, before responding flatly, "No."

When Sylvia Cross approached me about it in my fourth period, I gave her the same response.

Then it was lunch break and they could stare firsthand at the one who'd killed a guy in France, was extradited to Germany, spent several weeks in the squalid conditions of a German cell, eating rats to survive, fighting demented and depraved inmates, eventually paying off an official in order to risk a daring escape back to the United States.

By the end of the day, Eran was the most notorious student in campus history, taking the title I'd held since starting at the school. Even the faculty eyed him suspiciously. He took it in stride, seeming not to notice a single sideways glance or overhear a not-so-distant snicker. Thinking back, I realized he was astutely familiar with this scenario. Eran had never been one to tip toe a line and as a result he'd encountered fierce rumors and violent antagonism during several of his lifetimes.

"You handled that well," I said complimenting his resilience once we were standing at my bike at the end of the day.

"Huh?" he asked, perplexed.

"The amount of attention you were getting…" I hinted.

"Oh, that…I didn't notice it much." He shrugged. "My thoughts, for the most part, were on you."

I glanced up. "Me?"

"Sure," he said, slipping on his helmet so that his voice became muffled as he continued. "I was figuring out how I could get you alone."

My stomach burned as those words registered in my mind. He'd been thinking about spending intimate time with me? All day long? My confidence faltered then as the full weight of it hit me. I could tear apart Fallen Ones, whisk myself and others to the afterlife and back, but when it came to being intimate with Eran I went weak in the knees.

Noticing my reaction, he winked arrogantly at me, and then gestured to take a seat on my bike.

"What did you come up with?" I muttered shyly, as I slipped on the bike behind him.

"You'll see…" he teased.

I sighed in disagreement, not wanting to wait any longer. "Tell me," I demanded.

"Wait and see."

"When?"

"Soon, Magdalene." He reached his hand around and placed it against my thigh, the weight of it making me crave him more. Then he said the only pointed comment that could distract me from his hand. "You have a problem with patience, my dear."

In reaction, I scoffed and then brushed his hand off my thigh for emphasis.

Chuckling, he started the engine and by the time we'd made it to the house, I could not discern whether I was infuriated with him or impassioned by him. It wasn't until he slipped his arms around my waist just outside the kitchen back door did I know.

"Your impatience is one of your most endearing qualities," he said.

It wasn't one or the other. It was both.

4. FERNANDO VEGA

The next few days passed quickly and followed the same patterns as the first day back. Faculty and students continued to keep their distance from Eran and me, though the rumors started to dissipate in favor of Becky Monahan's reaction to alcohol at the latest party. Intermittently, Eran or I would find The Warden peering around the corner at one of us, ensuring we were keeping Ms. Beedinwigg's promise, and watch as a frown rose up in finding that we were.

Homework began piling up so Eran and I were the last ones to sleep each night, books covering the kitchen table, heads drooped over them. While we knew much of it all ready, having experienced some of it firsthand, the actual paperwork needing to be turned in was mountainous. The kitchen lights were the last ones turned off for the evening.

I began feeling stronger, I noticed. My muscles moved easier, their aches having subsided. My meal portions, which had been twice my regular amount, were subsiding too, my body no longer needing it. My appendages, oddly enough, itched to be released, which I complied with when I started lessons again with Ms. Beedinwigg.

Ms. Beedinwigg was surprised and exhilarated to find me at her doorstep midway through the week. She led me inside for a quick hello to Mr. Hamilton and then down the stairs to her underground training room. There, she had jerry-rigged the walls to support her frame and a system of levers and pulleys so that she could spar with me airborne. I'd thought my appendages would give me an advantage but after the first lesson, as we sprang from wall to wall and flew around the room in the midst of fighting drills, I found that she was nearly as good a fighter in the air as she was on the ground. Our trainings lasted only an hour but it left me physically drained and inspired me to keep working on my recovery, which also kept Eran happy.

My work at The Square the following weekend was especially fulfilling, knowing I would be leaving again soon. It seemed as if word had spread throughout my regular customers that I was back because every one of them stopped in for a quick message delivery to their loved ones. That night, I had over forty messages to deliver from both new patrons and regulars.

Of the new ones, I witnessed a few of the most dramatic afterlife habitats I'd ever come across. One woman had recreated every locale where she'd ever found herself happy while on earth. I found her sitting halfway between a vineyard and the Pacific Ocean, one leg in each realm. A man who'd been Italian in his last life had created an elaborate dinner party for a few hundred of his closest family and friends. I had to deliver my message following him around an enormous kitchen with ovens stacked five high and along both walls as he fluttered between them, delivering hors d'oeuvres as they came out. Finally, a little boy who'd passed on from a hit-and-run accident was, in my opinion, the most exciting. He'd created his afterlife as a continuum, moving from a land of dinosaurs to one filled with zoo animals openly wandering an expansive range to the Wild West with cowboys and

Indians roaming the hills. I'd had to chase him through two of his realms before catching him and delivering his mother's message. He smiled softly and gave me a discreet message in reply. "I love you, Mommy," he said and then, in typical childlike fashion, he returned to creeping up on a sleeping lion.

By the end of the first week, I felt fully recovered and the reminder that Fallen Ones still walked the earth made me more and more motivated to return to hunting. The thought became so pervasive that as Eran was washing up for bed on Sunday night, I lifted my bed mattress and pulled out the leather-bound book encapsulating all Fallen Ones dossiers. Opening it to the very next one I'd intended to kill, I sat on the edge of the bed, listening to the shower running down the hall, and quickly read the pages.

"Fernando Vega," I muttered to myself, my eyes reading quickly over his summary. "Mississippi…18 Hilbrook Way…no pets…no significant others…"

After I had consumed the rest of his information, I slipped the book back beneath the mattress. Directly next to it laid my black leather suit, neatly folded like a prized possession. Next to it, laid my weapons.

I stared at them for only a second before my body began moving on its own.

The next thing I knew, I had slipped on my black leather suit, secured my weapons in their respective places, and pulled open my balcony doors.

Without thought behind it, I lifted my shoulders then and my appendages sprang out. I extended them wide, enjoying the stretch. They reached outward, almost touching either side of the balcony, lengthening the muscles and tendons like others do with their arms and legs. A groan escaped as I allowed myself to feel the freedom of my fully-healed body.

As I stood there, assessing the night, my bedroom door opened, moaning against its hinges, and I knew Eran had finished showering. He was checking on me and, I was certain, he didn't expect to find me suited up facing open balcony doors.

Without turning, I stated, "I'm ready."

It may have been the resolute tone in my voice, my stance, or simply the feeling in the air but he knew without question that I was correct.

I heard shuffling behind me and then he was at my side, his appendages already unfurled and resting behind him.

He had given his unspoken agreement, I knew. And while I didn't need it, it was a comfort nonetheless. Although I would never admit it to him – even if he had some indication of it already – with Eran being amply familiar with recovering fighters, his concurrence that I was equipped to take on a Fallen One again meant that I wasn't fooling myself. That was reassuring.

What was not so reassuring was the fact that he would be accompanying me. Getting him even remotely close to danger was not a pleasant forethought. I was certain it was the same for him.

It was late so the street was quiet. Lights were off in our neighbor's houses and the only thing that seemed to be moving was the alley cat scampering across the lawn next door.

The air was clear, fresh tonight with almost a sugary taste to it. It made me wonder how the air was in Mississippi…

My wings pumped hard, lifting me effortlessly off the balcony and over the street. I soared higher, enjoying the cool wind on my face. I'd missed it, I realized. Elated to be in the air again, I spun like a missile through the night sky until I was far above the city. Using various ground markers – the placement of cities, mountain ranges, major highways – we found our way to Mississippi and along the river there.

The air was more humid here, I noticed, becoming noticeably more so as we dropped towards a small structure on the water's edge surrounded by acres of trees. Fernando lived in an abandoned house on the edge of the Mississippi River. Knowing this from his dossier, we simply needed to fly up river until my radar picked him up.

Our speed was somewhere between a bullet and an airline jet so it didn't take long before I felt the hair stand at the back of my neck.

That's when I stopped in midair.

Realizing it, Eran came to a sudden halt. He peered over his shoulder at me, questioning.

"I did as you asked..." I explained firmly. "I gave you warning that I was going to leave for a hunt and, against my interests, I've allowed you to escort me. Now, I have to make a request."

He nodded, hesitant and unsure where I was going with this conversation.

"I need you to fall back."

He opened his mouth to protest but I didn't allow it.

"Feel free to stay close, you can even watch, but do not interfere. This is my undertaking. Allow me to do it without intervening."

Even while I debated on whether I was deceiving myself in to thinking Eran would actually stay out of the fight I'd elected, I used my appendages to angle myself down towards Fernando's dwelling. Once there, I drew closer and circled once before landing on the river's bank.

The walls had long since given way to the weather that regularly crept up from The Gulf and entire boards were missing from every external wall of the house. Moss grew over the remaining ones, draping down from the roof and windowsill of nearly every window. There was no glass and no doors to prevent the elements from entering his home. Peering inside, I found few pieces of furniture, each one looking as if he'd bought them at a flea market over a century ago.

I might have felt sorry for Fernando if he didn't work as a hit man for mob bosses.

Eerily quiet on the bank of the river with just the wind in the trees and the lapping of the water on the shore, it made me wonder if Fernando had killed or scared off every living thing in the vicinity. The carcasses of dead animals piled against a tree told me that may very well be the case.

I stepped through the brush and closer to the house, noticing that it was actually well lit from inside. Kerosene lamps hung from the rafters giving the place a hazy, yellow glow.

Just as I was within a few yards from it, a giggle began from behind me, and the hairs on the back of my neck rose to their fullest height. It continued as I turned around, seeking the source in the darkness.

It broke in to intermittent snorts as my eyes found Fernando hunched against a tree. His hand was arched over his mouth as if he were ashamed of his giggling.

I stared at him, waiting for him to finish. Already my awareness level had been piqued, drawing in my surroundings through each of my senses. A mosquito buzzed from somewhere inside the house, the scent of rotting wood along the shore enflamed my nose, and, most interesting of all, Fernando Vega's hand was twitching nervously against his mouth. This one was unlike other Fallen Ones, powerful still, but scared.

"Maggie…" he said smiling through his giggles. "Such an honor…"

"Thank you," I replied almost curtly. I didn't feel nearly as impressed by him as he did with me and it didn't bother me to show it.

His giggling settled and then snuffed out all together. Still, he held on to his wide smile. "We crossed paths once...up in Montana."

I bristled. "Montana was where I was born."

His grating giggle returned. "And where you died."

"What do you know about that?" I asked firmly.

His giggling calmed until it was coming strictly out of his nose, quick and short wisps of air filling the silence.

"Me?" He slid around the tree and strolled to the next one, never narrowing or widening the distance between us. My appendages stiffened, preparing, although he didn't seem to notice. "I know all about it...all about it because I was there."

The hair at the back of my neck suddenly felt as if someone had taken them by the ends and were yanking them out. I ignored them. "What were you doing there?"

"Watching..." His head tilted up so that he peered at me from under his lashes, that hideous smile lurking beneath the surface of his expression. "Abaddon's plan was executed perfectly...and Gershom's timing of that vehicle collision was a work of beauty. Really, it was. In the middle of the night, between Helena and Billings...no one around to assist. It was just that no one accounted for your mother." He must have caught my look of confusion because he went on to explain. "No one knew before you two were separated, and she was sent to medical care in Helena and you to Billings, that she had set your death in motion, protecting you from us and from eternal death. Her one final hail mary..."

Anger roared through me then and I had to actively subdue it. He had no right to bring up such a personal matter and far less right to talk about it with such casual indifference.

"Careful, messenger..." he taunted, excitedly sniggering now. "Your guardian will sense you if you keep it up..." At the very sound of Eran's name, I froze.

Fernando, who was watching me closely, made a quizzical face. "And you don't want your guardian here, do you?" He didn't wait for my answer. "Is it the same one? The same guardian? When you died before as a baby, little Maggie, he was there too…watching…unable to help, having arrived after the accident had happened when your fate was already sealed." Fernando sniggered again and then continued. "He was so…wrought with pain…Interesting guardian, he is. Cares for you more than other guardians care for their wards. Maybe not more, just…different. It's…intriguing…" When I didn't respond, he continued, eyeing me curiously. "He was so distraught when you died and you…you were so thoughtful. It was almost as if you were expecting it."

I was still calming my rage through clenched teeth, unable to speak yet.

"And then you returned…" he said through his sniggering. "Fooling us all because you had returned as a human." His giggles deepened briefly. "A human…" he said in amazement, shaking his head, continuing to giggle. "A human with no power to protect yourself…You are amazing, messenger, to have lived as long as you did. It is an honor to finally meet you, however brief it may be." His smile, unwavering, began to irritate me. Then he spoke again and I forgot about it completely. "Such a treasure…and then to die by your own kind…" He seemed almost wistful about it.

I froze, realizing instantly that in all the centuries I had ever encountered a Fallen One I'd never heard that particular threat.

"I can assure you," I replied stiffly, "that will not happen."

He ignored me, shaking his head, his smile having sunk back in to his gaunt face. "You've caused more upset than you know, Maggie. This hunting excursion you've been on…killing off my kind…It has drawn attention to yourself. And they are not pleased…" He caught sight of my expression and must have found it to be apprehensive based on his following statement. "If you're thinking about running, I assure you that no one would blame you."

"I don't run."

"Stay…run…it doesn't matter," he said wearily with a shrug, his voice so low I doubted Eran could distinguish his words. This was a good thing because I didn't want him to know what Fernando relayed next. "If you continue your killings, they'll hand you over to us."

I began shaking my head in response, unable to comprehend that could happen.

"They'll hand you over to stop our kind from killing them. You've started a war, Maggie, one of retaliation from both sides…a war that can end only one way…with your death."

"That will not be the case."

Although those words ran through my mind, it was a voice behind me that spoke then and it was one that I could never in this lifetime or any other ever mistaken.

Eran stepped from the darkness stealthily, displaying his unique ability to sneak up on his enemies. His body was poised, even as he moved quickly across the ground, like a lion evaluating its prey.

"Magdalene…" he said, without looking in my direction. "Get behind me."

I opened my mouth to protest. This was my fight. He had no right to be here. And worse, his presence endangered him.

"We'll discuss it later," he said, having noticed my struggle. "Get behind me."

When I didn't move, he opened his mouth to speak again but halted when Fernando began giggling again. Apparently, he was excited to watch a messenger and her guardian bickering and it made Eran pause. Then, very slowly, his head tilted, a look of absolute disgust in his expression.

"It is incredible how annoying that is!" he said in astonishment. "Has anyone ever told you how annoying that is?"

Fernando had his hand arched over his mouth again, shyly, quietly sniggering. "Yesss," he stuttered, his answer trembling between his hissing laughter. "Yesss."

Eran rolled his eyes and then turned to address me. "Magdalene, get back…please."

Just then, during that moment of distraction between Eran and me, Fernando changed and I saw for the first time why he had been hired as a hit man by wealthy executives. In an instant, he stood to his full height and dropped his hand from his mouth to his hip where he'd stowed a handmade weapon, a gun, rutted by daggers for close combat. His sniggers were gone now, replaced with rigid and determined attention. In fact, I was still processing my surprise at his complete metamorphosis when he lunged.

I stepped aside just as Eran came forward, directing his own weapon at Fernando. Simultaneously, Eran's hand reached out to move me backwards and behind him, designed to protect me. That motion gave Fernando just enough leverage to take advantage of Eran's open torso and his gun exploded, the bullet racing from its chamber and towards Eran's waist. Evidently, Fernando wasn't aware of Eran's ability to control metal because he was stumped when the bullet stopped in midair and fell to the ground, never piercing his skin.

That shock became my opportunity and, immediately, I attacked Fernando, our bodies becoming entangled as I swept him off the ground and through the air. Suspended, we both sought for an opening. He found one and sliced a dagger from the side of his gun into my flesh just above my hip. It was shallow but I felt the sting nonetheless.

Then Eran was on top of him, spinning through the air, slamming against the crumbling rooftop of Fernando's dwelling. Boards flew aside, lanterns crashed to the floor, neither Eran nor Fernando noticing.

They had taken the fight out over the water by then and I sprang off the ground, intending to join. They moved fast, ramming through the wall closest to them and into the one room house.

With the broken lanterns releasing kerosene across the floor I entered the house following Eran and Fernando through the gap they had created and found myself surrounded by flames. Fire licked the kerosene, across the floorboards and up the walls, against one of which Eran had pinned Fernando.

Fernando was putting up a good fight, preventing Eran's blade from getting any closer to his heart. Then I reached them, took the handle and shoved it deep inside Fernando's torso. Its handle quivered as it sunk with Fernando's body to the burning floor below.

Eran, for the first time noticing we were hovering inside an inferno, retrieved his sword, grabbed my hand, and pulled us to safety.

"What were you thinking?" I demanded once we'd reached the middle of the river. My senses were still heightened and, despite his efforts a moment ago, I smelled the sweet fragrance of his body. It diverted my attention but only for a moment.

My appendages were making short, abrupt movements to help me stay aloft while his were flapping lightly every once in a while. Eran, clearly, felt he was in the right about having intervened.

"You said you'd stay back," I stated angrily, knowing it wasn't the response he was hoping for.

"I didn't say a word, Magdalene. You didn't give me a chance," he reminded delicately, but his tone didn't save him from my wrath.

"I didn't believe I needed to. This was my battle, Eran. Mine! You were supposed to remain at a safe distance."

"Safe distance," he scoffed. "You have no idea what you are asking your guardian to do. Do you know that Fernando Vega, that very man you attempted to kill solely on your own, has personally killed three messengers? Without any assistance from his own kind? There is a reason he took jobs as a hit man, Magdalene."

I understood what he was implying and yet it didn't register with me. I could handle myself. My only reaction was a tight pinch of my lips.

His shoulders slumped forward then, tired of trying to convince me to act with self-preservation. "Let's get back. If Ezra finds us gone again it'll hurt her beyond words." He started towards the clouds, slowly, ensuring I was following.

I wasn't.

He slowed his pace upward and then stopped all together. "Your desire…no…your obsession in killing our enemies…alone…takes precedence over any other thoughts or concerns. It dominates you, Magdalene, and anything that dominates you can hurt you." He paused then, closing the gap between us to place his hands on each side of my face. Peering at me through the night, shadows from the flaming remnants of Fernando's house dancing across his cheeks. "I'm-I'm frightened for you, Magdalene."

The understanding of his message was suddenly a palpable presence in my stomach, twisting my insides until they ached.

He was right. Every waking moment, every second I spent in the afterlife each night, thoughts cycled through my consciousness on how to exterminate them. I hated them because through cold calculations they had hurt…killed the ones I love. Now ever fiber in my body ached for vengeance. It was me acting with cold calculation to destroy them and I understood exactly what Eran was warning me against. If I didn't watch it, I would become one of them.

"I worry myself sometimes," I muttered, causing the creases in his brow to deepen. "I'm trying to control it. I-I just think that sometimes it controls me."

"It's all right," he whispered soothingly. "We'll work on it together."

I wasn't entirely in agreement with that suggestion. Working on it together implied he would need to be present as I hunted - something I wholly disagreed with. Yet, I knew, staring back at him that I would not win this argument tonight.

He kissed my lips deeply for a brief moment and then his wings flapped, carrying us higher. We separated but it was a struggle, our hands slipping from each other only at the very last second.

The flight back to New Orleans was silent, as I considered the best way to convince him to allow me to hunt alone. By the time we reached our roof I had considered countless reasons, each one making less sense than the last. I knew his reasoning, he'd used it before and it, unfortunately, was entirely logical.

He was a guardian. I was a ward. He would protect me at all costs...including my own desires to hunt alone.

As we landed on the balcony outside my room and my wings sunk back inside my skin, his hand found mine. It was warm, pulsating, and irresistible.

He didn't look at me when he began to speak, his head dropped, gazing at the balcony's wooden floorboards instead.

"Magdalene...when you died as a child, those Fallen Ones who attempted your murder were thought to have been the last of our enemies. We thought..." Shaking his head, he muttered, fury hidden just beneath his words, "I had thought we'd succeeded in their extermination. I was wrong." He pulled away and began pacing the balcony.

"You don't need to do this," I told him.

"Yes...I do. I need you to understand why I need to accompany you." Agony coursed through him then, an emotion so strong and swift it seemed to flow from him directly into my veins. His body seemed to cave against it for a fleeting moment before he recovered and continued on. "There, in Montana, after you were revived from the accident that had taken your infant life, I was assured you were safe and those Fallen Ones who took your life could no longer hurt you. Believing those were the last of our enemies, I stepped back...allowing you the chance to experience life on earth as you had always wanted, as a reborn, a human. And...knowing you have never wanted a guardian, I set my destiny aside and acted on your desires. I disappeared." His eyes met mine, filled with an anger that confirmed he would never forgive himself for making that decision. "I disappeared and unknowingly left you alone in a world littered with our enemies."

I placed my hand on his arm and he stopped his pacing. It was then I noticed the tremble that had taken over his body. I stepped closer, pressing my head against his chest, taking his hands in mine, hoping that physical touch would help heal him. Yet, it was my words that seemed to deliver some measure of solace. "I forgive you..." I whispered softly. "I forgive you..."

At that moment, a pained sigh escaped him, one that had been pent up for over a century. His hands came to my chin, pulling me away from him so that our eyes could meet.

"When I felt your radar, your fear again just a few months ago, I appeared just below that streetlight," he pointed to the yellow globe a few yards away. "And I knew you still needed my protection. But it wasn't until later, when I realized the Fallen Ones still existed - that they hadn't been completely decimated – when I knew just how much. At that point, I recognized the reality that we faced, that we were still in danger, and suddenly very little made sense. Everything I was certain of was gone. Your safety, my beliefs. So, you see, I get it. I understand your need to execute them. I face that overwhelming desire every day we are on this earth. The anger that is conjured at knowing my loved ones...that you...are in harm's way is irrefutable, undeniable to me. It drives me, just as it now drives you. But it's not as strong as you think, Magdalene. It will not own us. We will own it by choosing when, where, and how to destroy our enemies."

At the end, his speech conjured in me an awareness that had been hidden. When it surfaced, I couldn't ignore it. The intensity was too severe. We are in this together, together we are stronger, and together we will succeed.

"Together..." I murmured.

"Yes, together," he replied emphatic.

"And all this time...I never knew how it made you feel to guard me. I always thought you saw it as a job, a responsibility. But it is more..."

"So much more," he whispered, tensely.

"I understand that now."

Then, gradually, life began flickering again in his eyes. "Promise me, Magdalene, that you will not under any circumstances leave me and search out to destroy your enemies without my presence?" As if afraid I would decline, he added, "You may continue your hunting and I will stay aside but I reserve the right to intervene if I consider the risks too great."

"Well," I sniffed laughter, "Who could argue with that bargain?"

"Promise me, Magdalene."

I stood on my toes then and ran my lips along the curve of his neck, along his jawbone, coming to rest them just over his lips. I could hear his heartbeat, strong and sound, quicken as I intentionally brushed against him. "I promise," I whispered.

"Tease," he murmured deeply. I breathed in his woodsy scent, becoming intoxicated simply by the smell of him.

He slid his arms along my back and then picked me up swiftly, carrying me to the bed.

Laying me on top of the billowing mattress, he pressed his lips resolutely against mine.

"Get some rest," he said huskily after pulling away. "Tomorrow we hunt Fallen Ones."

He left my room then with a more relaxed stroll, one I was thankful to see. Only after he'd turned off my light and the sounds of him preparing to sleep drifted across the hall did I realize he hadn't heard…

He hadn't heard Fernando's warning…that our own kind would come after me if I continued my killings. The sane part of me realized that was a problem. The insane part of me refused to care. That part won.

As I rolled over to stare across my room towards the balcony doors, I was certain of one thing: I would continue killing Fallen Ones regardless of the obstacles, even if they came from the side I was defending.

5. FRANÇOIS GERARD

The following morning was a challenge.

After reviewing the next Fallen One's summary in the book of dossiers, I realized all I'd done is tease myself. I had to sit through breakfast and then through the ride to school with a nagging irritation. It felt as if very muscle in my body remained taut, impatiently waiting for tonight and the opportunity to hunt the next Fallen One.

After Eran pulled the bike into the parking lot, found a spot, and shut off the engine, I begrudgingly slid to the ground and headed for our first class.

My only consolation was that Eran was beside me and Ms. Beedinwigg taught our first period. Even though Eran noticed my mood, he didn't say a word about it. He knew me too well to bring up the subject. Although his presence gave me a small amount of solace, the salve to my wound, my mood didn't go unnoticed by Ms. Beedinwigg. At the end of first period, she called me to her desk as students filtered out into the hallway.

"I couldn't help but notice you were preoccupied this morning," she said quiet, her tone edged with suspicion.

"You also missed training last night…And that can only mean one thing. You're hunting again."

"Yes."

Her eyebrows lifted as she waited for me to elaborate.

"Last night was spontaneous. Tonight is planned."

She nodded thoughtfully. "Last night was Fernando Vega?" she asked, recalling my mention of where I'd left off in the book of dossiers.

"That's right."

"The one known for his homemade weaponry…Given you are standing before me without noticeable injuries, I can see who won."

"Eran fought him, actually. I didn't get the chance," I replied, consciously excluding from my tone the disappointment I felt.

At that declaration, her eyes darted towards the door, inspecting him from top to bottom. I half-smiled then, realizing she cared about him just as much as she did me. It was comforting to know.

Seeing no reason for concern, she redirected her attention back to me. "Well…you attended my class this morning and yet you've returned to hunting. That must mean…"

"Yes, I'm staying here…in New Orleans," I confirmed.

"You understand," she said pointedly, "your life is about to become more demanding?"

If she was hinting at reducing my trainings, I met her head on with that decision. "That's why I feel my trainings will need to be scaled down."

"Maggie, let's be honest. You've cornered me the last several sessions, have given poor Alfred nightmares with your swordsmanship…Don't you think it's about time you let us off the hook?"

A smile crept up in both of us then.

The relief was overwhelming. "I didn't know how to tell you…" I admitted, having been unable to find the words to explain to someone so dedicated to her craft that I no longer felt it was necessary.

She was now shaking her head at me. "Never hold back with me. I have fairly thick skin."

I rolled my eyes at that understatement.

Then she grew serious. "Maggie, at this point, the most help I can be to you is to assist you in your hunting. If you should need me…ever…I'm here."

While I knew that would never be the case, I replied, "Thanks for the offer."

"Now," she said, glancing at the clock over the door. "You're late for your next class."

I was, so late in fact that I didn't get a chance to tell Eran of our decision until lunchtime.

When that hour came, I couldn't have been more eager. He met me outside my last class just before we headed for the cafeteria and we remained agonizingly silent until seated at a table in the far corner.

After I whispered the details of my conversation with Ms. Beedinwigg, leaning in close so no one would hear, he sat back and reflected. As he did, his knee absentmindedly swung out, coming to rest against mine. It was a pleasant diversion. He was warm, as usual, and it took effort not to press back against him.

"Do you feel any Fallen Ones around?" he asked.

"No," I replied, a bit surprised. "I would tell you."

"Good," he stated and then placed his hand on my knee.

My heart leaped in my throat, feeling almost scandalous. He never showed affection in public, but that was likely because a Fallen One always lurked nearby. With all of them having fled the school a few weeks ago, Eran seemed to be starting to relax. I was thrilled by it.

So deep in thought, he didn't seem to notice my reaction. "With your training out of the way, we're free to hunt any night you are up to it."

"I am always up for it," I confirmed.

Noting my conviction, he asked with a grin, "How about we take it one night at a time? You might change your mind now that we'll be facing the more hazardous of our enemies."

"I won't," I said, and meant it. I leaned forward then and was momentarily distracted by our proximity but recovered quickly. "I know what we're up against, Eran. I remember it. I remember it all."

His head rotated towards mine, his eyes wide from my disclosure. "I didn't realize your memory recovered so fully…Never having come here as a human myself, I…I didn't know."

"It has and I know it wasn't pleasant before. It wasn't easy. I know it won't be now. But it's worth the risk. This world and the moral ones who've come here have a right to live safely. I won't stop until that goal is reached."

He stared at me, a glimmer in his eyes the only sign he'd heard what I said. Then he leaned towards me, our lips almost touching. "Do you know…your strength has always been a powerful aphrodisiac for me?"

I drew in a quick breath.

Despite having known this man for centuries, he still had an effect on me. Meeting him with the same vigor, I whispered softly, "Good to know."

Suddenly, the table shook violently and Eran was on his feet, his body poised for conflict.

Standing over the table with a look of uninhibited disgust was The Warden.

"Mr. Talor…Ms. Tanner. You will keep your hands off each other while on school grounds." His eyes narrowed even further and for a moment it looked as if he were entirely closing them. "Do you understand me?"

Eran, who by this point knew no possible danger could come from The Warden, relaxed his stance. "Not a problem, sir," he replied, holding in a chuckle.

The Warden stepped around the table and came within inches of Eran. Ironically, it was meant to be a movement to impress power over Eran but it failed miserably. At Eran's height, The Warden stood in his shadow making him look like a barking Chihuahua against a Great Dane. He must have realized this because he tilted his head back further so he could look down his nose at Eran. With a great deal of effort, given the cranked position of his neck, he struggled to deliver his threatening message. "You do realize Ms. Beedinwigg's job is on the line here? And that you and Ms. Tanner have a direct correlation to the amount of time she will be able to remain in her current post?"

"Yes, we've been told," Eran replied, showing no sign of uneasiness.

"Don't forget it," he stated snidely before spinning on his heel and marching through the cafeteria and out the door.

Just as it slammed shut, snickers could be heard across the cavernous room. Bridgette Madison, my least favorite person on campus, sat a few tables over, her mouth turned down with loathing. We ignored them all in favor of quietly remaining at our table until lunch was over. It really didn't matter what we did, or if we didn't do anything at all. Eran and I were the source of countless stories of gossip on campus and retained an infamous reputation because of them. That – I was certain - would never end until we left school permanently.

For the remainder of the day an aggravated impatience dominated me. I couldn't recount a single word any of the teachers spoke but I could tell you exactly how slow the clock in each classroom ran. It felt as if time was testing my fortitude.

Meeting Eran after each class, and more specifically after last period, immediately improved my day. Still, it was a very good thing Eran drove my Harley back to the house since not a single red stop light registered with me.

Dinner was brief: a few slices of bread, a thick piece of leftover ham, and a handful of potato chips. Felix thoroughly disapproved but was told to pipe down by Rufus, which didn't cause him to pipe down and instead set off an argument. However, it achieved the desired effect with Felix more focused on Rufus than on the meal Eran and I were practically inhaling.

On his last bite, Eran told them that we would be studying in my room tonight, not wanting to disturb the household by dominating the kitchen with textbooks. They waved him off in favor of continuing their argument, which had evolved to something on whether cheese could be considered a main food group all its own.

The truth was we had no intention of studying. This was Eran's ploy to keep our other three housemates unaware of our nightly plans. I didn't fully agree and mentioned it on our way up the stairs.

"There's no harm in letting them know the truth," I whispered, wanting to only raise my voice to normal levels once we were inside my room.

Eran closed the door almost entirely, leaving it open a crack to abide by Ezra's house rules, and then turned to me. "And there's no harm in keeping it from them either, is there?"

He was already at my bed, lifting the mattress, and pulling out my leather suit. Holding it up, he paused, his rushed pace halting for just a moment. "I really enjoy watching you move in this…"

I sighed and swiped it out of his hand. "It's not meant to be seductive."

"Intended or not…it is," he replied with his signature smirk.

I shook my head at him, retrieving and throwing him the book of dossiers, which he opened to review the next

Fallen One's summary. Although, we'd read through it earlier, a brush up couldn't hurt.

I, on the other hand, began to unbutton my jeans. The moment he saw this, he spun around and faced the balcony doors. Before I could mention how ridiculous his prudence was, he held up his hand, motioning me to listen.

"You may disagree all you want but, as a gentleman who has seen you naked just once, I am compelled to preserve your chastity."

"Uh huh…until you take it from me again," I pointed out.

"I didn't say virginity, Magdalene," he corrected. "I've already taken that."

The mere mention of our wedding night together made my cheeks burn as the memory of it coursed through my mind. As it turned out, I wasn't the only one affected by the remembrance of it.

While dressing, my eyes stayed on Eran, whose hands clenched against the surge of emotion running through him. He breathed through his nose, too, in an effort to release the pent up aggravation of not having been able to enjoy me in the same way since then.

I couldn't imagine what it took for a man to live over a century without having been given another night with his wife but it certainly said a great deal about his patience and persistence.

I cleared my throat, more to get his attention than to remove an obstruction. "Granted this isn't the best time to ask but I've wondered why it is you've never…we've never been together again?"

His back straightened and I got the distinct impression I'd offended him.

Tightly, he replied, "You're correct. This isn't the best time to ask."

"I'm sorry for bringing it up. I didn't mean to…"

He relaxed a little before replying, "I'm not insulted, Magdalene. I'm…frustrated."

Although I wondered what he meant, I didn't bother asking. He'd already mentioned this wasn't a good time to open up the conversation. But, I made a mental note to ask him about it later tonight and then finished dressing in silence. Once I'd attached the last weapon to my suit, I announced, "I'm ready."

Without turning, he strode towards the balcony doors and pushed them open. On the way, he collected his sword from the corner of my room, where he typically left it tilted against the wall, easily available in case it was needed.

I stepped up beside him and prepared to take flight. It was early spring which meant shortened days. This was good as it gave us the cover of darkness.

"You're certain you want to do this?" he asked, refusing to look at me, and instead surveying the street below to ensure it was vacant. It was a reasonable thing to do but his behavior told me something else. I got the sense my question had done more damage than I'd realized and I made a mental note that this was a sensitive subject for Eran.

"Yes, I'm ready."

"François Gerard will be well guarded. As a diplomat, he'll have a full security detail. We'll need to perform surveillance prior to entry."

"I understand."

He didn't respond immediately and yet he didn't move to leave the balcony. A few long seconds passed before he announced with strain in his voice, "I'll explain tonight…once our mission is over…why we've been together only once."

Then he stepped forward, leapt up on to the balcony railing, and sprang into the air.

I shook the uncomfortable feeling left behind from our conversation and then followed him up and through the night sky.

Our flight was quick. The brisk pumping of Eran's appendages for the beginning leg of it told me that emotions conjured by my question lingered with him. Only towards the end did his flight become more paced, steady.

Eran, being the better navigator of the two of us, led the way to François Gerard's residence, a brownstone in the heart of downtown Washington, DC. As he'd warned, there was a car parked outside the front door and armed men stood just inside.

Eran motioned towards the rooftop and I followed him there, settling down beside him.

"You go through the door," he said pointing towards the one designed for roof access. "By the time you find Gerard, I'll be at your side."

"What are you going to do?"

"I'm going to take care of the guards. Now go," he commanded just before springing into the air.

I opened the door and found a narrow chute, which I descended quickly. Opening the interior door, I found the hall lights to be on and orchestral music playing faintly from behind a closed door at the end of the hall.

My radar was already telling me that François was nearby and as I approached the music it grew more declarative. My senses were already acting up, picking up tobacco and expensive cologne. The swoosh of soft fabric told me that he had made a brief shift but hadn't actually moved from his spot. I knew this by the sound decibel and I knew by the angle of it that he must be across the room from the door.

True to his word, by the time I was standing at the door leading to François Gerard, Eran was at my side.

"All clear," he motioned.

I nodded and then kicked in the door.

Inside, François stood at the window, a pipe in his mouth, a silk robe draped over his slender body. It appeared he had been waiting for us and I got the impression he'd just watched with mild amusement Eran derail his security entourage.

"Humans…" he stated with repulsion. "Useless…"

His accent, interestingly, was undefined and I judged this to be because he had been a world traveler for the last four hundred years. It made him perfectly suited to become a diplomat.

"Have you noticed how they chew?" His lip curled up in disgust. "Without class…spitting…slavering…"

I stood before a man who had worked for kings, barons, presidents and who had been given the opportunity to forge alliances between competing nations. He had instead concocted reasons for conflict and it was easy to see how he could do so without questions of morality.

"Maybe if you had spent your time helping them-" I began but he didn't allow me the chance to finish.

"There is no helping them. They are extinct," he said with brazen hinting. He turned to face Eran and me then, one hand on his pipe, the other tucked through the silk belt around his waist which kept his robe closed. "That is what you fail to see, Maggie. You are defending an extinct race. They are the English Wolf, the Dodo bird, the Caspian Tiger…though far easier to kill. I know as I personally slaughtered the last one of its kind. Just as these creatures had their time, the humans have had theirs. And yet you fight so tenaciously to defend them. My dear Maggie…why?"

"So you know who I am…" I stated, ignoring his question.

He smiled sympathetically as one does with a child. "I know everything about you. I take special notice of my enemies, paying good money to be kept informed. You did an impressive job throughout Nevada, Arizona, ridding it of my cohorts." He smiled at me then, the pipe still protruding from his mouth. "Claden Markett, I thought, might get the best of you though." He waited for me to admit the truth and then openly acknowledged it himself. "It was good that your guardian was there to assist…"

"Don't underestimate her abilities, Gerard," Eran said, coming to my defense.

"Or do," I said, playfully suggesting he let his guard down. All of us knew it wouldn't happen.

He smiled at Eran and me. "I've heard you have…shall we say…a unique relationship. A guardian and ward who argue as much as the two of you should possibly be separated? Yet you've remained together…" His eyes took on a knowing gleam. "It makes me curious…"

"Feel free to speculate," I muttered, my attention was now focused on the hand looped around his robe's belt. It appeared to be flexing, preparing for movement.

I wondered if Eran saw it too.

"There's no need for it," said François. "I have a full account of your clandestine love affair. While I've kept that account to myself, it has kept me pleasantly entertained on many evenings."

Eran stepped forward, fury radiating from him, prepared to defend my honor. But he stopped himself, which I knew was the result of his promise to allow me the victory of the kill.

"You couldn't have believed it would remain a secret forever…" François suggested, emboldened by Eran's halt. Then he must have seen something – a flinch, a blink, the whiff of an uncertain expression – because he added, "You did…foolish lovers. It is no wonder you relate so well to humans. You think like them."

François casually took a slight puff from his pipe and then changed the subject to something far more concerning. "In fact, your love for each other is the very reason why I've made preparations. I've known that it would only be a matter of time before you reached me on your list...your book of dossiers."

Despite my best efforts, I recoiled. François did keep himself well informed.

"So I've informed your kind, the Alterums, of your efforts to annihilate my kind." He paused and stared thoughtfully at the ceiling. "I believe they understood the consequences of my message."

Eran, clearly sensing the danger hidden in François's discourse, stepped forward then. "Stop speaking in circles, Gerard. Explain yourself."

François scoffed, offended by Eran's tone, but he answered nonetheless. "I've informed the Alterums of the dangers in allowing your lover's hunting to continue. Having delivered the message personally, I can reassure you that it was taken seriously."

Eran glanced at me, though I couldn't be sure why. I refused to move my focus from the hand, still flexed and waiting, at François waist.

"Since then," he went on, "I've been waiting for your arrival. Although I have to admit, Eran, I'm slightly disappointed. I believed you would know me well enough to bring your army instead of your lover. This battle will be won far too easily."

The hand at François's waist suddenly flew aside, releasing his robe, and exposing a cache of weapons. Taking a saber and a sword from their sheaths, François strode across the room but never completed his advance. Midway across, his appendages appeared from beneath his robe, lifting him into the air and flapping so aggressively they sliced the silk robe to shreds.

François hung in the air, chest barren, arms extended, weapons readied, a hideous grin stretching across his face.

"Thank you...for allowing me the honor of killing you," he stated with genuine sincerity.

Eran and I were airborne immediately, our own weapons ready. By that point it was too late. The trap had been sprung and we entered it easily.

At the very moment we reached a certain height, blades flew from opposing sides of the room, slicing through the air and catching both Eran and myself.

It was all the distraction François needed. He was suddenly on top of me, slamming me against the door I'd just entered. His saber was at my neck just as quickly, the cold steel coming to rest against my skin.

It didn't stay there long. He was thrown backwards as Eran took hold of François's body and hurled him at the window he'd just been peering through.

It cracked against his weight, remaining intact enough for him to launch from it and back towards Eran.

Another trigger was released, sliding aside hidden compartments in the ceiling, and blades dropped from above, daggers ready to impale any of us who came too close. One nearly nicked Eran but he caught their movement in time and shifted from its path.

François still had his arrogant grin when he reached Eran. As they collided, spinning backwards, head over heels, I came up from behind, enraged and ready to end that grin.

Eran, facing me, sent me a signal, a slight lift of his chin towards the ceiling where the daggers gleamed. I caught his motion and prepared myself.

Suddenly, Eran's hips rotated, swinging his leg out and across François's, causing him to tumble upwards. Picking up the momentum, I grabbed François's shoulders and shoved him upward impaling him on the daggers designed to protect him.

He hung there, steel points protruding from various places throughout his body, blood sliding down the points and dripping on the hardwood floors. His head hung limply towards the ground, eyes closed, breathing raspy.

"Well done…" he exhaled. The last of his breath released just as his appendages slipped back inside his body.

Eran, drew in a deep breath and turned to me with pride. "He was correct…Well done."

"Thanks for the assistance," I said, turning back to François. "But I'm not looking forward to the clean up…"

A drip of blood landed on the floor, splattering into the growing pool.

"Better than having to deal with an international investigation," Eran commented, already moving in to peel François's body from the ceiling.

After the room was put back in order, Eran approached the window that François had been peering from when we'd arrived and the same one his body had slammed against during the fight, leaving a halo of cracks around the center. Without hesitation, Eran broke the glass entirely, allowing varying slivers of it to fall to the ground outside François's townhouse. Eran then took François's body and soared out the window to the spiked fence lining the property below. He then impaled François on to it directly below the window.

His solution was simple, almost elegant: The authorities would deduce his guards were delinquent in their duties while François had committed suicide.

I met Eran outside.

"Ready for another?" I asked, recalling the dossier of the next Fallen One.

"Tomorrow…tomorrow we'll up the ante to two."

"And from there, one additional each night until sunrise," I proposed.

Eran simply shook his head and I knew it was because he didn't know whether to chastise or ignore me. He chose the latter and crouched, ready to spring into the sky.

"Shall we?" he asked.

I nodded and followed him.

For the moment, I was fine with returning directly to New Orleans. There was something else plaguing me, an unanswered question. Once we were safely back in my room on Magazine Street I wasn't going to hesitate to ask.

New Orleans was damper than Washington, D.C. I recognized this before landing on the banister of my balcony and stepping down to the floorboards. Eran, who followed behind for safety reasons, did the same and came up beside me.

It was silent on our street, a stark contrast to the wind that had whistled in my ears caused by the speed of flight only moments earlier. The silence was calming and a welcoming part of our night.

Instead of entering my room, I allowed my appendages to slip back in place and took a seat on one of the plastic chairs at my banister. Eran did the same.

We watched the night, listening to the Cajun music play down the street and the foghorn on the edge of Lake Pontchartrain, our feet propped on the railing, enjoying the change of pace.

It was surreal to realize we had just been engaged in a battle with an international diplomat, one that royalty and the elite had relied on for so many years, and one that we had ultimately killed. It was freeing, and odd, to know that his colleagues would no longer be able to rely on his honed skills of manipulation to cause catastrophic outcomes. They would now need to rely on their own inept abilities, reduced in practice by a few hundred years.

As we were each contemplating the revelation that we had changed the future for the better, I glanced at Eran, who was staring at his hands clasped in his lap. While he didn't appear to be deep in thought, I still had the uncomfortable feeling I was going to disturb him. I debated it only a moment and then my curiosity won out. "You mentioned earlier...when I asked about why you'd never made an advance towards me again after our wedding night…you said you were frustrated. You also said you'd explain it to me…"

He grinned to himself. "I was waiting for you to bring it up."

"Then you must be ready to answer it," I implied, although cautiously.

His head dipped forward in a weak nod. "I am."

I waited for him to continue, watching as he prepared himself with a deep inhale before explaining.

"My ability to regenerate…to heal quickly, has been both a blessing and a curse. It has kept me alive…here in this dimension…long after you had gone and allowed me to hunt our enemies on my own. While I understand this is the way it must be, it is a source of…inconvenience to say the least. I would prefer to…well, you know what I prefer."

"No, I really don't," I urged him on.

He blinked in surprise. "To be with you, here or in the afterlife."

That simple reassurance caused a swell of warmth to grow in my chest, as if a blanket had been wrapped around me.

Noting my content smile, he went on. "As you know, instead, I dwell here until my body grows weary and erodes, until it can no longer sustain life, and I then die and return to the afterlife where I can exist with you again… at least until you choose to return here," his hand swept absentmindedly out towards the street. "That is how it had always been. Then something changed between us. We admitted our love for each other and we became husband and wife. That night…our night together…" He paused to meet my eyes and I couldn't deny the intense passion flowing behind his. "That was the most incredible experience of my existence. Nothing else comes close." His head dipped again and he fell back in to his world of memories. "I was, in fact, hoping to experience it again the night you went missing. The night you were taken and...and tortured by Abaddon and his followers...in the clearing outside Gettysburg." He drew in a deep breath, waiting until his thoughts cleared before continuing. "And then you were gone, murdered by my own hands-"

"Eran...stop," I pleaded but he continued on.

"Murdered by me." He grimaced, his body suddenly shaking at the memory. "And when I saw you again in the afterlife-"

"I remember...I was there waiting for you," I said, hoping to transition his memories to something positive.

It didn't work.

"There was no ignoring what I'd done. That feeling...the stark awareness...the memory of hurting you was...It was too much."

"And you withdrew from me...I remember." I placed my hand on him, a soft but firm hold that I hoped would be comforting.

"And so you did something I would never blame you for...you returned here...as a reborn, a human, forgetting your past. Escaping it...and escaping me."

"No...never..." I stated, aghast.

"It is all right. I understand," he said, his sincerity undeniable.

"No, you don't," I declared softly. "I came back here not to escape, not to forget you. I would never," I swallowed back the lump that had grown in my throat. "I would never want to leave you, Eran. I came back as a reborn to finally fulfill my need to experience life as a human. Memory loss is simply a side effect of it. And I chose that specific time to return because you needed space...time to recover from me."

He spun towards me, his eyes wide with disbelief. "All this time...that's what you thought? That I needed space?"

"Yes..." I whispered, confusion washing over me.

Releasing a quick breath, his shoulders sagged. "Never, Magdalene. You are my life…" His eyes rose to mine then, amazed and perplexed at the same time. "I think…we need to work on our communication…"

Despite the situation and the bitter reality we'd just unearthed, his response, so understated, caused a tickle, one that quickly turned to laughter. Within seconds, a smile broke through the sorrow etched in the gorgeous contours of his face, and a moment later he was laughing alongside me.

When our laughter calmed, I drew in a breath and then answered my own question. "So that's why we have never been together again…There has never been an appropriate time to do it…"

"Exactly."

"So much time…" I mused sadly.

We fell silent, computing what we could have gained if we could have remained together, if we could have simply acknowledged our feelings with each other.

Then he stood halfway, rotated, and slid me from my chair on to his lap. Enjoying the feel of his solid body, I hugged him closer before asking, "You've been enticed by my presence for…?"

"Over a century," he calculated quickly and then shrugged before confessing, "Well, longer than that. I was in love with you well before I announced it. I just wouldn't admit it to myself."

I considered how much time that must feel like and, after understanding it, I was compelled to speak gently when asking my next question. "Any ideas on how to make up for lost time?"

His eyes were still on the rooftops across the street when he smiled. "I'm working on that…It's all about finding the perfect moment."

"The perfect..." I said, aghast. "How about we forget the perfect moment and take advantage of the time we have?"

"Breakfast in the morning, folding laundry, grocery shopping. All of these can be rushed. Lovemaking, Magdalene, should not be. The planning of it included."

I slumped back in my chair. "Now, you're being a tease."

He pushed himself up with a groan. "And for once, I'm not trying to be."

His hand took mine and he guided me to my feet. "At the risk of leaving you enticed," he smirked at the use of my word, "we need to get to bed. You have a calculus test tomorrow."

I didn't hold back my groan. "How is it we are tasked with saving the world...while still being required to maintain a high grade point average?"

"Just lucky, I suppose," he said with a grin.

We were in the middle of my room by that point. His hands had dropped to my hips, the unspoken desire to simply cast aside Eran's plan to wait hung in the air. His lopsided grin told me that he was contemplating it too. Only after he leaned in and grazed his lips across my forehead did I know that his better judgment – the one I continually fought against – had won again.

"Good night, my love."

I sighed deeply, trying to express my dissatisfaction. "Good night."

He glanced over his shoulder on the way out of the room, his smoldering stare taking me in until we could see each other no longer.

6. SUMMONED

As the rest of the week passed, Eran allowed me to eliminate an additional Fallen One each night, accumulating to a nightly total of four.

Oddly, I noticed that while I began each hunt with vigor, a powerful desire to annihilate as many enemies as possible, at the end of the night, on our final flight home, there was no closure. There was no peace. I only secretly noted the thickness of the remaining pages of the book containing the Fallen Ones' dossiers. Although it slimmed each night, it told me there were multitudes left, and I still craved to find them.

While this constant reminder weighed on me, I went about my classes with relative ease. Having the ability to recall multiple lifetimes on earth allowed me a certain measure of aptitude during tests. Since I'd never particularly struggled with my grades, scores came back relatively the same (although slightly higher at times) without a single mention from my teachers. The only issues I'd encountered were turning in papers on time.

In fact, Eran and I were hastily finishing a report on the disintegration of a tribe in South America when a knock came to the front door.

He and I were at the kitchen table with Ezra in her office down the hall. She was the first to address the fact we had a visitor, entering the hallway and heading for the door. Rufus and Felix came down the stairs just as she passed by the landing. Eran and I, however, stayed at the table.

The door opened to a quiet, firm voice that reminded me of an old Native American saying: Talk softly, carry big stick.

The instant that voice drifted into the kitchen, Eran's head, which had fallen back towards the book in front of him, snapped up.

"What?" I whispered.

He shook his head, telling me that it wasn't safe – or appropriate - to explain now, and continued listening intently.

Ezra responded kindly to the visitor, as was her usual way. "Please, come in. We have coffee brewed."

Heavy footsteps followed shortly after, growing louder until they reached the kitchen door.

Eran was already facing the entrance, intense concern etched in his features. I had to spin around, however, to get a look at the one of the few guests to ever set foot in our home.

He towered over the rest of us, Rufus included, having to bend at the waist to avoid hitting the top of the kitchen door frame as he passed by. When he stood to his full height again, his skull barely missed the kitchen ceiling. The rest of him was equally as massive. His jaw, thick and knobby, jutted outward above a neck that rivaled the size of a horse. His arms hung limply beside him, ones that could have been mistaken for tree trunks if they weren't clothed in billowing cotton sleeves. Two incisions were made in his shirt directly between the shoulder blades and immediately my curiosity grew.

He was one of us.

His eyes stood out too, though not for any of the reasons given.

They were pinned on me, unwavering and unashamedly evaluating.

I held his gaze and stood, walking directly up to him. "Maggie," I announced, extending my hand.

"Peter," he said with a European accent I couldn't place. When he took my hand, it engulfed mine, the entirety of it disappearing all the way to above my wrist.

Eran was suddenly beside me and I got the sense it was for the purpose of protection, which confused me. Peter wasn't a Fallen One. My radar was at rest.

"Peter, it has been a while," Eran said cordially, though an astute ear would have picked up the fact it was laced with uneasiness. I glanced at him, wondering when Eran could have met this man when I had no recollection of it. It was a rare occasion when Eran left my side. "What brings you to New Orleans?"

"An assembly," he replied, coolly.

The room's tension suddenly escalated. Glances were exchanged. Breaths were held. Ezra set the mug she'd been pouring coffee in onto the counter, not bothering to finish filling it.

When Rufus broke the silence, saying what the rest of us were thinking – at least in his own way – the tension rose again. "Ah, bloody hell," he muttered.

"Language," Ezra cautioned.

"Well, for once, I agree with him," said Felix.

It was telling that Rufus didn't flinch at that acknowledgement.

Ezra stepped forward, determined to calm the situation with reason. "An assembly to discuss what in particular?"

"The topic will be unveiled when the assembly commences. Your presence is requested in London."

She nodded slowly, thoughtfully. "When?"

"Tomorrow evening."

Ezra's lifted an eyebrow but still her reply was agreeable. "We'll be there."

Peter nodded, and moved to leave, though not before his attention paused on Eran and then on me. It was quick but it didn't go unnoticed. There was a purpose behind the movement, a sense of curiosity, a lingering thought, a suspicion of something maybe?

Then he was gone down the hall, his long legs carrying him faster than a human and swifter than most Alterums.

The mug intended for Peter somehow found its way to Ezra's hands and, as the front door closed behind Peter, we stood silently in the kitchen until Rufus returned from escorting our guest out.

"How is it that you all know him and I don't?" I asked Eran, perplexed that I could be the only one without an introduction until now.

"I believe we've only met him once before," said Eran, waiting until the rest had shown their agreement. "Peter was sent out to assemble Alterums on only one other occasion. You were preoccupied, so to speak, during that time."

My brow creased in confusion. "Preoccupied?"

"You chose to deliver messages rather than address the call for an assembly…which was called, in fact, to address the very thing that was – at the time – hunting you. You may remember it…You were in London and it found you in a quiet alleyway-"

"The Elsic…" I murmured.

"Exactly. We had been called to assemble to be made aware that it had escaped and to form a hunting party. When I discovered the purpose behind our congregating I left and went in search of you."

"And nominated yourself my guardian," I recalled.

The side of Eran's mouth lifted in a gentle smile. "Because it was abundantly clear to me by that point you needed one."

I ignored that assertion in favor of asking, "Do you think another Elsic has escaped?"

"Possibly," said Ezra. "It was only a few weeks ago we found the Elsics had been released from imprisonment." Everyone simultaneously bristled at the remembrance of it, which Ezra noticed but didn't deter her from summing up her thoughts. "While most stayed in the caves in favor of getting a piece of Maggie, one or two may have sought freedom."

Rufus crossed his arms and leaned back against the refrigerator, deliberating. "There's been rumors floatin' 'bout too many humans dyin' out 'round 'bout Paris…"

"That's right," Felix exclaimed, nodding furiously. "I heard it too."

Rufus's brow creased in suspicion. "Who woulda told you?"

Felix's jaw fell open. "I have informants too, you know."

"Ain't seen any of 'em…" he challenged.

"Well, who told you?" Felix retorted.

"Coupla lads I keep in contact with back from the orphanage," said Rufus offhanded. "Who're yer…whatdya call 'em? Informants?"

Felix's mouth pinched closed for a moment. "You don't know any of them."

"Just like I said…I ain't met any of 'em." Rufus was purposefully riling Felix, and enjoying it.

"All right, boys," Ezra stepped forward, her warning and the very size of her creating a barrier between the two. "There are more important matters at hand. Such as…will we be attending this assembly?"

The room went quiet as we stared apprehensively at each other.

I opened my mouth to speak, a slight movement but one that Eran caught. His hand came up to my elbow to quiet me before I could release a word in favor of going and I glanced at him, questioning. Yet, if he saw my confused reaction, he didn't respond to it. His attention remained on the others.

No one else seemed to notice us because not a second passed when the three of our housemates agreed simultaneously to attend. When Eran and I didn't confirm we'd be joining them, they looked to us and waited.

"Aren't you going?" asked Felix, as if it were abominable that we would choose to stay behind now that the rest had made their decision.

"They'll be staying here," Ezra said, having already made her assessment.

Felix's head swiveled back and forth between Ezra and Eran. "Staying? And miss the biggest assembly of this century? Of the past seven centuries?"

"That's right," Eran replied plainly. "We'll be staying."

Rufus, too, seemed to be surprised but he kept it to himself.

"Tomorrow morning, gentlemen," said Ezra, "tea and crumpets for breakfast."

"I can handle that..." said Felix, contemplating.

Ezra drew in a deep breath and stifled a yawn. "I think I'll get a little rest. Tomorrow is sure to be a big day. Lots of reunions..."

Felix gasped and made a quick leap in excitement. "A reunion...Of course...Patrick will be there...Johnathon...Ricardo...And I'll have to visit with Ellings..." His voice trailed behind him as he left the kitchen making a mental list of who he'd need to catch up with while in England.

Rufus watched him leave, frowning. "Blimey…Little bloke's got no idea what's in store fer 'im. If the reason fer us congregatin' is as big as I think, won't be time fer chattin'."

"If nothing," said Ezra, briefly placing a kindly hand on Rufus's shoulder as she passed by him on her way out of the kitchen, "it will be an interesting excursion."

None of us had any idea how true that statement would be.

She stopped at the door, absentmindedly. "We'll be back as soon as possible."

"We know," replied Eran.

I realized Rufus was watching us now and turned to meet his stare. "Eran and I will be fine," I stated. "There aren't many Fallen Ones in the area any longer." I didn't bother mentioning it was because I'd eradicated them from most of the southern states.

"I know it." He shrugged, embarrassed to have been caught with his thoughts so openly transparent. "If anythin', you'd be the ones savin' us." We chuckled at this and then he headed for the stairs.

I waited until hearing his bedroom door close before I spun to face Eran. "So, are you going to tell me why you stopped us from leaving with them?" I asked, perplexed at his behavior.

He responded with his signature smirk. "Why? Don't you trust me?"

"Absolutely and irrevocably. But I'm curious as to why we're staying. It's only the second time in history Alterums have assembled."

"Yes, and the first time they assembled we missed it and all went well," he reasoned.

"True…" I conceded. "But it doesn't mean we couldn't attend this one. Everyone will be there, including our housemates."

"That's correct. Everyone will be there," he replied patiently. "And we'll have the house to ourselves."

"Yes, we will," I agreed.

He waited for me to come to the same conclusion he had several minutes prior. "And we'll have the house to ourselves," I said again, allowing the reality of it to sink in.

Eran had a glimmer in his eyes as his arms slipped around me. "The house will be empty…and we will be alone, Mrs. Talor."

As my excitement grew, I felt a smile creep up without consciously initiating it.

"What did you have in mind?" I asked.

"You wouldn't want me to spoil it by telling you…" he insinuated.

My eyelids fell to a playful glower.

"You have nothing to worry about, Mrs. Talor. I have it covered."

Maybe it was the word 'cover' or the realization that in less than a full day Eran and I would be intimate again. Whatever the reason, my mind was suddenly focused on my closet and the fact that I had nothing but jeans and t-shirts to seduce my husband.

"Magdalene?" Eran was saying, pulling me back to him. "I'm a little concerned by your expression. If you don't want to do this, we can-"

Already, the pain of giving up this opportunity was evident in him.

I cut him off before he could finish his thought. "No…" Then I repeated the word more vigorously for emphasis. "No."

"Oh, I see," he replied quietly, saddened. "You want to take the time to hunt."

My head pulled back a bit surprised that the idea hadn't even occurred to me. That was a good sign. My obsession hadn't entirely taken over. Eran still came first.

"Not at all. I'm not going to allow a Fallen One to intrude on our night together. I was…" I laughed at myself, slightly uncomfortable. "I just need to find a lingerie shop."

Eran blinked. "That's what you're concerned with?"

"Well, yes. You haven't seen me…unclothed…in over a century. I want you to enjoy what you see…when you finally see it."

He tilted his head back and released a bellow of laughter. "Magdalene, you can wear whatever you want but it isn't simply your body that I'm attracted to – although it certainly is attractive. It's you in your entirety that I love. No piece of clothing is going to change that."

My lips wavered as I tried to subdue a smile and failed. "Nonetheless…"

His body shook with another bout of laughter and then settled. "I am so in love with you." By the time he said those words, he was calm again. The only signs of emotion were in his eyes, which were blazing with passion, and the ache of desire that seemed to radiate from him with such intensity it took our breaths away.

"If I kiss you now, I won't be able to stop myself," he concluded in a murmur, more to restrain himself than to disclose what he was thinking.

"I wouldn't stop you if you did," I admitted softly.

He drew in a stifled breath, his chest swelling with the craving to be with me right here, right now.

His gentlemanly side won out, though it was clearly after a strong internal struggle, and he dropped his hands from my waist.

Clenching his teeth against the pain of his decision, he stated, "When we're alone…When we're alone tomorrow…"

I nodded, absorbed in my own struggle to contain the passion racing through me.

He took my hand and led me upstairs, stopping at my door to kiss me good night...on my forehead, unable to trust himself with anything more.

"Tomorrow..." he whispered against my skin, gently tightening his grip on my hand.

When he released it, we turned and stepped into our rooms, each of us closing our doors much slower than usual, having no idea, no premonition of what was to come.

In fact, I fell asleep quickly and before long I was back in the Hall of Records, where I awoke every night without fail. This time, however, I didn't stay long.

Something forced me awake only a few hours later. I found myself back in my body, laying bundled beneath the covers of my bed in New Orleans. Unable to immediately detect whatever had disturbed my sleep, I listened motionless, barely breathing. I heard nothing but silence, saw no movement, and felt only the weight of my bedcovers. Then it came.

A chime I'd heard just one time previous rang through the house. Yesterday, when Peter had arrived, he'd used the doorbell and it was the sound I was hearing now.

We had another visitor.

I stood and slipped on a pair of jeans and a sweatshirt before heading downstairs.

Eran was already at the door, which was now closed, and standing before him was Ms. Beedinwigg and Mr. Hamilton, both wearing serious, concerned expressions. While Eran had apparently just gotten out of bed, wearing only jeans and displaying a muscular bare chest, our guests were dressed as if it were the middle of the day and they were out running errands. A quick glance at the clock on the fireplace mantle told me it was 3 o'clock in the morning so clearly that wasn't the case.

"We have reason to believe it involves Maggie's efforts to kill the Fallen Ones," she was saying as I made it down the last step. When she caught sight of me, she crossed the room in two brief paces. "Maggie, we need to speak with you."

The urgency in her tone did not sit well with me.

We returned to the parlor, Eran coming to sit directly next to me, a hand placed protectively on one of my knees.

"Eran has informed us that you know an assembly has been called."

"Yes, that's right."

"What you may not know is that they will be discussing your actions against the Fallen Ones."

"Yes," I replied again, just as plainly.

The three of them shared glances before Eran asked, "Did you know about this?"

"I didn't know about the assembly."

"But you knew something," Eran plied, knowing me too well to give up so easily.

I shrugged. "Someone mentioned the Alterums weren't happy about my work."

Eran's eyes widened as he moved back for a better look at me. "And you didn't bother to mention it…"

"No, it wasn't qualified information," I explained.

His lips pinched closed in a clear indication he was irritated with that justification but he didn't respond to it.

"Well," Mr. Hamilton drew in a breath, seemingly attempting to ease his distress, "it's qualified now."

No one spoke for a long minute.

"Since it is, do you plan to continue your hunts?" asked Ms. Beedinwigg, clearly nervous about my response.

When I didn't respond, Eran prompted me. "Magdalene?"

I felt the side of my mouth turn down in a frown as I gazed towards the unlit fireplace. "Somewhere out there are Fallen Ones who are hurting the innocent. They have been allowed to walk freely inflicting harm and perpetrating acts of violence for their own amusement.

We've allowed them to do so because of guardians like Eran. Now the guardians themselves are at risk. How can you ask me to stop something that should have been started so long ago?"

No one could deny my argument made sense but Eran did make one point that clearly influenced the outcome of our situation. "What we do not know is whether they'll be discussing in favor or in opposition to Magdalene's actions."

"That is why I'll be there," Ms. Beedinwigg stated. "To ensure they find in favor of your hunting."

My eyes were suddenly on her. "You'll be there at the assembly?" I asked, astounded.

"I'll be working behind the scenes, with my relations who can deliver the message to the assembly. Humans aren't permitted in the event."

Mr. Hamilton spoke up then, asking for reassurance on the one topic I hoped would be forgotten. It really was too bad he excelled in the art of damage control. "Will you refrain from your hunts until the assembly has made their decision?"

Again, I felt the frown rise up. Irritation riled me and I had to draw a breath to calm myself. He was asking me to decide between my obsession and the want of others. The challenge I had was that my obsession was, at its core, meant to help those others. It was painful to witness those acting in self-defeat. Still, my hunts seemed to be causing more trouble for those I'm helping than our actual enemies and that, in some small way, defeated my purpose.

"A few days rest couldn't hurt..." I said, noticing the sadness in me as I wavered in my mission.

Yet, it did the job. There was an obvious relief felt around the room.

"Excellent," said Mr. Hamilton. "Ms. Beedinwigg, I have a jet waiting for you at the airport."

She stood and headed for the door as we followed.

"Maggie, Eran, it may help to have your presence at the assembly when they call the decision to vote."

"Or it may hinder it," said Eran. "I'd rather not take that chance. I think your message will be effective if you're able to deliver it through those with authority."

"I have a few in mind..." she hinted coyly. With her hand on the door knob, she turned to me. "Alterums, as a group, can be equally as defensive as the Fallen Ones, if threatened. As much of a challenge it will be, please restrain from changing your mind while I'm gone."

"I won't," I reassured her. "Eran, I'm sure, will make certain of it."

He smiled mischievously as she left, which must have been some measure of comfort to her.

As the door closed and Eran and I were alone again, I said, "I can't sleep, too much adrenaline, and I don't want to be alone."

Eran's eyes gleamed back at me. "You're in luck. I have no pressing engagements."

I smiled and headed back to my room. "The sun will be up, which means so will Ezra."

"If you're suggesting we need to keep our voices down, don't worry. They left an hour ago."

Spinning around, I asked, "We're alone in the house?"

"Yes," he replied not showing a single sign of apprehension at our new found freedom.

I, on the other hand, instantly felt self-conscious. Confidence, I reminded myself as I continued up the stairs. Instinctually, I began to sway my hips with each step and then told myself to stop. It didn't make me feel confident. It made me feel like a floozy. Trying to project self-assurance felt more awkward now than when I wasn't aware of it.

At the top of the stairs, I began to notice the silence surrounding us. There was no brewing sound coming from the coffeemaker in the kitchen; Rufus's snoring wasn't rumbling through the house; Felix's light wasn't on beneath his bedroom door. All common signs of our house being occupied were gone and the realization of it weighed heavily on me.

This was something I'd wanted, encouraged, and now it was here and I didn't know what to do with it.

Just as we reached my bedroom door, Eran's whispered voice came from behind me. "Relax, Magdalene. This evening…you'll need to wait until this evening." His hand came over my shoulder and pushed my door open for me.

I laughed at myself as I heard his chuckle from behind. He then took my hand, walked passed me, and led me to the bed. Laying down and pulling me beside him may have caused my heart to leap into my throat if he hadn't confirmed his plans for intimacy were set for the end of the day rather than the beginning.

Instead, we rested next to each other as the sun rose and gradually brightened my room. I kept my eyes closed, nudged against his solid chest, enjoying every moment of it. Occasionally, his fingers drifted slightly over my skin, along my arm, down the curve of my neck, along my collarbone, connecting with me in a way other than I'd anticipated on my walk up the stairs, though one just as sensual. My body responded with shudders, uncontrollable messages telling him that he was successful in his temptations.

At some point, I felt his breath tickle my neck as he murmured, "We should get to The Square soon."

I groaned and stretched, allowing my arms to fall across his body. "Is it that time already?"

"It is…" he affirmed. My eyes were still closed but I could hear the laughter in his voice. Evidently, he enjoyed knowing that his teasing had an impact. He rolled out of bed and headed towards his room. "Downstairs in twenty minutes?"

"Thirty…today."

He chuckled and left my room. I then dressed, slower than usual, and met Eran downstairs. He handed me a cup of coffee as I entered the kitchen, which I guzzled until empty. We were at The Square a few minutes later.

Instead of lugging my chairs and sign on my Harley Davidson, I chose to simply take a seat on the edge of the wall in my usual spot. Without my sign informing tourists I was actually a vendor, it restricted the number of customers. Not that it mattered much. It was a quiet day with far fewer sightseers than usual. This allowed me and Eran extra time to exchange long looks, each one more alluring than the next so that by the time the sun set I was strongly anticipating whatever Eran had planned.

Over a quick lunch break, I slipped in a store at the edge of the French Quarter that boasted mannequins in lingerie, selecting a translucent black negligee with matching accoutrements. The fact that I exited the store with a bag small enough to carry a jewelry box caused Eran's eyebrows to rise and a wicked smile from me.

On the ride back to the house, he leaned against me more than usual, which I returned with full appreciation. In fact, by the time we reached the shed and locked the bike up, my heart was beating harder and adrenaline coursed through my veins.

Our walk to the kitchen's back door was unhurried and silent and I was certain he was predicting what tonight would bring as much as me.

The house was hushed as we entered; a peculiar sensation and one that reinforced the fact that we were completely alone. My hand was in his as he led me down the hallway and up the stairs to my door, where he paused.

"How much time do you need?" he asked in a hushed tone. His breath had quickened, I noted. He was stifling his excitement as best he could.

"Only a few minutes." I would be as quick as possible.

"All right," he said with a nod.

I turned then and with one hand on my bag of seduction and the other on the door knob I entered my room.

The first thing I detected was that my French doors were open and that a line of Alterums stood just inside, their backs hunched, their wings extended. The next thing I noticed was the sound of Alterums racing down both ends of the hallway…directly towards Eran.

7. ASSEMBLY

The Alterums charged me as I stopped just inside my door. The ones in the hallway barraged Eran.

The fighting was brief. They far outnumbered us and while they were fully prepared we were unsuspecting. Eran and I accomplished a few good hits, taking down three of them total, but in the end they had one contrivance we didn't.

A net made of thick cabled fabric landed over me just as I took down the third attacker. It cinched tight, taking my legs out from under me. Just as my body hit the floor, the cables cutting painfully through my side, I saw another one drape over Eran.

It was dark by the time our attackers had finished restraining us. No words were spoken during the course of the fighting or afterwards, when they heaved the ends of the net over their shoulders and carried us out into the night. Their cause for assault made no sense to me and I knew from experience that demanding a reason for it would go unanswered. These Alterums were on a mission and it didn't include explaining it to us.

As they kidnapped us, Eran in one net and me in another, I tried to judge from the geography below where they were taking us. It wasn't until we reached the Atlantic seaboard did I have an inclination.

Not long after, I found us over London, Big Ben shining brightly against the lightened sky. It was almost dawn so I figured they would need to touch down soon.

Beyond London, in the countryside, directly over the ruins of a disregarded stronghold, they began their descent. As we approached, a part of one turret fell in and away, creating a concealed entrance in the roof. I was dropped through it just as Eran was released in to another across from me.

Gravity drew me hard and fast toward the ground and I landed with a thud, striking the air from my lungs. Heaving, I pulled the net from me, drawing in deep breaths with little relief. The ache of my fall permeated my entire body, a deep powerful awareness that despite my capabilities as an Alterum I still suffered from some limitations here on earth.

After several tries, my lungs began functioning fully again and I stood up, my wings snapping out from behind me.

If anyone dared to be in my vicinity at that time, I'm uncertain whether I could have contained myself. As it was, I was alone, left inside the circular column with no visible doors or windows. I knew of only one exit but despite incredible force and multiple tries no amount of slamming against it would allow it to budge. In the end, I leaned against the cold stone wall, bent on regaining my strength to try again, while wondering if Eran were doing the very same thing.

It was dank and cool where they held me captive, something I appreciated after my exertion in trying to break free. It was also dark with barely enough light to see my feet with the sun that streamed in through various broken stones. Apparently, the turret had once held a staircase, which had long ago been taken down, leaving spaces in the stones. I wondered at what point in history it had turned from a place of defense in to a prison cell.

Flitting lightly, I used my appendages to lift and hover at the same level with one of the gaps. It was large enough for one eye to peer through to a courtyard below.

Not much had changed in the time since it had been a fortress. The ground was still dirt; the stone walls remained with pockmarks from earlier damages. The only sign that it was the twentieth century was where the drawbridge would have been. In its place was a massive steel door.

Evaluating my prison, I realized this was the perfect meeting place for Alterums. The open courtyard allowed for easy access to flight, the stone walls held some form of protection, and the very location of it, in the countryside, gave it some privacy.

The courtyard was empty for a few minutes and then a rutted wood door opened and a woman marched out. Although I wasn't able to hear her, the waving of her hands told me she was barking orders at someone above her, apparently on overlooks I couldn't see from my vantage point.

The woman was portly with a round face and eyes that narrowed even though the sun was behind her. She wore a business suit which appeared out of the norm given her surroundings.

She headed directly for me.

A door, one carved so well in the wall it was impossible to see before, suddenly opened as I landed on the ground.

"Maggie, come with me," she ordered.

Apparently, she was used to others following her commands because she spun around and walked two paces without waiting for my response. When she noticed I wasn't behind her, she turned at the waist.

"Gentlemen, collect her."

Two robust men entered the door, their wings out and ready for conflict. I prepared my stance for the coming fight when one spoke under his breath.

"Please, don't struggle. You'll be with Eran soon."

When I met his eyes, I was surprised to see the pleading in them.

Still, my desire was to struggle, to fight my way out of their grip, and release Eran from the turret across the courtyard. Only the promise that Eran and I would be together again made me withhold my aggression.

As they took my arms and led me across the courtyard, the anger I felt boiled over.

"Need to use your bodyguards?" I hissed at the woman ahead of me. "Don't you have the courage to fight me outright?"

She stopped and her head swiveled halfway towards us. Her face was barely visible, limited by the angle, but I saw the scowl she wore. She scoffed then. It was the only reaction I got from her.

I was led through the same door the woman had entered the courtyard from and down a flight of stairs, through several hallways, and finally down a second flight of stairs. There were no windows at this level, the passageways lit only by flickering candles, so I knew we were underground.

We stopped at a wooden door, the woman's hand on the door knob as she prepared to open it.

"We do not tolerate misbehavior at assembly, Maggie. This is your only warning." The woman said this plainly as if she couldn't care less whether I caused a disturbance or not. She was focused on a mission. In fact, they all seemed to be.

Then I recognized the word she'd mentioned: assembly.

"Eran and I were kidnapped in order to be at the assembly?" I was in shock. "Why didn't you just ask us?"

"You aren't here to vote," she snapped, scornfully. "You're the defendant."

That message sunk in as she opened the door revealing something I had least expected.

An underground circular chamber had been dug below the fortress with steps and seats running the entire circumference of the room from ceiling to floor. Candled chandeliers hung above, casting an eerie light on the hundreds of Alterums mingling loudly below. A thunderous hum of unintelligible noise nearly shook the walls, immediately quieting as the woman led me to the center of the room.

Collectively, those in attendance took their seats, preparing to watch the proceedings to come. While the men released me, the stern woman took a seat at the edge of the stage I now stood on.

A man of twenty stood almost immediately and stepped to the center, though he kept his distance from me.

"Maggie, you may retract your wings. There is no need for them here."

I wasn't so certain and when I kept them extended, he shrugged and turned towards the audience.

"We have been in discussion for nearly twenty four hours. As time has passed, we can be assured that our enemies are amassing. In an effort to come to a decision quickly, Ms. Barrett has suggested we hear directly from the one who has caused the trouble we are in discussions over." He motioned towards the woman who had brought me to the chamber.

I felt my anger flare again and my eyes become slits as I evaluated the woman. She sat proudly defending her decision to take Eran and me as prisoners. Worse, those around her patted her shoulders, supporting her efforts.

"Maggie," said the young man, prompting me.

I stood silent, searching the crowd for Eran, Ezra, Rufus, Felix, anyone who might be in support of me. What I saw instead were frowns, scowls, hatred from my own kind. They were of all ages, all ethnicities, and both genders. Their dress was just as diverse with a smattering of business suits, jeans and sweatshirts, sarongs, Rasta beads and dreadlocks, ushankas, Native American shawls. Every walk of life was represented. The one unifying commonality was that they were all Alterums.

Fernando Vega had been correct. My hunting had drawn attention to myself. Thinking back to his other warning instantly made my wings snap straighter in reaction. He'd mentioned a rumor to deliver me to the Fallen Ones, to sacrifice me for the safety of the rest.

"Maggie," said the young man again, standing briefly to urge me to speak and then taking his seat again beside Ms. Barrett.

"It may help Maggie to hear why she has been brought to the assembly," suggested an older woman whose hair was graying and whose eyes held the sense of mature experience.

Ms. Barrett stood then and entered the stage, glaring briefly at the older woman who'd just spoken as if Ms. Barrett had been directly criticized. Loudly and firmly, she recounted, "She is here before us to defend herself. Alterums are dying at an alarming rate by the hands of Fallen Ones directly because of her actions. Her killings have caused our enemies to unite and attack our kind. We are in danger because of her."

She strolled back to her seat where a book, even from this distance, was easily recognizable to me.

She picked up the Fallen One dossiers, the one the Beedinwigg's had spent generations compiling, and held it up for the chamber to see.

"What I have in my hand is information on every Fallen One ever to have existed. It is Maggie's information source, her way of finding her enemies and destroying them. Its very existence is a danger to us all, an undeniable threat when in the hands of someone like Maggie." As she reeled off her speech, she spun around theatrically until she was again facing Maggie. "And that is why it is better off that we destroy it before it destroys us."

She lifted herself into the air then, swooping up with her arm holding the book high over her head, her legs bent out behind her. When she reached a chandelier above, she did something that spurred equal amounts of panic and rage in me.

She placed my book in the flames.

Thoughtlessly, I soared towards her, thinking of only one objective: retrieve the book.

My body had never moved so fast and yet, despite my incomparable efforts, I didn't reached it, her guards catching me well ahead of time and dragging me back to the earth.

My voice reverberated off the walls, something I didn't consciously identify as coming from me. I released only one word, thick with horror in watching the only thing that gave us an advantage over our enemies become entirely consumed in flames.

"Nooooooooooooooooooo!"

Ms. Barrett spun towards me. "What do you have to say for yourself?"

When I didn't respond, my chest feeling as if it had caved in from the loss of such a valuable resource, she stepped forward to within inches of me. "Nothing?" she beseeched, and it was clear she was almost content with my silence. Again, she addressed the audience. "Maggie has no defense, proven by her refusal to speak up. Yet she has endangered each one of us, provoking our enemies and sparking a war. There is only one solution to this problem. They have told us they will retreat if we give them what they desire, what they have always desired. Give them their nemesis…" Immediately the crowd began to murmur, steadily growing in volume until Ms. Barrett concluded her message in which the chamber erupted in commotion. "Give them Maggie!"

Then it all became clear to me. Ms. Barrett hadn't kidnapped me to attend the assembly. Her mission was to hand me to the Fallen Ones.

In the midst of the din, I drew in a breath filling my lungs to their depths. All that was flowing through me, in words and emotion, was suddenly released; and when I screamed my message it resounded off the walls, catching the crowd by surprise. "WHAT HAVE I DONE?"

The crowd reduced to a murmur and then fell still entirely.

"What have I done?" I repeated, stepped towards Ms. Barrett, who instantly retreated. "I have killed our enemies. You've heard the stories…you've known the Alterums…you know the crimes our enemies have committed…you know what they will continue to do. I didn't start this war. Our enemies have been at war with us long before I made any effort to eradicate them."

"So you admit it?" Ms. Barrett demanded with her eyes widening.

"Admit what?" I retorted. "That I wish to defend myself – and all of you – because you refuse to do it yourselves?"

Spinning around, I spoke to the chamber. "I have visited this dimension over the last five hundred years and what I have witnessed of Fallen Ones is nothing less than murder, thievery, crimes too atrocious to recount. In the midst of it, I focused solely on delivering messages to those on the other side, some of them…some of them coming from those who had been attacked by the Fallen Ones." I stopped and stared in to the eyes of those so intently focused on me, speaking passed the lump that had grown thick in my throat. "For that I am ashamed. Delivering messages is no longer good enough for me. I am not content to stand idly by as the lives of innocent Alterums, innocent humans are consumed by our enemies." I turned then and marched across the stage to Ms. Barrett. Standing directly in front of her, seething with rage, I noted and enjoyed how she leaned back, away from me.

In the brief moment of my pause, I heard a voice speak up. It was proud and unyielding and it came from the older woman who had confronted Ms. Barrett earlier.

"And so the hunted became the hunter."

I responded so resolute it was without question. "Yes."

Ms. Barrett's eyes snapped open and then just as quickly narrowed to slits. Clearly, she didn't anticipate such an honest and unshakeable affirmation. Opening her mouth, she began to speak, but I didn't give her the chance.

"Ms. Barrett is correct. Our enemies have united and that will be their strength. They will come at you with force, likely in waves of attack, as has been their strategy in the past. You can no longer hide or turn a blind eye. None of you are safe. Do not let Ms. Barrett's actions or the actions of this chamber divide us. That will be our weakness." I swung around, throwing my arms out to the chamber, imploring them to action. "Are you prepared to fight them alone? Can you protect yourselves and those you love alone? There is only one way to defeat them. Come together…not in assembly but in force. Come together and defend yourselves."

As the chamber exploded with voices, Ms. Barrett's shoulders dropped and rolled forward. By instinct and by witnessing the signs of an attack, my wings snapped outward, spanning across the stage.

A second later, I was on my back, my wings being crushed beneath me. Writhing, I fought the two bodyguards Ms. Barrett had brought as they bore down. Then, just as quickly as I was on the ground I was lifted up.

Ms. Barrett stood in front of me now. The smirk on her face told me that her deception had worked. She'd never had any intention of releasing her wings. She knew there was little hope in winning in a physical battle against me, so she'd used her manipulation to get what she wanted, tricking me in to thinking she would attack so that I could be restrained and no longer incite the crowd towards my way of thinking.

"I told you," she said snidely. "We do not tolerate misbehavior."

With a quick gesture from Ms. Barrett, I was taken from the chamber. Her bodyguards led me down a flight of stairs to a hall directly beneath the stage. There, what I saw made my chest crush inward.

Barred cells made of fused stone lined both sides of the room. Inside each one was someone I knew and loved.

The moment he saw us, Eran sprang to his feet, wings extended, seething through the bars that kept him imprisoned.

"Release her," he demanded, his chest rising and falling rapidly in anger.

They ignored him, dragging me towards a cage at the end of the row. I was taken passed Ezra, Felix, Rufus, Ms. Beedinwigg, Mr. Hamilton, Alfred, and even Magnus, who had assisted us in our battle against the Elsics only a few short months ago. Ms. Barrett had found and captured everyone who could have been any help to Eran and me.

One of her bodyguards opened the door and I was shoved inside while the lock was secured.

Beside me was Ms. Beedinwigg, who was already at the bars separating us.

"Are you hurt?" she asked.

"No, are you? Are any of you?" I stepped forward, my hands coming around the cold stone bars.

She breathed a sigh of relief before answering. "Not yet." She went on to add something that caused the breath to catch in my throat. "Although I'm not certain about Eran's army."

"What about his army?" I asked, tensely.

"We've been told they are in the cells below us."

I felt my face fall in reaction to this news. "Then there's no one…no one coming for us…" I deduced.

Ms. Beedinwigg couldn't muster the words to answer me, instead choosing to slowly nod her head in confirmation.

Knowing no better time to break the news, I revealed, "The book of dossiers is gone. Ms. Barrett…" I swallowed back my body's refusal to speak the words and went on. "Ms. Barrett burnt it."

Absolute dread swept across her face as she collapsed against her cage.

I fell back too, allowing my hand to slide along the bars; giving myself time to digest all that had happened, to contemplate a way out. The bars, while cylindrical, were rutted, which briefly commanded my attention. "Stone cells?"

She lifted her eyes, which now reflected a depth of sadness I'd never expected to see in this woman and then she rolled them weakly. My assertive, inspired mentor was slowly giving up. "Stone cells to counter Eran's ability to operate metal objects," she explained. "They thought of everything."

I remembered back to all the times he'd turned the lock to my French doors without having to touch them, always having considered it a blessing.

Anger coursed through me then. "Why are you here? What cause do they have to hold you?" I demanded.

Then I knew without having to be told. Ms. Barrett was the cause. She'd deceived them just as she'd done with me in the chamber. This was the case for all of them, with the exception of Eran. He had been taken captive because of me.

"I'm so sorry," I muttered, falling back against the stone bars, the weight of what I'd done squeezing the air from my lungs, pressing against my chest with excruciating pain.

Finally, I realized what I had done. In an effort to save those I loved I had only succeeded in hurting them, imprisoning them, threatening their safety, and very likely threatening their lives.

All I'd ever done was implicate others, drawn them to the treachery and dangers that permeated my existence. I felt my head shaking against the reality of it but there was no denying it.

I was the one who endangered others. I was worse than our enemies, my friendship coming with strings attached that yanked them in to my world of deceit and despair.

"No…" I heard myself mutter before everything around me fell away.

All I was aware of – the cell, my loved ones, the ancient castle prison – all of it became a surreal existence and then inexplicably disappeared entirely. I was consumed by a void. A vague awareness of elements around me entered the void and then quickly fell away…Something told me that I had collapsed against the end of my cell and that same thing gave me an understanding that my name was being called. But, none of it could breach the misery that consumed me.

Gravel crunching…

Whispers…

Water sloshing…

I wasn't sure how long I laid there until my eyes reopened, adjusting and blinking to clear the blur from them. My side ached but it wasn't until I shifted did I recognize that the stone bars lined the floor of my cage and I had been lying across one.

That movement caught the attention of Mr. Hamilton, in the cell across from me. He aggressively waved at Ms. Beedinwigg, who had never left my side of her cage.

"Maggie?" she whispered harshly, trying to wrestle my attention back to her.

That whisper caught the attention of Ezra who alerted Rufus who then alerted Felix. Magnus, whose cell was closest to the door and directly from Eran, tried to alert Eran but there was no need.

He'd already felt me coming back.

"Ms. Beedinwigg," I said quietly, crawling towards her to lean against the bars separating us.

She bent down and placed a comforting hand against the side of my head. "Yes?"

"Earlier you said they'd thought of everything in preparation for our imprisonment."

"Yes?" she urged, more excited.

"Well…not everything." A grin began to stretch across my face, something that felt uncomfortably good given our situation and the consuming desolation I'd just escaped.

"What are you trying to tell me?" she asked.

"Pass a message to everyone for me, especially Eran and Magnus. They're going to need to be the first line of defense. Tell them…" I felt my smile deepen. "Tell them to be ready."

"Why? What do you have planned?" Ms. Beedinwigg was already beginning to break a smile too, hope returning to her.

It was astounding how that simple gauge of happiness invigorated me further.

"There's one person they didn't get to, one person who's free that I can trust," I said.

Her head jolted back, astounded. "Who on earth would that be?"

I gave her a wicked smile. "Oh…he's not on earth."

Drawing in a deep breath, I enjoyed the feel of cool air in my lungs, reinvigorating me. It was affirming to know that my energy was returning. I would need it too.

First things first, I told myself. First…I would need to subdue that rising energy and fall asleep. Sleep was the only way to the one who could save us.

Working on finding the most comfortable position I narrowed my awareness to the feeling of exhaustion still with me. Very soon after, my breathing became more rhythmic and my muscles went flaccid.

The instant I felt the warm, soft breeze so common in the Hall of Records, my eyes snapped open. It was as if someone had gently caressed my cheek, telling me it would be all right.

Of course there was no hand comforting me and so I was on my feet before I could focus on my surroundings. In fact, it barely registered with me that there were two men hovering a foot above the ground directly in front of me. They halted their conversation in favor of watching in amusement the commotion I caused.

Now on my feet, I flew down the hall towards a particular pocket containing a particular scroll. Moving along the wall faster than I'd ever done before, I reached the scroll and grabbed for it. It unraveled and I swept my finger over the name of the person I needed so desperately at that moment.

Without pause, I was swept away to the edge of a stream surrounded by towering pine trees. Overhead, the sky was a clear, deep blue, nearly matching the rocks lining the stream's floor. Spotted along the shore were massive boulders, seemingly dropped there from far away as no mountains were visible nearby.

It was uncanny to be on a heightened sense of purpose, a rush to accomplish what I'd come to do, in such a serene setting. Momentarily, I felt as if I were intruding but shoved it aside. There were more important issues to consider than my discomfort in being intrusive.

Besides, it was deserted here with the exception of one person. Lying on the top of a boulder was Gershom, his hands folded beneath his head, his legs crossed at the ankles, his eyes closed in a seemingly peaceful rest, one that I was about to disrupt.

"Gershom," I yelled as I approached him.

The tranquility shattered, he sat up in a rush, rotating at the waist in search of my voice. When he found me, he pushed himself to a standing position, hands on his hips.

"Maggie, this is my time to relax…to meditate. Do I come screaming through your room in New Orleans whenever I need you?"

"No," I admitted and then countered quickly, "But that's because you can't. Listen, I need your help."

"Why am I not surprised?" he said, exhaling through his nose in irritation as he leapt from the boulder.

I ignored his mood and walked up to him. "Everyone I know is being held captive."

That got his attention. Immediately, his face tightened and his eyes drew in sternly.

"Abaddon?" he charged.

"Alterums."

His eyes widened but he said nothing, waiting for me to explain.

I did and by the end his expression steadily changed from amazement to dread. When I finished, he turned from me, his hand to his mouth in worry.

"Maggie, do you understand what this means?" he asked under his breath, coming to terms with the reality of the situation they were in. "The Fallen Ones will be attacking a people at war within themselves. I've seen this before, Maggie. It…It will be catastrophic…"

"This is why I need your help," I stated, taking hold of his shoulders to rattle his attention. "I need you to release us…so I can get to the Fallen Ones before they get to everyone else." For influence, I added, "You know as well as I do that once the Fallen Ones recognize their strength in numbers, they'll terrorize not only those Alterums who are left but all human beings as well. Gershom…we need you down there."

I felt his shoulders slump beneath my hands then as the weight of what I was asking came over him. It was a request no one in the afterlife decided on easily and evidently his initial instinct was deep trepidation.

"To release you would require physical aptitude…which would require me to fall back to earth…" he inferred.

"Yes, it would," I confirmed hesitantly.

He sighed, openly adverse to the thought.

"What about Eran's army?" he asked suddenly optimistic.

My hands fell from his shoulders, increasingly losing hope of motivating him. "They're imprisoned too," I said quietly desperate as I waited for Gershom to accept that he was the only answer. "We need you, Gershom. There is no one else who can help us."

"I think you have greater faith in my abilities than I do…" he said shaking his head, a frown stationary on his face. Then he shook his head in amazement. "Whoever would have thought I would be the one to help save civilization?"

I drew in a deep breath, releasing it in a rush of relief.

"I'm not sure I can help as much as you think but I'll try…I'll do whatever you need." He turned towards me, still tenuous. "Exactly what is that, by the way?"

I didn't bother containing my grin, which didn't make Gershom any more pleased.

"Do you know where the Alterum's assemble?" I asked.

"That's where they're holding you?" Again, the feat seemed insurmountable to him.

"Yes, get yourself together, Gershom. You must have been in more secure strongholds than that one," I encouraged.

"No, Maggie, I haven't," he replied, frowning again.

"Oh…well…" I muttered. Having no further words of encouragement, I laid out the plan instead. "We need you to enter the fortress without being seen, find the key to unlock our cells, and then locate us. We're being held directly below the assembly stage. Eran's army is detained below us." I paused, allowing the plan to soak in and then asked for firm confirmation, "Can you do that? Can you get to our cells without being seen?"

He lifted his eyebrows at me. "I'm a tracker, Maggie. How do you think I found you in New Orleans before most of the other Fallen Ones could? I can find virtually anyone…" he declared proudly, "…certainly those who don't know I'm coming. No, getting through the fortress won't be a problem."

Good, I thought. He would just need to find them before they found him.

"Well, let's get on with it," he said, no more happy about it than he'd been a moment ago. At least, however, he was moving.

Our appendages weren't needed here but in our haste we both used them. Gershom fled to a place we'd both been many times before, the very same place we greeted others on their return from the other dimension and the very same one where we left in our fall to earth. I, on the other hand, returned to the Hall of Records, it being the only place I could think of that might help me get back to sleep…and to my body on earth.

Once in the hall, I noted that it was vacant, not that it mattered. It was vast and yet somehow voices did not echo here. They seemed to be absorbed through the stone walls, protecting its perpetual solitude. Lying down on the bench I always awoke on, I did my best to calm my nerves, slow my breathing, relax the body I held here in the afterlife. This last element in particular was a challenge.

To say it was trying to occupy two bodies simultaneously in different dimensions would be an understatement. While all others had the benefit of leaving their bodies behind on earth after they had passed and filled the body they held here in the afterlife, I wasn't given that option. As a messenger, it was a necessity to have 'shells' in both dimensions. On this side, in the afterlife, it wasn't as difficult to maintain since this shell didn't require feeding, bathing, or any of the other upkeep needed by bodies on earth. On the other side, my principal obligation to that shell was to protect it from the Fallen Ones, which continually proved to be a battle in and of itself.

When I'd been on the road a few weeks ago hunting, my primary concern was to find a secure place to sleep. Without knowing Eran watched over me, it had become my responsibility to ensure our enemies couldn't locate and kill me while I was asleep and occupying this body in the afterlife. I wasn't certain what would happen to my soul in that case but I had no inclination to find out.

My thoughts shifted then, to those waiting for me on earth. My mind took me through a tour of memories of my loved ones sitting in their cages. Eran paced the cell like a confined lion, while still keeping a watchful eye on me. Ms. Beedinwigg sat against the bars, her legs bent, her arms resting across her knees. Her head was tilted back deep in thought. The rest wore grim expressions, emanating nervousness that was so palpable I could feel it in the afterlife.

They were scared, each one of them, and they had a right to be.

"Maggie…?" Ezra called out in the darkness.

"Wake up, Mags…" Felix urged.

Something dug in my back hard and cold, which I vaguely recognized as the bars lining my cell's floor.

"Magdalene, wake up, my love." This last voice was more insistent, thickened with an English accent, and the very sound of it pulled me out of my slumber.

When I opened my eyes, I found Eran kneeling over me, his hand cradling my face, concern etched in his dazzling eyes.

"It's all right," I murmured. "I'm all right."

Eran pulled me to a sitting position while remaining knelt beside me.

"I was just returning from the other side," I said, still a bit groggy.

"I hadn't seen you wake like that before," Eran said, his eyes still evaluating me. "You were…shaking."

"Oh…" I breathed laughter. "My thoughts weren't pleasant as I drifted to sleep."

Using my hands, I pushed myself to a standing position.

"Are you sure you're ready?" Eran inquired.

"Yes," I stated firmly. "Gershom's coming for us. I need to be prepare…Wait, how are you in my cell?"

Eran grinned, relieved to see my awareness had returned. He then stepped aside to reveal those behind him: A portion of his army who had been imprisoned in cells below us, Campion, his first lieutenant included, having fallen earlier to protect us; my housemates gawking expectantly to see if I was all right; and…Gershom at the opening of my cell. From his fingers dangled the stone keys custom designed for our captivity.

"How did you...?" I began but he nodded his head towards the door and I followed his motion.

Standing there, acting as lookout, was the older woman from the assembly.

"You don't have much time," she whispered urgently, again peering around the corner of the doorframe.

That message got us moving.

While passing Gershom, I said, "Good job. How-How did you know she would have the keys?"

"I didn't," he said with a shrug. "I evaded the guards, made it to the door of your confinement and found Evelyn here... She was already unlocking it."

The rest of us turned to her in unison, eagerly waiting for further understanding.

She glanced over her shoulder briefly. "I disagree with your imprisonment...and I'm not the only one. But it will take time, or something calamitous, to convince others. Until then, once you've escaped, stay hidden. Gershom will remain with me so that he can locate you when it is safe."

"Sounds like a solid plan," Felix agreed. "Now...if we could just find our way out..."

"I'll show you," Gershom offered and I was pleasantly surprised to see him finally embrace his role as sentinel. "Since I'm the only one with the ability to sense others coming...it's just logical."

"Thank you," I said, placing my hand on his shoulder to show further appreciation. Then I spun towards the woman who had released us. "And thank you, Evelyn, for all you've done."

"Well...it isn't over yet," she replied and then nudged me out the door. "Get going..."

I followed Gershom with Eran directly behind me and the rest of our entourage behind him. We lined up single file down the hallway, keeping our footsteps light to prevent them from echoing.

119

We took several hallways and two flights of stairs before we were back on ground level. Our group had just reached the door to the courtyard, to freedom, when I halted.

"No…" I whispered, furious.

Eran was frozen by that point, tense and alert. While his eyes were on me, I knew he was listening for the same telling sounds, the same confirmation as me.

"What?" Ezra whispered from further down the hallway.

Already my hand was on the back of my neck…where I felt the unmistakable sign of Fallen Ones advancing.

"They're coming…" I said, "and they're coming fast."

8. INVASION

Fallen Ones typically attack alone with stealth invisibility or in small, inconspicuous hordes. At times, when the need has called, they congregate and send progressively larger flanks into battle on intervals. This assures them the advantage of terror as their victims witness an ever growing army while giving them an understanding of how their victims fight and the tactics they use to defend themselves.

There was no need for either of these strategies to be employed for the Alterums.

Alterums had no tactics.

Most of them had never learned defense, having come to earth with the innocent belief they would be safe from harm given the advantage of their supernatural ability.

They had never considered the possibility of an invasion by Fallen Ones. This couldn't have been clearer when Eran opened the door to the courtyard as the first wave hit.

The Fallen Ones came in silent just as dusk had arrived and it appeared they had discarded their previous tactics in favor of an all out bombardment. Their winged bodies blacked out the sky almost entirely as only the whistling sound of air moving across their wings and succeeding grunts from their victims filled the air.

The guards positioned as sentry were tossed aside like fabric dolls as Fallen Ones landed on the turrets and climbed over the useless stone walls, using their grey wings for flight as well as leverage when shoving aside the fortress's defenders.

"The armory," Eran urged as he closed the door and turned from it. Just as he did, its metal lock fell in to place; as I was certain he did with the rest of the fortress's exterior doors. The look he gave me confirmed what I thought. The frail wood doors would do little to obstruct the Fallen Ones but may buy us some time. We needed to get to the armory quickly.

Evelyn, who had followed behind us, whispered hastily, "Come with me."

It probably would have been difficult to find if it weren't for the rest of the Alterums heading there too. Rounding the last corner, we found a throng of them desperate, shoving, terrified as each tried to enter the one room weapon storage. Some had sprouted wings and were hovering haphazardly above the crowd, attempting to enter the door from above to no avail.

Ms. Barrett was shoving her way through the crowd from the opposite side when she caught sight of us. Her jaw fell open in offense at seeing us free and she began pointing in our direction, shouting madly. If I read her lips correctly, she was screaming, "Remain calm! Remain calm! They came for Maggie!" The incensed crowd, however, drowned her meager voice and we turned our attention back to the matter at hand.

"This won't do," Ezra called out over the pandemonium.

"If they find us here," Campion yelled, "we'll have rounded ourselves up nicely for them."

Eran nodded sternly, surveying the situation.

Evelyn strode through our cluster, gesturing for us to follow her.

She led us through a number of passageways, the crowd's noise growing fainter from behind with each turn, until she shoved open a door to reveal a small but tightly organized room on the other side.

"Ms. Barrett's office," she announced, entering. "I think it'll take her a while to get here considering she was on the other side of the mob."

Rufus snorted. "I'm thinkin' she's the least of our problems."

"Indeed," Evelyn said as she and Ms. Beedinwigg stepped up simultaneously to an armoire.

"Eran?" Ms. Beedinwigg called for his attention, which had been directed down the hallway.

Without a word from him, the armoire's lock turned, initiating a unified 'thank you' from Evelyn and Ms. Beedinwigg.

When the door opened, it revealed what we all hoped. Apparently, Ms. Barrett had an appreciation for weapons. Her cache inside the armoire included artillery from all areas of the world.

Ms. Beedinwigg immediately commandeered the sai while I took hold of two swords, giving one to Eran. By the time each of us had made our selection, the armoire was empty.

"What's the plan?" asked Felix, clearly hopeful that there was one.

We stared from one to the other and then Eran, who had continued to keep watch at the doorway, showed his ability to plan an offensive strategy in the most dire of situations. "The Fallen Ones will want to maintain a perimeter while the remaining forces raid the fortress, looking for Maggie. I will take the perimeter, quietly

eliminating their guards. The rest of you will follow
Campion and wait…"

"Wait?" Evelyn demanded, stepping forward in
disagreement.

"…wait until the Fallen Ones have surrounded the
Alterums at the armory and are focused on seeking Maggie
in the crowd. Then you'll surround the Fallen Ones and
incite the Alterums to fight back from inside the huddle."

Understanding now, Evelyn nodded. "And suffocate
the Fallen Ones until they have nowhere to fight or to
run."

"Correct," Eran replied firmly. "Are we ready?"

Without uttering a word, each of us headed for the
door, our weapons out and readied for battle.

I was the first in line and mentally preparing myself for
the worst when Eran halted me. "Where do you think
you're going?"

I glanced at him. "To fight."

He appeared momentarily stunned before his
expression transformed to firm opposition. "You're
staying right here." When I opened my mouth to argue, he
didn't give me the chance. "It's too dangerous out there for
you."

My mouth fell open, amazed he would propose it. "It's
dangerous anywhere right now and if you think I'm going
to hide while others die during a fight that I caused-"

"I'm not asking, Magdalene."

The rest of the room was silently watching now, which
irritated me. They should have been down the hall already.

"They have come here because of me, Eran."

"You are not responsible for this," he countered.

We were at a standoff, neither of us willing to bend to
the others request.

Rufus growled in frustration then and stepped forward.
"I'll keep 'er safe."

I turned towards him, openly offended, which Rufus ignored.

"Thank you," said Eran with a firm nod before disappearing through the door.

By the time the room had emptied, I was clenching and unclenching my fists, my jaw clamped shut and grinding.

"Ah...calm down," Rufus muttered.

I exhaled loudly, never having been more slighted. "You are my friend, Rufus."

"Aye, that I am. Now...if ya so much as leave me side, I'll kill ya meself."

"Excuse me?" I said, perplexed as to what he was insinuating.

"'Scuse yerself. I mean it, Mags. Ya need ta stay close ta me."

I still didn't know what Rufus was implying but I nodded agreement nonetheless.

When we left the room, I was exhilarated and confused, having no idea where Rufus was headed until we reached a staircase to the lookout lofts.

"Don't know what yer boyfriend's thinkin'," Rufus mumbled, disgruntled, "but he ain't goin' ta last long without someone watchin' his back."

I didn't bother holding back the smile that surfaced. It might very well be the last one I have. It faded soon enough, anyways, once we opened the door.

Outside, Fallen Ones circled a few stories above the fortress. Along the lookout, additional Fallen Ones commanded the walls, watching for anyone who might attempt to breach the perimeter. I didn't bother to count them but they far outnumbered us. It was discouraging until someone slid over the stone wall, grabbing one on the lookout platforms and pulling him over the edge.

Eran, I thought to myself. You're about to get some assistance, whether you want it or not.

Rufus and I slipped along the wall of the lookout, intentionally staying in the shadows, until we reached the first Fallen One.

He was just over Rufus's height with the same brawny physique. His wings were out but not extended, telling me that he was comfortably self-assured in his new surroundings.

We were going to challenge that…

Carefully waiting until no other Fallen Ones were looking in our direction Rufus then reached out and pulled the one we'd pinpointed back to the shadow.

My weapon, already drawn, slid across its throat, decapitating it.

Even severed, its mouth opened, preparing to warn the other, but Rufus caught him first. His hand clamped over the Fallen Ones mouth, suffocating it until it passed out. He then handed the head to me.

"Finish 'im off," Rufus whispered.

Knowing I was the only one who could ensure a Fallen Ones ultimate death, I placed my hand over its cold, thick lips until we were certain it wouldn't revive again. We then moved on to the next.

Eliminating them was not easy. As was the case with all Fallen Ones, they were vulnerable each in their own way. Rufus and I had to discover what every one's vulnerabilities were and most importantly we needed to do it quietly.

Whether by luck or skill, the remaining Fallen Ones were oblivious to our actions, quietly circling from their posts above. The only one who did notice was Eran.

I looked up just in time to see him pull another one of our enemies over the wall and our eyes met. His grew wide and his jaw jutted out but he continued with his task at hand until it was done. Then, he found a way into the shadows that hid Rufus and me. By that point, we had eliminated every Fallen One on the lookouts.

When Eran emerged from a window next to me, his eyes said everything going through his mind, and it was not pleasant.

Rufus handed me another limp body and I quickly did my job to send him to a permanent death. Being the final one, Rufus motioned to us, asking if we were ready for the next onslaught.

I nodded in agreement but, even with my head turned away, I was convinced that Eran refused. Instead of getting the attentions of the Fallen Ones above, he and Eran launched in to an unspoken argument using rapid and sharp hand gestures.

The disagreement turned out to be futile. They had forgotten one pertinent element. The Fallen Ones felt me just as easily as I felt them, their radar being the same intense electrical volts I experienced.

Although I couldn't be certain, I believe that as I grew more agitated while waiting for the two of them to finish their silent debate, the Fallen One closest to me suddenly picked up on the swell of emotion that began coursing through me.

She swiveled her head from right to left and quickly back to the right again. Not seeing anything of consequence, she looked down and then up.

Then she knew right where to find me.

Almost leisurely, she spun around in midair, a deep and widening grin stretched her flawless skin. In her eyes wasn't the excitability I'd seen in other Fallen Ones at the prospect of claiming the life of their kind's archenemy. She had the eyes of an immoral warrior who had suddenly picked up the scent of blood. Her goal wasn't fame.

Taking my life would be its own reward.

Without waiting, and midstream between another one of Eran's refusals, I launched myself from the lookout and collided with the woman.

This set off a chain of events so rapid I didn't catch all that happened. Eran and Rufus set out in opposite directions, tackling the first enemy closest to them. Within seconds, the remaining Fallen Ones surrounded me but were slowly picked away, one by one, by both of my protectors. All this took place as I did my best to get the upper hand with the woman I had engaged.

What seemed like minutes passing were likely hurried seconds and before I knew it, the woman's limp body was falling to the ground below and Eran and Rufus were hovering on opposite sides of me.

The sky was clear now. The fortress had been freed…from the outside.

Eran rotated to face me. His fury was ebbing away, I saw, as he moved to take my face in his hands.

His breaths were coming in short gasps as he brought his forehead to rest against mine. One shuttering exhale told me everything he felt…terrified of my involvement in the battle and gratified we'd survived it.

"I suppose," he said, his breath brushing my face, drawing me closer, "asking you to stand back from the battle inside would be out of the question."

I pulled back slightly. "To the armory."

As if he already knew my answer, he nodded quickly after. "Stay close to me," he stated and then led us over the edge of the wall and through a window below.

Inside, the stench of battle filled the air, seemingly inflamed by grunts echoing off the walls. The lanterns, some downed along the way, lit the passages until we reached the center of the conflict.

There, bodies littered the floor, most still moving, shuddering. Only a few Fallen Ones remained uninjured and they were now being dealt with by the massive number of Alterums still alive.

After seeking the crowd for our housemates, Gershom, Ms. Beeginwigg, Mr. Hamilton, Alfred, and Magnus to confirm they were alive and healthy, I turned to Eran.

"Watch over me as I get to work?"

"Always," he affirmed.

I then went about purging the Fallen Ones from their bodies and to eternal death. With a dedicated focus, Eran and I worked our way efficient through the injured, picking our enemies from the piles, until the last one was eliminated.

In the end, over a hundred bodies scattered the ground, half of them Alterums.

Noting this, my reaction was slight but I felt it. My lip quivered, something that took me by surprise. My emotions had always been locked down, shuttered from others, and certainly never exposed in a room full of strangers. But, there I stood, holding back the onslaught of tears threatening to stream down my face. Alterums, ones I never met before, had suffered a great punishment, one that was meant for me.

It felt as if my chest was crushing in, the air squeezing out of me when I felt a hand on my shoulder. It was Eran.

Only then did I look up and what I saw was bittersweet.

Alterums lined the walls, covered in blood, a mixture of their own and the enemies they'd maimed. They had been silent, watching Eran and me work meticulously and exact until I finally lifted my head.

Their expressions, however, weren't filled with hatred or blame for having been responsible for the loss of their friends. To my astonishment, they reflected admiration.

It stilled the breath in my chest.

This should have been enough to tell their thoughts but then they spoke in motion, conjuring in me a tumultuous swirl of feelings so intense I continued to struggle for breath. Starting with just one, we were approached and hands were placed on us in thanks. Progressively, every

Alterum in the passageways touched our arms gently in silent gratitude, their faces quivering in reaction to what they'd just gone through, tears leaving clean tracks down their faces.

The great ones, those who had witnessed countless lives in this dimension, who held powers far more potent than me, who were respected by just as many souls here as in the afterlife, joined the procession. They placed their hand on me with a firm purpose, one that told me to take comfort. They didn't hold me responsible.

There was no sound, other than the scuff of feet along the ground as they shuffled forward, but there was a sentiment and it was powerful. It flowed through us like a hot, fluid stream, uniting us, making us whole.

Even those more potent in their unique abilities than Eran or myself.

Later, I reflected on this quiet but potent expression of thanks by the Alterums and knew it was the most humbling experience of my existence. At the time, however, my thoughts centered around one realization...

The calamitous event Evelyn had forewarned would be needed to rally the Alterums had just taken place.

9. BARGAIN

Over the next few days, the fortress was repaired, the bodies were removed, and new sentries were positioned at the lookouts. A routine, a normalcy began again, one that Eran and I and my other prison mates were now allowed to participate in.

Only a few Alterums, it appeared, adamantly refused to comply with the rest. Ms. Barrett and her guards were suspiciously absent over these first few days.

As I freely roamed the passageways, it was hard not to notice the surreal dichotomies within the fortress walls. The ancient kitchen was equipped with state-of-the-art cooking equipment; meeting rooms were lined with antique canvases alongside plasma screen TV sets; and a heating and air conditioning system had been retrofitted inside the primeval stone walls.

Eran and I had been given the largest bedroom, or chamber to use a term more familiar to the century in which the fortress was built. We spent every night there, my head on his taut chest and my arm strung across his torso. He fell asleep each evening with his hand laid gently on my head, as if an inch apart would be too painful for him.

We overlooked Ezra's disapproving eye while knowing it was ever present each night we disappeared upstairs and every morning we reappeared downstairs.

I wasn't sure if it was Ezra's reaction to our sleeping arrangements or something else but Eran had not made a single attempt to go any further than holding my head to him. Still, I noticed the reaction in him each time I sat down on the edge of the bed and slipped beneath the covers. Each night, he drew in a sharp breath and then his body would stiffen, almost board-like, until morning came. I didn't tempt him, although the idea of it nagged me throughout the night, but I didn't hold back either. On more than one occasion, I nuzzled my lips to his neck and kissed lightly and then increasing passionately until I heard him muttered tightly, "Magdalene..." Then I would begrudgingly acquiesce and lay my head back against his shoulder.

On the third night this habit became more than I could stand. Rolling back against my pillow, I released a frustrated exhale and felt my face twist to a frown.

Unable to ignore it, he briefly broke his rigidity, risking uninhibited reaction to sharing a private bed with me, and rolled towards me to whisper delicately in my ear, "Not long, Magdalene...We've been patient. I think we can refrain a bit longer."

When I heaved another discontented sigh, he chuckled through his nose and then groaned, equally as bothered. "If I don't get my mind on something other than the privacy of our room..." He rolled towards me, propping his arm on my pillow, and peering down at me through the dark. He watched me for a moment and I got the distinct impression he was absorbing the memory of every detail of my face. Then he focused entirely on my lips before asking, "Do you remember our kiss just before you left for this lifetime on earth?"

Instantly, my muscles tightened. I did recall it and it had been unexpected by both of us.

When I was silent, he quietly recounted it, a light smile lifting his lips. "You appeared at the cabin…in a huff, I'll add. And you had every right to be upset with me. We were existing between this life and our last. I say existing because it certainly wasn't living, what you and I endured."

I nodded, that time running vividly through my mind. It was unheard of in the afterlife to live in despair and yet Eran had, while overcoming the upset in having taken my life in Gettysburg, and I had as Eran separated himself from me during his recovery. Time is not thought of in the afterlife, not in the way it is considered or dominates here on earth, and yet that duration was the longest I'd ever experienced between lives.

By this point, Eran's smile had faded away. "Being apart from you was punishment I hope to never suffer again, self-imposed or otherwise. I had worried…" He suddenly looked uncomfortable. "I had worried that your love for me might have weakened and that possibly…you found someone else."

"No," I whispered, my head lifting from the pillow, closer to him, in response. "No, Eran."

"I know that now but…" He shrugged and allowed himself to progress through the discomfort. "I wasn't sure of it then…That was difficult, to say the least…My worry of it didn't end until you appeared on the dock." His eyes glossed, recalling a far happier memory. "You wore a white dress I'd never seen before…Your hair was down, flowing in the breeze and glistening from the daylight…You seemed to be glowing, Magdalene. The sight of you…" He finished with a trembling sigh, unable to express what it had done to him in words.

I smiled, familiar with that reaction.

"You marched right up to me and without a word took my face in your soft hands and…with fire in your eyes…you reached up and your lips landed on mine."

"Were you surprised?"

He chuckled. "To say that would be an oversimplification. It woke me up, Magdalene. I'd been living in a void, a cave, while trying to deal with the turmoil inside me. But your kiss, soft but so firm, brought me back to…well, to life. I suddenly smelled the fresh air, heard the birds in the trees, felt you on my skin. Your hands on my face were so delicate but…determined. I felt that. You, Magdalene, brought me back to life."

While my heart fluttered, I played it off teasingly. "I had no idea what my kisses do to you."

"No…" he agreed reflectively. "You have no idea…"

"That kiss was unplanned," I admitted, and his eyebrows rose, questioning. "When I arrived and saw you on the porch…The sight of you filled the emptiness in me that had been so present during that time. I couldn't stop myself."

"I am truly thankful you didn't. There is no telling what might have happened if you hadn't broken the spell I was in." He tried to hide the shutter that shook his body but I still felt it, our bodies lying so close.

"My leaving for this lifetime was prompted by your seclusion," I explained. "I couldn't live without you any longer. And thinking it was safe to return here, to earth…thinking it safe from the Fallen Ones, I-I came to replace the pain of your distance with a distraction."

"Well, you certainly found one," he replied, frowning playfully.

I rolled my eyes. "Now that is an oversimplification."

"I always wondered…why did you come to the cabin in the first place?"

"To see you one last time…before I departed."

He nodded, understanding. "Couldn't help yourself?" he asked, smirking.

My jaw fell open and I playfully attempted to shove him. He caught my hand well before it made contact, drew it to his lips, and tenderly kissed each of my fingers. When he'd finished making my stomach turn flips, he didn't release my hand. Instead, he held it and placed it against his chest, the warmth of it calming me instantly.

"When you did leave," he said quietly, "I followed you. Well…I tried to follow you."

"Really?" I asked, intrigued. "What do you mean…tried?"

"I went looking for you…after you chose to launch yourself from the porch and flee from me without a single word," he said, lifting his eyebrows insinuatingly at me.

I sighed and gave him the answer he hinted for. "I was…nervous."

"I see…" he replied. "Please try to overcome that in the future."

"I promise to try."

He accepted that statement as enough for the moment and continued on. "When I didn't find you in your realm in the afterlife, I realized where you'd gone. Back to earth. But, I thought you had planned to fall during this lifetime as you'd always done with each lifetime prior. So, I fled to the steps where we fall for earth. And I waited there, not knowing you were already in the womb. When I realized that you were gone, I…" he let his voice trail off, the unmistakable sound of regret tainting his beguiling English accent.

I slipped my hand up his cheek, enjoying the feel of his skin against mine. "Eran…" I whispered, pulling him from his thoughts. "I'm here now."

"Yes, you are," he said, drawing me closer, sliding me against the bed sheets towards him.

Our lips came dangerously close to touching and in reaction his breathing staggered. His eyes traced the features of my face before he released me and rolled on to his back.

"Speaking of distraction...I need another topic of conversation."

I laughed and moved closer to him again.

"That wasn't exactly what I was thinking," he warned.

"I know," I replied softly. "I'm only getting comfortable so I can get to sleep."

My head landed gently on his chest again, rising and falling with his breaths, which were gradually becoming more regular.

"Sleep is a good idea," Eran murmured. "We leave tomorrow. We'll want to be rested for it."

"Right," I said. "Tomorrow..."

The last thing I felt before I awoke in the Hall of Records was Eran's hand rubbing my arm, gently and with the purpose of touching me without allowing it to go too far.

The next morning, I no longer felt Eran's hand. Where he'd been laying was now a cold, vacant spot with an indent where his body had been.

I lifted myself up and found him at the narrow window, one hand holding back the drape.

"Is something wrong?" I asked, ready to heave myself out of bed.

"Not exactly..." Eran replied, though his tone was suspicious.

I stood and walked to the window, only to find myself pleasantly surprised.

In the courtyard below, the Alterums had paired up and were now sparing with each other using wooden swords. They were haphazard, slow, and contrived motions, but they were trying.

Neither Eran nor I openly critiqued them but we both knew that if a single Fallen One were to suddenly land in the middle of them, not a single Alterum would survive.

We found later that we weren't the only ones to notice.

While preparing to leave, Eran, me, and our friends collectively entered Ms. Barrett's office, which continued to remain mysteriously unoccupied, to replace the weapons we'd taken from her armoire.

Ms. Beedinwigg, standing at the window overlooking the mock fighting practice taking place just outside, commented, "It seems they could use a little guidance."

She glanced over her shoulder to find Eran and me nodding in agreement. "Could we be leaving too soon?" she offered.

"These are the same Alterums who imprisoned you," Gershom reminded, tenuously.

"And the same that are allowing us to walk freely now," Ezra countered.

The room fell quiet then as we individually assessed what it would mean to stay or to leave. Those Alterums outside hadn't given us freedom. We'd taken it. They could just as easily imprison us again. The only reason they didn't haul us back to our specially-designed cells was because we'd saved them from a fate they didn't believe was coming. Now they did and were preparing feverishly for it.

Still, I couldn't help but realize that I had brought the fight to them. Yes, the Fallen Ones had preyed on them, and humans, for centuries, but it was my actions, my hunting that had drawn our enemies to the fortress. It was my actions that would make them return.

"Maggie Tanner?" said a voice behind me.

Shaken from my thoughts, I rotated at the waist to find two men and a woman standing at the door.

"Maggie Talor," I corrected, sensing the pride flushing Eran.

The woman stepped hesitantly through the door, revealing Evelyn behind her.

"They've come to ask if you'll deliver their messages to the other side," Evelyn explained, clearly hopeful I would agree. "Time moves so slowly here and their wondering how their loved ones are faring."

I scanned the rest of their faces finding expectant hope there too.

"Uh…sure…" I said, looking around the room in preparation, hearing sighs of relief in response. "Eran, do you mind if I…"

He smiled knowingly. This hadn't been the first time we'd been prepared to leave when someone had overcome their timidity to ask me to deliver their message.

"Thanks," I said. "It should only take a minute. There are just three of them."

"Um…" Evelyn stifled a smile. "It may take a while longer."

She motioned for me to approach the door. When she did, I peeked around the corner and found a line forming down the hall.

My jaw dropping, I didn't know what to say. Then Eran's hands came over my shoulders, squeezing lightly, comfortingly. "It's all right. I'll wait," he said against my ear.

I sighed in gratitude. Then I said something completely unexpected, something I had never realized before. "You seem to wait a lot for me."

Not certain whether he took my comment with my unintended sexual undertone or not he whispered, "You're worth it."

It only took a moment longer for the rest of those in the room to agree to wait too, although they thought it would be best to wait outside the room and allow my customers their privacy.

When the room emptied, I sat in a wingback chair similar to the one I owned in New Orleans and motioned for the first one in line to sit in the wingback chair opposite me.

One after another, the Alterums outside Ms. Barrett's office entered, gave me their message, and left but not before giving me a mention of support.

"I'm glad you're all free."

"Wish I had spoken up in support of you..."

"...embarrassed at my behavior."

I didn't bother to question their sincerity. It was apparent, and welcomed.

A few hours later and with over twenty messages memorized, I took a brief break to glance out the window, the same one Ms. Barrett had been peering from earlier. There, in the courtyard, I found her, my housemates, and Eran's army coaching the Alterums on the art of warfare, their expressions holding the same gratitude as the ones requesting their messages be delivered.

All this gratitude couldn't last long, I figured, and sure enough, it was disrupted.

The day wore away quickly and the sun had just disappeared over the edge of the fortress's walls when my final customer entered the room.

She was the last one I expected to see and my reaction was nothing less than open hostility. I was on my feet before she had the second foot through the door.

"Please," she said, gesturing me to stop, as if she were concerned I would cross the room towards her. "Please stop. I'm here to apologize."

Eran, having sensed my discomfort, raced down the hallway and through the door in seconds.

"Magdalene?" he inquired, coming through the door.

"I'm okay," I told him. "Though, I'm not sure for how long."

Ms. Barrett's mouth snapped shut but she seemed to consider that my statement was deserving because she chose not to address it. Instead, her eyelids closed briefly and when opened they revealed a redefined sense of purpose.

"I was wrong," she said, bluntly. "Wrong to have made accusations against you and your friends-"

"Family," I stated. "These people are my family."

She conceded. "Your family. I was wrong to have incarcerated you all. I was also wrong to have suggested we deliver you to our enemies." Her lips pinched closed, ill at ease with recounting her actions. "I am deeply sorry." She released a deep breath and moved across the room to take a seat in the chair opposite from where I stood.

Eran and I watched her speculatively.

Once seated, she began again, her forehead in her palm, her eyes downcast. "I was out of options. Having no idea what else to do...Unable to formulate a single plan that might protect us. Trying to keep the rest of us...the Alterums safe is just...mindboggling." She lifted her head then and leveled her gaze at me. "I understand now that I imprisoned the ones best equipped to defend us...you and your family. In doing so, I endangered the very ones I was meaning to protect." Shaking her head, she continued wistfully, "Regardless, incarcerating you was wrong. I just...I just didn't see any other option. You deserve better treatment from us. You deserve better treatment from me."

"There are other options," said Eran, remaining in the room but having relaxed his pose. "Look outside."

Ms. Barrett half-stood and then leaned forward towards the window, her jaw dropping a moment later. Then, slowly, a smile crept up.

This was unexpected, since I was beginning to wonder if she had it in her to smile.

"They'll return," I warned her and she fell back in her seat. "Our enemies are preparing as we speak. I can guarantee it."

"I know...I know. That is why I made a trip to your residence."

I was suddenly on alert again. "Our residence?"

"Yes," she replied plainly, showing no sign of noticing my apprehension. "In New Orleans. I brought something back with me, something I hoped would prompt you to stay a while longer. I left it in your chamber upstairs but I'll tell you what it is now...Your combat suit."

"Combat suit?" I reiterated, confused.

"Yes, the suit made of leather...with weapons secured from it. I found it in your room."

It was then I unequivocally understood Ms. Barrett. Clearly, she lacked any social skills, but this wasn't her most distinct trait. What stood out among the rest was her tenacity. Nothing would stop this woman, social mores and trespassing included, from protecting the Alterums. Ironically, we both had the same goal. We were simply going about it in opposing directions.

Eran recognized this around the same time I did and released a long and resounding laugh in reaction. It startled Ms. Barrett but by the end, as it dwindled down, she smiled again, faintly, but it was there.

"So...will you stay?" she asked, insistently.

I looked towards Eran, who shrugged in response. The decision was left up to me.

"On one condition," I stated. "As we prepare the Alterums for the Fallen Ones return, I will continue my hunts."

She nodded agreement without flinching, which I took as a good sign.

"And I will select the top candidates to accompany me."

She bristled at this request but after a pause nodded again, hesitantly.

"Then we will stay…until this fight is over," I concluded.

"And when will that be?"

I knew she was asking when I expected the Fallen Ones to strike with full force but that wasn't the answer I gave her.

As she waited for me to respond, I stood and stared out the window at the Alterums fighting vehemently, dedicated to their lesson.

"When every one of them is eternally dead."

10. RAID

That night, I left the fortress, although not for New Orleans. As the rest retreated to their bedrooms and the hallways grew silent, Eran and I were busily preparing for the evening hunt.

I pulled on my black leather combat suit and attached the weapons I would be bringing while Eran collected an alternate sword from Ms. Barrett's armoire.

There was one vital piece missing from my hunts now. The book of dossiers, which Ms. Barrett had burned in order to prevent me from further hunting, was now gone. Thankfully there was another solution.

Earlier in the day, I'd pulled Gershom into a private study and told him that his help was again needed, explaining he was the only one I knew who could track down our enemies, who could help us locate them.

Again, he'd nervously declined but in the end he conceded and then left the rest of the day to prepare his nerves.

Gershom, having lived amongst the Fallen Ones for several centuries, had every right to fear them. He had seen firsthand the terror they'd inflicted and this time there was a possibility he'd be on the receiving end.

When we met in the courtyard well after sunset, I could see that he'd been unsuccessful in calming himself. Eran and Campion detected it too and strolled away, giving us a little privacy.

"Gershom," I said, placing a hand on his shoulder for comfort. "You're leading us there. You're not coming inside." He didn't seem to grasp my meaning so I clarified, "The fighting will be inside and you'll be outside."

Gershom gave two quick nods, agitated head shakes really, and I second guessed whether he should come along at all.

"Outside," he muttered. "I'll be outside."

His utterance gave me some measure of calm. "Yes, Gershom. You'll be fine outside. You'll see."

Eran, who'd been speaking to the portion of his army which had taken up nightly lookout positions, returned to us with Campion at his side.

"So…how are we doing this?" Eran asked, repositioning his sword sheath to unobstructed him from flight.

"We'll follow Gershom until he finds one. He'll get our attention, tell us the exact location of the Fallen One, and then he'll remain safely in the sky while we attack."

Eran nodded with his full attention back on us. "I still believe we should postpone until the Alterums are ready to provide support. Simply putting it on record."

"I'm not waiting," I replied flatly.

He sighed quietly. "Then I suppose we'll do the best we can," he stated, reluctant and slightly disgruntled. "Ready?"

I turned to Gershom. "Ready?"

He only nodded, again, two quick quivers.

"Most of them have likely heard of the attack here and will be more diligent," Eran stated in warning, his wings spreading out behind him, preparing for flight.

"Yes, I considered that," I replied plainly.

Gershom didn't say a word, choosing to stare back, tensely.

The four of us rose through the air then, Eran, Campion, and me falling back to allow Gershom the lead. We then trailed Gershom towards London's gleaming cityscape. Once there, I split my attention between Gershom and the city below. Even from above, I could recognize streets I'd walked back in the 1300s and it was especially poignant to fly over the street where Eran had rescued me from an Elsic and immediately after declared himself as my guardian.

Only one element of our relationship had changed since then. I still declined the need for a guardian, and always would; the distinct difference was that while he had always been the one to fight our enemies, it was now me who instigated it. He wasn't particularly enthusiastic about this evolution in me but I refuse to give him, anyone really, a say in it.

This was my destiny. I would live it as I wanted.

A swell of empowerment washed over me just when Gershom began to slow to a hover. The rest of us slowed to linger beside him, though he didn't acknowledge us. He was focused on a warehouse directly below, one on the edge of the river.

A thick mist rolling through the network of streets below nearly engulfed the building and made the streetlights encircling it glow wide, extending to the surrounding structures. The tops of cars protruded from the haze and lined along the edge of one street told us that the building was not vacant.

"Everything all right, Gershom?" asked Eran, confident but alert.

"There," he said, pointing to the same building Eran and I had figured he'd been evaluating. "Second floor, northwest corner. She's not alone."

"More Fallen Ones?"

Gershom shook his head tenuously. "Humans…around thirty of them."

"Humans?" I said more to myself. They didn't spend time with humans unless it allowed for an opportunity to take advantage of them.

"We'll try to remove them safely," said Eran. "Magdalene, please stay within my sight."

I glanced at him under my lashes.

"Please?" he implored.

"I'll try to remember that," I conceded.

"Good enough," he said. "Now let's go see what this one's up to. Circle a few times for surveillance first."

I barely caught the last part of his instructions, the wind already picking up and obscuring his voice as I dropped towards the building.

He caught up to me easily and gave me an annoyed look. I ignored it because we'd just reached a set of windows exposing the second floor.

Campion remained above, acting as sentry from the roof, so it would be just me and Eran executing the Fallen One.

I liked those odds.

The loft inside was spacious, filled with expensive furniture, oversized artwork, and a crowd of what appeared to be fashionable elite. Music thumped through the windows where they held either tumblers or flutes in their hands while waiters dressed in black suits weaved handheld platters through what appeared to be a thriving party.

One woman in particular stood out from the rest. Not because of her white hair wound in a foot-tall beehive or the flowing, low cut gown she wore.

She caught my attention because the moment she entered the room and started down the stairs, the hair at the back of my neck began to rise. At nearly the same time, her radar went off too, stopping her midway down the steps. Her expression, previously relaxed, darkened; her eyes alone taking on a rage that would have chilled her guests had they been watching her. They swept the throng below, unable to pick up any sign of me and then, very slowly, she lifted them to the windows.

One side of my mouth tilted up in a coy smile and I knew she'd seen me, immediately spinning around and marching up the stairs, her stride hurried and clumsy now.

As she went up, I dropped down, feeling the hard pavement meet my feet in a rush. Eran landed at the same time as me and was already at the wide metal door.

Before pulling it open, he asked quickly, "Do you feel any more?"

Knowing he was asking if my radar had increased, a warning of the presence of more than one Fallen One, I shook my head. "She's alone."

A glimmer came to his eyes and knew exactly what he was thinking, because I was thinking the same thing: This one is going to be easy.

It turned out, we were very wrong.

Inside, the first floor was completely vacant with a single set of metal stairs lined the wall directly to our right. Beyond them was a cavernous and entirely vacant room. The music and voices drifting down the staircase, the only signs of life, might have seemed welcoming in this environment. But, that would be true only if we'd come for another reason, one that didn't include killing their host.

By the time we reached the top step, our appendages were already back in place so when entered the crowd in search of the Fallen One, I was surprised to find someone place a hand on my back…directly where my wings extended.

It was cold, like that of a Fallen One.

"Now this ensemble…" I heard a feminine voice stating in an English accent as I spun around. Before me was a skeletal man wearing a skin-tight, polka dotted one-piece. He ignored my abrupt maneuver to focus on my one-piece suit.

His eyes slimmed as he evaluated it, a finger lightly touching the side of his lips. "The leather's nice…and the slits in the back…they do add something. But these weapons…" He frowned and clucked his tongue, deep in thought. "It's a bit too…antagonistic. Don't you think?"

"Yes," agreed a slender blonde next to him. "Antagonistic…Yes…"

She too was evaluating me now.

"Do they have this in my size?" asked the man, sincere curiosity driving him. "And possibly in red?"

I took a glimpse at Eran, who was stifling a laugh by keeping his eyes on the stairs we were about to ascend.

Because I hadn't answered yet, the man asked, solemnly, "It's a one-of-a-kind, isn't it? I knew it." He shook his head, his lips pinched in disappointment.

"Tell us…" said the woman, leaning in as if she were going to ask something gravely important. "Who's the designer?"

Leaning forward, I looked them both in the eyes before whispering, "Me."

In unison, they sprang back, their jaws falling, drawing in a stunned gasp. Then, slowly smiles spread across their faces.

"Well done," said the man. "Well done."

I tipped my head cordially at them and then moved on through the crowd. Eran had spotted the woman through an open door at the top of the stairs.

When we reached that room, she was just ending a phone conversation. As the door opened, she turned expectantly to face us, wearing a devious smile now.

Something was wrong. I couldn't place it but I felt it. This Fallen One had gone from self-assured to nervously angry to mischievously pleased.

She was up to something.

"Maggie…Eran…Welcome," she said, unhurriedly. "I wasn't expecting you but there is room for more at my party."

Something in the way she said this made me wonder exactly why she was holding this party at all. There was an ulterior motive I couldn't quite place yet.

By this point, Eran had closed the door behind us and all three of our wings were out. Then, as Eran and I unsheathed our swords, she slid her hand beneath her desk and withdrew a small handgun. We were all now equally defensive and waiting to see where it would lead.

Only a few seconds passed when, seeing no reason to hesitate longer, I stepped forward.

She quickly looked out the window and then back to us, something that both Eran and I noticed.

"Expecting more company?" Eran inquired.

"Truthfully…yes. The fact your pathetic little fortress still stands was an alert that you survived and would continue to come after us…and, as a matter of recourse, we've agreed to call in support whenever either of you were spotted. Seeing as how my friends were going to arrive later anyways…"

"Arrive later?" I muttered.

She seemed appalled. "Of course. You don't think I'd let those dirty, wretched humans in my home without a good reason…" She scoffed and then grew excited. "Truth be told, I'm overjoyed you're here. My small gathering will be the talk of the century. Everyone will know you were killed and that it was done at my party. I will be revered…" She drew in a deep breath in anticipation. "And once my friends and I take care of you, we'll celebrate using them." She waved her hand towards the lower level, her eyes eager and expectant.

I vaguely noticed her motions, my concentration centering on her last words instead. They made a shiver run down my spine, which quickly transformed to annoyance. "I have no hope for your kind any longer. You have no compassion."

"For them?" She laughed cynically. "No."

"And that will be your downfall."

I started across the room again with Eran moving forward directly next to me.

He spoke for the first time, low and contemptuous. "I have a feeling your friends will be arriving a little later than you'd like…You are alone in this now. Prepare for eternal death."

She seemed to agree with Eran, her finger squeezing the trigger of the gun she held a second later.

The shot cracked through the room and was met by screams from downstairs. Footsteps rushing down the metal stairs to the first floor and the squeaking of the metal front door opening, told us that her guests were fleeing. Ignoring them, I searched for where the bullet had landed.

In my heightened state, I'd heard it whiz passed my ear, break through the plaster of the wall behind us, and lodge in the wooden support beam.

Eran was inspecting me so I shrugged to show I felt no pain and simultaneously we stepped forward.

The woman's aim hadn't been precise for a reason. She was using it as a distraction, already withdrawing another weapon. This one was a thick steel chain. At the end of it, an array of knives protruded from a center point so that no matter where it hit, the victim would be severely injured.

"Fernando Vega sent this to me," she explained reflecting back to that time. "Always good with the tools, Fernando was…"

"Not anymore," I stated.

She didn't seem to appreciate my humor, taking the chain in her other hand, lifting it, and circling it above her head as if it were a lasso.

I wondered for a moment just how good she could be with the device when Eran stepped in front of me. He'd already deemed her worthy of it.

As she released the chain and the blades sliced through the air towards us, Eran shoved me back and fell to the ground.

It soared over our heads, cutting a swath through the door behind us, sending shards of wood across the room.

Eran was now on his feet, giving her no time to recoil the chain. As he lunged for her, she brought the chain forward, yanking it so that the knives would catch Eran from behind.

I saw this coming, stepping up and seizing it before it reached Eran. Wrenching it from her hands, the chain slid across the floor to land limp, harmless in the corner of the room.

The woman was defenseless now.

Eran wasted no time in incapacitating her. He'd finished his task by the time I could cross the room. One arm was around her neck, the other restraining her. As her breathing became progressively more laborious, she struggled to remove Eran's sword from her chest, her hand not quite able to reach it.

Then, just as quickly as her eyes shut, the life ebbing from her, her lids opened again and life returned. Eran's sword slowly, gradually ejected from her torso and fell to the floor with a dull clang.

She tossed her head, sweeping the hair from her face as if she were relaxing on the beach and not moments from death.

Then she smirked and explained her confidence. "Impaling isn't effective on me."

Anyone who has fallen comes to earth with their own set of defenses, their own paranormal powers which can protect them from danger. This woman's friends were coming, our time was running out, we needed to figure her vulnerability quickly.

I glanced back at Eran. "Drowning? Suffocation? Electrocution?"

While I was offering these as suggestions to Eran, I was also watching her reactions, stopping only when she flinched.

"All right...Let's see if this will be," I said, crossing the room to where her knifed weapon had exposed the electrical components in the wall.

Sweeping my legs out from beneath my body and using my appendages to hover above the ground, I took the exposed wires and returned to her.

My eyes met Eran's and I knew he understood my intentions when his appendages quietly stretched and pumped once, lifting his feet inches from the ground.

"What's your name?" I asked her.

"Paula," she sneered. "May my name haunt you."

"Paula, there is something you need to know with absolute lucidity. It is your choices that have brought you to this point. You are here because of your actions. You will be leaving because of your actions. I am simply the messenger."

With that I impaled the electrical cords through her torso.

Eran smoothly drifted around her as the body he once held fell to the ground gyrated until the nerves succumbed to the electrical currents.

The lights blinked, lingered on briefly, and then flicked off permanently.

In the still darkness, I asked Eran, "Do you hear that?"

"Wings…" he whispered. "Are you ready?"

Once I nodded, he took Paula's chain and threw it through the oversized window behind her desk, shattering it. We slipped through the shards and into the cool night air, lifting ourselves to the flat roof above.

Campion was already facing their direction, his stance unyielding and his expression firm. Without taking his eyes from the sky, he commented, "Looks like our party is just beginning…"

There we waited, swords drawn, facing the approaching onslaught.

The thumping of wings cutting the air steadily grew louder until we saw the bodies appearing in the distance. They approached in a single line, forty of them, and they flew with determination.

Watching them, I realized this hunt no longer appeared so easy.

As they drew closer, I scanned their faces for signs of weakness, fear, trepidation. None of these were evident, their entire beings projecting only one feeling…rage.

The hair at the back of my neck snapped wildly, trying to gain my interest, warning me.

"Stay calm, Magdalene," Eran warned.

"I'm not anxious…" I said. "I'm eager."

He sighed in frustration, preferring me to engage some type of self-preservation.

That was impossible. Adrenaline pumped through me, faster and faster, until the line of Fallen Ones landed in unison on the rooftop. Then it dissipated, my muscles absorbing the rush, containing it for the fight to come.

That was when I heard the chuckle.

"'Ello, Messenga'," said a cordial voice in a thick Australian accent, one that teased my memory.

A man stepped closer, in front of the group, dressed in a black suit, his hair slicked back, diamond cufflinks glinting in the dim light.

"Sharar…" I mumbled, surprised, despite the situation.

Eran and Campion took a quick look at me, gauging my comfort level with this particular Fallen One.

"'S been a while," he stated with mock sadness. "No more deliverin' messages in Jackson's Squa'?"

"Those have been postponed in the interest of exterminating you."

The group chuckled boldly, which I disregarded. "It looks like we've disturbed your plans for the night." I motioned towards his suit.

He lifted his shoulders in a deep laugh and then explained to his cohorts, "This one's observant, blokes. Best keep yer head 'bout ya."

My lips lifted in a half-smile.

"Ay, took me away from me party," Sharar confirmed. "Notta wurry. Happy to be the one ta take down the last messenga'."

My smile widened considerably then. "Your confidence is inflamed, Sharar."

"We'll see 'bout that." This statement was delivered with a considerably darker tone, something the rest of us picked up on.

Suddenly, all weapons were drawn. The collision came seconds later, a sweeping and organized alignment against us.

Using my heightened awareness, I was able to eliminate three of them quickly, which only seemed to free up space for the rest. Eran and Campion made a circle around me, one of flying bodies and spraying blood. They held off our enemies as one after another tried to breach the circle.

Then Sharar came through the group, his arrogant grin now stone cold determination. Lip curled up, wings out, arms stretched, he reached me.

He was faster than me, his hand coming around my neck before I knew what was happening.

His fingers had just begun to squeeze when his eyes glassed over and his mouth went slack. As he fell to the ground, Eran stood behind him, withdrawing his sword from Sharar's neck, the pointing having made its way entirely through to the other side. I finished him with my own swipe across the throat. Eran took a moment to ensure I wasn't injured, scanning me from the feet up, once and deliberate, before turning back to the fight.

Eran, a far better fighter than me, debilitated five more. Campion removed four. As they fell by their swords, I followed up, ending their lives eternally.

The prospects appeared dim as the remaining Fallen Ones hacked away at us, looking for an opening to get at me.

Then something happened that didn't quite register with me until the movement stopped.

Bodies were being thrown aside, one by one, as someone from the outside worked their way in. In the midst of the chaos, I didn't get a good look at the one intervening, trying instead to assist.

When the last Fallen One had taken their final breath, I turned to face the person who had stepped in on our behalf.

Eran had his hand extended, thanking the last one I would have least expected.

Gershom's head was tilted down, bashfully accepting Eran's appreciation.

"What?" he asked, slightly uncomfortable, as if he'd exposed a secret. "I don't like to fight. I never said that I couldn't." Then his brow creased and his expression changed to concern. "Maggie?"

Eran was already at my side, his arms around me, carefully holding me up when I realized that warm blood now spread down my side, pooling beside my combat boots.

In the heat of battle, one of our enemies had landed a precise blow, one directly beside my heart.

As Eran inspected my wound, I searched his face for any sign of relief. There was none. In fact, there was only one way to describe his reaction: rigid determination.

"Eran?" I heard myself say just as the blackness closed in.

11. THE IDEA

"Will she be all right?" The voice was drawn out, languid, slow and unrecognizable.

Cool wind crossed my skin, layered with dampness and causing my body to quiver.

"Is it a mortal wound?" The voice inquired.

Wings, rapid, rhythmic flapped around me.

"Shut up and fly, Gershom." This voice was Eran's and it was undeniably nervous.

My eyelids, thick and heavy, drew open in time to catch sight of Eran's muscular arm and, beyond it, stone walls. They closed again and soon after I noticed my body jostling from side to side. Searing heat flashed up my body, so intense I held my breath against it.

The darkness came again, swallowing me whole. The sounds fell away, dying down slowly as the sound does with a carnival ride when it comes to a stop.

I was jostled then, my body constricting against the shocking movement. Eran was on the ground, running.

"The door," he commanded.

We didn't stop so I knew someone must have followed it.

Then I was surrounded by sheets, pillows, and blankets and someone was tugging at my wound, irritating it.

"No," I heard myself moan as I rolled away.

Someone shushed me just before I fell back to the deep, dark void.

When I awoke, the pain was gone. The severe injury to my side was nonexistent, and I moved with ease, breathing deeply and without restriction.

Opening my eyes again, I found the peaceful hall I knew so well surrounded me. Beneath me was my stone bench, the soft breeze moving around us.

Sitting up, my first thought was encouraging.

I hadn't died yet. This, I knew with absolute certainty because I hadn't passed through the tunnel I recalled on previous trips to the afterlife in which my body had stopped working all together.

This was good news. As they healed my body in the other dimension, as it recuperated there, it seemed I would be spending my time here.

Then I paused, realizing for the first time how it must feel for those who knew loved ones fighting for their lives. Having been given the ability to transport myself between dimensions, I was never restricted in being able to communicate with my loved ones. But here, right now, I had no way of telling them I felt perfectly fine. A void separated us, inhibiting us from speaking and leaving us both to wonder how the other was faring. It felt so unfair for them, and now for me and Eran.

Oddly, I was surrounded by loving entities and yet, looking back, I couldn't remember a time when I felt more alone.

"I'm here, Eran," I said softly. "And I'm all right."

Knowing he wouldn't get the message, I resigned myself to the situation and stood up.

Scanning the pockets before me, I realized there was really only one thing I could do...I'd make the most of my time and deliver outstanding messages.

Alterums had lined up early in the morning asking me to deliver messages for them, something I readily agreed to. When I started, I didn't stop, working one message after another to pass the time, stopping only intermittently at Eran's cabin to visit with Annie and Charlie.

In the afterlife, time remains consistent and irrelevant. No clocks, no common sleeping patterns, and no rising and falling of the sun mark the passing of time. Because of this, I had no idea how many days went by on earth while I worked.

My thoughts were permanently torn between earth and messages with images of Eran bent over my bedside and Ezra pacing the floor in her room, anticipating the announcement that I had reawakened.

The moment did come and when it did, it was sudden.

Walking down a beach with glistening violet sand alongside a man with silver hair and a deeply lined face, I had been disappointed when our conversation came to an abrupt halt.

The man's name was Dominick and he'd approached me in the Hall of Records, interested in learning how Eran was faring on earth. Our conversation carried over from the hall to his realm in the afterlife where we strolled along a quiet beach.

Dominick appeared to be ninety but occasionally he would stoop, pick up a rock, and skip it across the water with the agility of a teenager. His stride was effortless, hands clasped behind his back, his toes barely leaving prints in the sand.

At some point in the conversation, I'd mentioned my frustration with Ms. Barrett, whom he seemed to know. In fact, he knew just about everyone I mentioned.

"You'll need to guide her," he urged me. "All of them. They need your assistance, Maggie. They may be old souls, wise beyond that of a human, but that is precisely what endangers them. They know what awaits them here in the afterlife, the tranquility. It subdues their preservation instinct and gives them reason to ignore the reality that they would endure significant pain at the hands of a Fallen One. I believe only Ms. Barrett, having personally encountered one before, knows the full extent of the damage they can bring."

"Ms. Barrett has had an altercation with a Fallen One?" I asked, stunned.

"In her first and only life yet as a human…But she remembers it well."

"So that's the source of her fear," I mused.

He agreed with a solemn nod. "She's young still, learning our ways. Her existence only began just over one hundred years ago. It's one of the reasons she's there as an Alterum. She feels safer with ulterior powers while evaluating how humans interact. Her first visit to that dimension wasn't easy for her. But know this…even as she learns who she is, she does mean well."

"Yes, I can see it." I agreed, reflecting back to my epiphany that she and I both carried for the Alterums but showed it in different ways.

"Eran will be of assistance. He's had a bit of time in both dimensions," he offered. "But of course you know this already." He gave me a knowing grin.

I laughed lightly at the understatement.

"I figured as much," said Dominick, holding his hand out to an incoming wave and with telepathic force prevented it from reaching us, carving a dry path through it.

"How long have you known Eran?" I asked, realizing I was shifting the conversation and not particularly caring.

"Long before you," he sighed paternally. "I trained him."

My jaw falling open, I swung my head up. "You…"

"Yes, he was my student, more of a prodigy to be honest. He excelled at warfare and because of it I didn't question his decision when he chose to become a guardian. And I certainly didn't question it when he chose to relinquish his former ward to another guardian in favor of guarding you."

That statement sparked my curiosity. "Why is that?"

He sighed and tilted his head up to gaze at the translucent blue sky above and the heavens beyond it. "Those of us who have lived in both dimensions multiple times were the first to recognize it. I suppose we had the experience to understand what we saw. The love that you and Eran share differed in its intensity and resilience, far beyond anything we'd ever witnessed before."

"I guess I don't entirely understand," I said, contemplating.

"My dear, you two are the original soul mates."

I felt my brow creasing as I absorbed Dominick's meaning. Then, my eyes widened and I drew in a sigh of amazement. "We're the-"

My sentence was never finished as I was transported back through the space that separates each dimension.

Before my eyes were open the throbbing ache reached my consciousness.

Groaning, I moved my hand to the wound intending to press against it and subdue the pain but another hand seized mine and stopped its course.

"Not yet, my love," Eran whispered. "Pressure will only reopen it."

The sound of his enchanting, English accent gave me the motivation to wake fully.

"Eran," I whispered, a smile pulling at my cheeks as I took in every fine detail of his handsomely-chiseled face.

He gently lifted my hand to his lips and kissed my wrist.

"Magdalene…" he murmured against my skin, tickling me with his breath.

I giggled lightly but didn't pull away. When he lifted his head, he was smiling and there was serenity in it that calmed me instantly.

"I missed you."

It took only a second before we realized we'd each said it simultaneously and our grins deepened.

I attempted to shift closer to him only to notice I was tethered, the movement yanking on something attached to the middle of my forearm.

"What…" I muttered, going in search of it.

It only took a second to find the thing causing the restriction. A needle was injected in my arm, secured to a tube which wound up and over a metal stand where a bag of fluids hung.

Eran cleared his throat uncomfortably.

"How long has it been?" I asked.

"Seven days. You were asleep for seven days." His voice was wistful, heartrending. Then his hand dropped, carrying mine with it, but he wouldn't release it, still needing to feel connected to me. "You're healing well. No sign of Fallen Ones and you'll be impressed, I think, with the progress the Alterums have made."

"They're still training?"

"They are. I've even convinced Gershom to share his skills."

"You're joking."

He shook his head. "Gershom's been holding sessions twice a day. He's a wealth of information on the Fallen Ones…having been one at one point."

I imagined he would be. "And you? What have you been doing?"

He leaned back, avoiding the question. "Don't worry about me."

I assessed him closely, noting his disheveled hair, groggy eyes, and the clothes he wore – which hadn't been changed since I last saw him.

"You haven't left my bedside once, did you?"

"Magdalene, don't worry-"

"Eran," I stated. "You can't do that to yourself. I don't want you to do that to yourself…not for me. You need to-"

He cut me off with a kiss, one that started out intending to simply end my rant but turned passionate, tempting.

"Now…" he said behind his signature smirk, having gotten the appropriate response he sought in quieting me. It was charming and antagonizing at the same time. "Now that I have your full attention, did you find Dominick?"

Grudgingly, I answered him. "Yes."

"And did you ask about Ms. Barrett and how to handle her?"

"I did."

"And?" he urged, knowing I was intentionally withholding answers until I was reassured he wouldn't sacrifice himself to be stationed at my bedside again. "All right, Magdalene. I'll make sure to take a five minute break at times."

"Thirty," I demanded. "At least."

He moaned reluctantly. "Fine…thirty."

"Thank you," I said properly placated. "Yes, I did find Dominick and he was very helpful. Ms. Barrett has suffered at the hands of Fallen Ones before so he suggested we delicately guide her. In fact, he suggested we guide all the Alterums."

"I assumed as much. They aren't known for their preservation instinct. I was actually inspired by the number of Alterums who stayed and have been learning to fight."

Eran's gaze had drifted towards the window where below I could hear Rufus bellow a command only to immediately follow it with, "Ahh, blimey…That force ain't goin' to do nothin' but tickle yer enemy. Use yer weight! USE YER WEIGHT!"

Eran chuckled and shook his head at Rufus's training style. "Of course, they might not stick around."

I laughed with Eran before we fell silent again and then I opened my mouth to speak before realizing what I was doing.

"He also told me…" I began to say, allowing my voice to trail off.

"Dominick?" Eran inquired. "What else did he say?"

I swallowed, realizing I was anxious to acknowledge it, to even mention it.

Eran turned to face me fully, sensing the discomfort with what I was holding back. "Magdalene? Whatever Dominick said was in our best interest to learn."

"Right…Right." I said, reminding myself he'd been Eran's mentor. "He said…I don't know why I'm having such a tough time telling you."

Eran was growing increasingly worried now, which was precisely what should not have been happening given that Dominick's news was positive.

In an effort to erase the nervousness from Eran's expression, I blurted out, "He said we were the first soul mates."

Silence filled the room then as Eran only blinked in reaction. Then he leaned forward and took both my hands in his own. "Magdalene, why was it so hard to tell me? Why so uncomfortable?"

I opened my mouth and closed it twice before answering. "Because I don't want anything to change between us. I've always known what I felt for you was too intense…too powerful to be anything different. But you…I didn't know how you might react. But you don't seem…surprised…whatsoever. Did you-Did you already know?"

"Yes," he replied plainly.

"But how?" I asked in amazement. "Did Dominick tell you?"

"He didn't need to, Magdalene. I felt it just like you. I knew you were missing me when you were on the other side these last seven days. I knew you were speaking to me…"

"You heard me?" I asked, bewildered.

"Felt would be more accurate."

The breath caught in my throat took a second to dislodge. "So you've always known?"

"I always knew the intensity of my emotions for you but it took me a while to understand them. Only when I tied them in with our ability to feel each other's reactions did I grasp what it meant." Noting my confused stare, he went on. "We feel each other because we are uniquely bound to each other, Magdalene. We are two pieces to one whole and because of it somehow what we feel transcends space and time."

He leaned further towards me until our lips almost met and then he stopped, an inch away. The pressure in him was undeniable as his breathing staggered and he swallowed hard.

"I…" he exhaled sharply, his breath tantalizing me. "I need you."

"It's the same for me…"

He groaned loudly and sat up, tilting his head to the ceiling, fighting his desires. "And that's why I'm refraining." As if to cement the statement, he said again, "I'm refraining."

As he stood and moved to the window, he repeated it twice more. "Damn bad timing and injuries…" he muttered, staring outside, his teeth clenching so tight I could see the edge of his jaw protruding.

From below, we heard Gershom shouting commands, his tone taking on a growing level of confidence. Other than the sparing in the courtyard, there was no other sound and the room began to weigh heavily on me. So, I shifted and dropped my legs over the bed and pulled the needle from my arm.

"What do you think you're doing?" Eran asked, already crossing the floor towards me.

"Getting up."

"Oh no you're not."

"Yes, Eran. I am."

"No…you're not." This voice was equally as determined but it came from the doorway where Evelyn now stood. Just behind her was Ezra. Both of them wore frowns.

"Eran, get her back in bed," said Evelyn marching towards us.

"Doctor's orders," Eran said, smirking as if he'd just won a bet.

"Doctor?" I asked, confused.

"Evelyn's the house healer. She's the one who stitched your wound," Eran explained in my ear as he gently forced me back to my pillow.

"And it was a nasty one at that," said Evelyn. "You'll be recovering for the next few days."

"In bed?" I exclaimed.

No. There was too much to be done. There were the hunts to pick back up, the Alterum trainings, preparation for the next attack by the Fallen Ones…

"That's correct. The next few days, you're going to spend the time healing." From this declaration alone I could tell how stubborn Evelyn could be. "I don't want that injury to open again during a battle and render you useless. It puts you and those around you at risk."

It was also hard to argue with her logic.

She was at my side, inspecting the healing process as Ezra stood at the edge of my bed and Eran by the window.

When Evelyn replaced my bandages, she stood and seemed pleased. "Coming along nicely. We'll check it again in a few hours. Get some rest."

I groaned. "There is no way I'm going to rest." I was too anxious. There was too much to do.

As if waiting for the opportunity, Ezra grinned and stepped forward. "Excellent, then you'll have time for studying." She placed a hand on the stack of books piled on the table beside my bed.

I wondered why I hadn't noticed them before. Probably deliberate denial.

"Scowling at them won't help," she said. "And it's better than playing catch up when you get back to school."

"Right…" I muttered under my breath. "Right…"

Ezra placed an advanced Physics book on my lap and then patted my arm, encouraging me.

At least Ms. Beedinwigg will be pleased I hadn't forgone my schoolwork.

"Well," Ezra sighed, appearing satisfied with herself. "I have to run. I'm needed in the kitchen."

"The kitchen?" I asked.

"Isn't that usually Felix's domain?" Eran asked, following my line of thought.

"Yes, I'm playing mediator. Felix has harangued the poor cook to let him prepare one meal and the cook is not happy with the selection."

"What is it?" asked Eran, already stifling a grin.

Ezra was at the door by then but she paused to peer over her shoulder with an amused smirk. "Braised cow tongue with lemon pepper mousse." She giggled then. "Poor man has no idea…"

We watched her leave, just as amused as she was, but when the door closed the room seemed to absorb tension. Then Evelyn looked at Eran curiously.

"Now that Maggie is awake…and given that she's healing well…may I ask what your plans are?"

"I'm not sure what you mean."

She walked to the window where Eran stood and pointedly glanced down to the courtyard.

"They could use your help."

Eran's head turned to me.

"Don't worry about me. I'm fine. Good enough to get up…" I hinted, to which Evelyn responded with a glare.

Eran watched the action below for a few long seconds and then said, "Maybe an extra hand may help."

With that, Eran became the Alterum's newest instructor. I was happy for him and the fact he wouldn't be sitting around pining at my bedside.

"Excellent. I'll go inform them. Now…it looks like there's someone else here to see you," Evelyn announced as she left the room, squeezing by Gershom, who was peering around the edge of the opened bedroom door. He seemed to be nervous about something but for the life of me I couldn't understand what it might be.

"It's all right," I coaxed him in. "We're all fully clothed."

He sneered at my joke and stepped inside.

"How are you feeling?" he asked, stopping a few paces in.

"Fine. If it weren't for the monstrous ache in my side I'd be running a marathon."

"Well, at least her sense of humor is back," he said to Eran.

"Not sure that's an entirely good thing," Eran teased.

I playfully glowered at Eran who simply winked back jovially, acting both annoying and charming at the same time.

"So…no wooziness? No fever? No shakes?"

Gershom's interest in my recovery was a little too keen for me to take his question lightly.

I squinted my eyes at him.

"Why are you asking, Gershom?" Eran pressed, also suspicious.

"Well, I was thinking…" he said, hesitant, cautiously stepping forward. "After you got hurt, Maggie…Maybe your nighttime hunts aren't such a good idea in-"

"Oh, not you too?" I asked, offended.

"Let me finish," he insisted in a rare show of confidence.

When my mouth snapped shut in shock he continued, his tone firm, demanding attention. "Maybe your nighttime hunts aren't such a good idea in the way you are approaching them. Maybe…we should make the best use of them. I mean if we're going to put ourselves in danger shouldn't there be a reason for it?"

"There is," I declared and expected to continue but this time he cut me off.

"Yes, to kill the Fallen Ones," he said, taking the words right out of my mouth. "But shouldn't we be centering on the most dangerous ones?"

"You're referring to Abaddon," Eran speculated.

"Yes."

"That's fine in theory, Gershom, but in practice it's nearly impossible. We have no way of finding him," Eran explained.

"The book of dossiers was burnt," I pointed out.

"Yes but…there must be another way to find him."

I immediately sat up in bed.

"Do you remember, Maggie, when you visited your past lives?"

"Yes," I said, reflecting back to just a few weeks ago when I relived parts of my lives while learning what to expect when Fallen Ones attack.

"Well, have you ever tried to visit anyone else's past lives?"

"Noooo," I replied slowly. It never occurred to me the scrolls would allow it.

"Maybe it's time you tried," he ventured.

"What exactly are you proposing, Gershom?" Eran asked.

He stepped forward again, gaining more assurance as our interest increased.

"We need to find Abaddon...I think we all agree that he's the instigator behind the attack and we know equally as well that it won't be his last. It's only a matter of time. Having been a part of his group for a period, I know him well enough to estimate that he's amassing an army to accompany him. The only way to stop him is to find him first. And while we may not know his whereabouts here on earth...maybe clues, unintentional ones, have been left in his past...clues that may lead to where he is now. If...and I'm not sure if it's possible but if Maggie can visit his past life-"

"No!" Eran was on his feet, swelling with anger, filling the room with tension. "Absolutely not!"

Gershom, taken aback by Eran's reaction, leaned away in nervousness.

"Eran, please calm down," I said, placing a hand on his arm.

"I won't allow it," he stated, flat, adamant. "No..."

"The choice, Eran, isn't yours," I reminded him softly.

His head swung down in shock. "You don't know what you're...you can't agree to it...it would be...it's too much..."

Despite his message being broken and delivered through stunned fury, I understood what he meant.

"I can agree with it and I will survive it."

"Survive?" he posed. "In what way?"

"You're being dramatic," I said calmly.

"With every right to be."

His emotions drained, he lifted his fists to plant them on his hips, shaking his head in disbelief. "I can't agree to this, Magdalene. I won't."

"I don't think you're hearing me…You don't need to."

"Because you're going to do it anyways," he finished my thought aloud.

"If it helps to find Abaddon, yes. I'll do anything to make you…everyone I love…safe."

He knelt down beside me, laying his hands on mine, which were folded loosely in my lap. Staring up at me, he was desperate. There was urgency, a stark anxiety in him that I couldn't ignore and I felt my heart tear before I looked away.

"Please," he implored. "Don't do this."

I closed my eyes against the pain of denying him. If I only had a choice…

"How can you ask me not to do it? I'm the only one who can."

Understanding flickered behind his eyes.

"Eran, it has to be me," I repeated. "I'm the only one with the ability to reach the Hall of Records…and Abaddon's scroll of past lives."

He awakened to the realization of what Gershom and I had been trying to tell him. There was a reason why Gershom hadn't gone to anyone else, asking them to crawl inside the body of a villain. No one else could.

Defeated, his head fell, absorbing the reality of our situation. None of us took it lightly, understanding that it wouldn't be easy for me. But it was necessary. If it could give just one idea of where Abaddon was hiding it would be worth it.

Eran stood quietly and moved to the window, staring out but not truly seeing anything at all.

"Where did Abaddon die last?" I asked Gershom quietly.

He glanced at Eran, hesitant and uncertain of what reaction might spur when he answered. It was silent as a morgue now. You could hear a pin drop…from outside.

171

Refusing to take his eyes off Eran, he said, "Abaddon mentioned once that he was the only one of his close group not to die in Paris, France. His mortal life ended in what is now considered Austria."

"What city?" I persisted.

"Salzburg."

I grinned at Gershom. "Half the battle's over," I said, trying to be encouraging. "Now I just need to find his scroll."

Eran snorted from the window, his arms crossed, his body leaning away from us. He suddenly realized he'd heard enough, spinning abruptly and marching from the room.

Gershom, who'd stepped far from Eran as he left, stood uncomfortably in the corner.

After giving him a wavering smile, I said, "I'll do it tonight."

"If you're up to it…" It looked like he wanted to say more but clamped his mouth shut until he reached the door. There, he turned and quickly declared, "It was just an idea…"

"A good one."

I watched him leave, fighting the feeling that I'd just agreed to something that I would deeply regret.

12. A DEATH REVEALED

That night, I nervously awaited sleep, watching the sky outside my window darken far too quickly. I was thankful for my housemates, once again, who distracted me with a tray of food specially prepared by Felix.

"Boar's rump with brandied mushrooms," he boasted, placing the tray in my lap. "They have great meat over here."

He was nodding convincingly until Rufus rolled his eyes at him. "Sure do…till you prepare it."

"Rufus…" Ezra warned.

He frowned but reluctantly ended his teasing.

I'd already taken a bite by then, chewing cautiously, allowing my palate time to discern the flavors.

"You know…" I said, pointing my fork at the lump of meat. "It's pretty good."

"Cause you haven't eaten in seven days," said Rufus.

Felix sucked in a breath, offended.

"Rufus!" Ezra chastised in Felix's defense.

"Well…she hasn't…" Rufus shrugged, unable to understand what all the fuss was about.

Ezra sighed, aggravated, and initiated a subject change. "Which one are you working on first?" she asked, pointing to the stack of untouched books on the table next to my bed.

"None," I replied, unashamed.

Rufus snickered and received another fierce look from Ezra and an elbow to the ribs from Felix. Despite their disapproval and his annoyance with them, the two of us shared a grin.

"You're already behind. I can guarantee it," she warned. "You'll be back in school before you know it."

The mere hint of New Orleans made the room quiet, everyone succumbing to their own desires to be back there again. Only my metal fork clanging meekly against the plate filled the void.

"Any ideas when that'll be?" Rufus finally asked the question on everyone else's mind.

All eyes were on me then.

The truth was we were close.

I considered telling them about my plans for the night and the hope of finding a clue to Abaddon's location but I quickly decided against it. I'd seen how unnerved Eran and Gershom had become when I agreed to it. Why put them through the same distress?

"Time will tell," I replied simply.

Although they weren't entirely receptive to my vague answer, it did placate them. Ezra patted my knee supportively. "I'm sure it will."

"I...I'm sorry you're here. All of you." I dipped my head, shaking it against the reality of our situation.

"We're here because we want to be," Felix declared, partly insulted and partly trying to pacify me.

"N' that's the truth," Rufus stated firmly. "Don't miss that humidity one bit."

"Or the mosquitoes..." added Felix.

"Or the principals," said Ezra with a smirk.

I gave them a weak smile, appreciating their effort, and then the door opened.

Eran entered. His glower from earlier gone, to my relief.

"I think that's our cue," said Ezra, heading for the door.

Felix held out his hand to me and I placed my plate in his palm. He nodded, approving that it was now empty and followed Ezra out the door.

Rufus hung behind a bit, shuffling restlessly from foot to foot. Once Ezra and Felix were out the door, he approached me sheepishly.

In a tone low enough it was clearly meant for only my ears, he said, "Don't go worryin' 'bout us. You've got enough on yer mind."

Then he left the room, sending a firm glance in Eran's direction. "You know I don't need to say it," he mentioned on his way by Eran.

"Because you know I'll already do it."

Rufus nodded back, appeased.

When we were alone, I asked, "Don't need to say what?"

He shrugged and came to sit beside me.

"Don't need to say what, Eran?"

"He…He was telling me to take care of you."

Rufus…my giant friend with a gentle heart…

Nonetheless I sighed in irritation. "They're worried about me…"

"We all are," he admitted, scooting himself to lean against the bed's headboard.

"Well, I wished you'd all stop."

"Yeah…that's not going to happen so you might as well get used to it."

When I didn't respond, Eran took my hand from my lap and held it. His fingers were strong, slipping through and intertwining with mine. They were a comfort even through my annoyance.

"And I wish you'd reconsider your plan tonight."

"Eran, you know I can't do that." I drew in a deep breath not wanting to reopen the discussion. "There's no happy end to this conversation."

He nodded slowly, agreeing while deep in thought.

"What you will see…What you will feel…It will be…" he paused, cautious, deliberate, while keeping his eyes down and focused on our linked hands.

"Horrifying," I finished his sentence and his hand flinched around mine. "I know. I'm prepared."

"Not for this. No one is ever prepared for it."

I got the distinct feeling that we weren't talking about some vague possibility any more. We were discussing something more concrete, something that had actually happened.

"Do you want to tell me about it?" I asked, keeping my eyes on him, watching for any sign that would tell me what he was thinking.

He didn't respond immediately, taking the time to think it through. Finally, after what seemed like several minutes, he answered. "No, no…It…The scroll, I mean, might…skip over the…event."

So now several things were clear to me. Eran knew of something horrendous in Abaddon's past that I was not privy to and whatever it was had left Eran branded enough that it hadn't been forgotten.

"When…" I paused wondering whether I should venture further down this road and then realized I needed to ask, whether Eran answered it or not. "When have you and Abaddon been together without me being there?"

"Once…Magdalene. Only once."

That was enough confirmation for me. What Eran was remembering unnerved him enough that I knew I shouldn't push him. Instead, I tilted my head to lean my cheek against his arm. But he lifted it, coming over my shoulders, and pulling me in and cradling me against his side. I draped my arm over his solid abdomen and his other hand came up to run his fingers along my forearm.

We remained like that for an undefined amount of time and then he spoke again.

"I'll be here when you wake. Right here, Magdalene."

"I would hope so. Otherwise I'd have to tell Rufus you didn't hold up your side of the agreement," I jested.

Eran sighed wistfully, having no interest in my joking. "He does love you…They all do."

"And I love them. None of this would be worthwhile otherwise."

"Yes…of course." He was silent for a moment and then he turned to stare down at me. "You are more important than anything in my short existence, Magdalene. More important than life itself. I work so hard at keeping you safe and when I fail…"

I couldn't tell him that it wasn't his responsibility, that the decisions I made were my own. The idea of it simply wouldn't register with a guardian, and certainly not Eran, whose entire existence centered on protecting me. Guardians were different. They were, for lack of a better term, mystical zealots bent on a single purpose, one that controlled every action, almost every thought.

There was really only one way to respond and console him. "Just help me recover. It's all I ask."

"Of course I will," he said, his voice restrained.

I would have had to have been emotionally blind not to see what was truly bothering him then. It was not the aftermath or what would happen to me when I woke that concerned him. It was the very experience going through it.

As if hearing me grasp the reason behind his worries, he added, "Magdalene, just remember that tonight…you are surrounded by those who love you."

I yawned and straightened my arm across his belly in a stretch, trying to pass my actions off as calm and casual. The problem was he knew the truth.

I actually felt very unsettled.

That discomfort stayed with me until my lids closed and my breathing grew heavy and I was again back in the Hall of Records.

Before my eyes were even opened, I missed Eran.

He was my rock, my support in so many ways. As much as I thrived on my independence, I felt lost without him. The loneliness was overbearing and unforgiving, and there was only one thing I could do about it.

Get up, I told myself.

At the pace of dripping molasses, I sat up. Despite myself, I heard Gershom's words in my mind, telling me where Abaddon had died last and that irritated me. My subconscious was actually propelling me towards something that was possibly very dangerous for me. Eran and Gershom had known it. Why didn't my own mind? Of course, I knew the answer to that question. My mind put in to practice my motivations, and my motivations were to keep everyone else safe.

Shoving aside that uneasy feeling I'd been battling, I stood and, using my appendages, lifted myself and fluttered to the 'S' section of the records.

Not allowing myself to pause any longer, I found Abaddon's scroll and unrolled it.

What startled me first was that I had a difficult time finding Abaddon's name. I searched it hurriedly at first and then had to go back over it a second time, contemplating whether Gershom had been wrong about the place of death.

Then I discovered why I'd missed it.

Unlike other lives who had visited earth multiple times, Abaddon had not. His time on earth was noted with two lines in the midst of many.

Abaddon Rautenstrauch – Died Salzburg, Austria April 8, 1530

Abaddon Rautenstrauch – Fallen Salzburg, Austria April 8, 1530

I was thrown by this for two reasons. Typically I would see the word 'Previously' just prior to a list of preceding lives. On this scroll, under Abaddon's name, there were none. But what shocked me more was the fact that he had fallen on the very same day of his return to the afterlife.

This was not common. I had never seen or heard of any other soul being evicted from the afterlife immediately after their earthly death.

Then it hit me deep enough that I couldn't move a muscle. My wings froze in mid-flap, causing me to drop slightly until I overcame my shock.

Abaddon had only come to earth once and during the course of that life he'd committed an act so atrocious it had thrust him from the afterlife to the discomfort and anguish of an unending lifetime on earth. And whatever that act had been, Eran had witnessed it.

With even more hesitancy, I lifted my index finger and swiped it across the first line of Abaddon's name, bracing myself for what was to come.

I was actually surprised when it worked. As I had experienced before, a tunnel rose up and I was shot through it, leaving the peace and comfort in the Hall of Records.

Everything changed then.

Before I even recognized where I was, I noticed how I felt.

Cold…

Empty…

Angry…

I would have shivered against it if I'd had any control over this body I was now in.

When I did focus in on my surroundings I realized that Abaddon was laying on his back, his short, stubby legs in the air. This seemed peculiar until I felt Abaddon open his mouth, draw in a breath, and scream.

It was shrill and piercingly loud. Immediately, a woman entered the room, dressed in a colorless, unembroidered dress. She was frantic, shushing Abaddon as best she could. When she spoke it was in German but I could understand her clearly.

"Hush, little one. Hush or your mother will come."

Just as she finished her request, the door opened again and another woman entered. She was older and wore an elaborate dress, detailed with an intricate design.

She approached the bed where Abaddon lay and peered over.

Her brow was creased with worry as she bent down and soothed Abaddon's belly.

At her touch, his arms flailed and his scream grew louder, rattling the bed frame.

"Anya," said the older woman over Abaddon's screams. "What do I do?"

Anya shook her head. "I-I don't know…"

"Could he be sick?" she asked, desperate.

Anya shrugged. "I don't see how he could be. He's been this way since…birth."

The woman sighed in despair, her face drawing in and her eyes clenching closed in torment.

As if waiting for the right moment, Abaddon drew in a breath again and screamed, this time from the depth of his lungs, and both women stepped back, frightened.

Then I felt it, something that disturbed me beyond words.

Abaddon was enjoying this anguish, a pleasure tickling from within him.

He opened his mouth and released another curdling cry causing the older woman to reach for Anya's hand in despair.

As their tears began to fall Abaddon cried louder still, the tickle expanding inside him.

Then I was yanked from Abaddon's infant body and back through the tunnel.

It was calm here, peaceful; but it was only a brief respite before I landed inside Abaddon again.

Voices, angry ones, shouted around me suddenly. Staring straight ahead, through Abaddon's eyes, I found him watching chaos unfold within a small group a short distance away. It was dark but those on the mob carried torches illuminating a platform with a rope dangling above it.

Someone was being carried through the mass, a man whose arms were bound and unable to defend against the mob's fists and kicks. He ducked as best he could but he'd ended up bloodied by the time he'd been hauled to the platform.

As two men lifted him and another two placed him under the rope, a fifth man read a decree.

Again, it was in German but I was able to translate without trouble. This man was about to be executed for engaging in a clandestine affair. Apparently, the affair was with the daughter of a noble, specifically a Hochadel who had the authority to impose a death sentence.

Instinctually, my heart softened for this man.

Love was this man's crime? And he was to be killed for it? How did it come to this point?

The decree never explained. Instead, as the sentencing came to an end, the crowd turned to face Abaddon.

"Sir?" said the decree reader.

Abaddon's head turned then and I found a portly man standing next to him. His mouth twitched uncomfortably and his eyes were downcast as if he was deep in thought.

I was absolutely certain that this man's answer would either save the lover or condemn him to death and that he didn't take the decision lightly.

Abaddon, sensing the man's hesitation, leaned towards him and whispered in his ear.

"He soiled your daughter."

Four words. Those four words, drew that man's head up and with undeniable conviction, he announced his answer.

"Death."

Sickened, I realized what Abaddon had just done. He'd secured the lover's fate.

The victim, whose neck was now constrained by the rope around it, struggled hopelessly.

"No…" I screamed inside Abaddon. "No!"

Every part of my being wanted to rip through Abaddon and release this man. It wasn't fair. It wasn't fair! When I couldn't I tried to turn away but Abaddon's eyes remained locked on the situation, unblinking as if he refused to miss a single detail, that tickle of excitement rising in his belly again.

A trap door below the victim's feet opened and his body dropped through, causing the crowd to draw silent with only the squeak of the rope filling the air.

I was yanked again back to the tunnel and cast to Abaddon's body again, later in life.

A brawl was taking place inside a pub where Abaddon sat in the corner. As fists flew and tables were crushed, he idly drank a mug of something warm, fermented, and filling. It took just a second to realize what Abaddon was doing.

He was enjoying a beer while watching a fistfight rage around him.

Abaddon chuckled at times, engaged as if it were a source of entertainment. After a few minutes passed and the ruckus died down, I sensed him turning his head, evaluating the men sitting to his right and then to his left. Finally, he lifted his hand and snapped his fingers, gaining the attention of a burly boy no more than sixteen. With only his fingers, he motioned for the boy to join the fight. Following the order, he did and shortly after the fight picked back up to full chaos.

At each juncture in the fight when it showed signs of dying down, Abaddon repeated this process, snapping his fingers at one of the men beside him and instructing him to fight, escalating the diminishing conflict back to anarchy.

When there were no more men left, he stood, mug in hand, and strolled over the bodies to the bar. There, a barkeep and possibly the owner, cringe against the back wall.

Abaddon rested one arm on the bar and used the other to gesture sweepingly across the room. His eyes followed and I could see the devastation.

Tables and chairs were gone, just splinters of wood now. Glass and dented metal mugs scattered the bloodied wooden floor. Windows were now jagged pieces of broken glass, allowing in the frigid night air.

"Next time," said Abaddon in German, his voice controlled, subtle, "It won't be just your business."

He then stepped across the bodies towards the door. Those who had been sitting beside him, the ones who had entered the fight at Abaddon's command, were the clear winners. They'd crowded together in the middle of the room, surveying their results and counting the bodies until Abaddon was nearly to the door. But at the sound of Abaddon's finger snap they seized their banter and quietly followed Abaddon out the door in a huddled mass.

As the cold air hit Abaddon, I was pulled from his body and dropped back in at a later date to witness another atrocity. This time, Abaddon arranged an abduction. The next, a mutilation. One after another, I was shown parts of

Abaddon's life, standing as resistant onlooker to the crimes he endorsed and set in motion.

There were three elements I noticed in each of them. First, never once did he commit the crime himself. He enjoyed being a spectator far too much to dirty his own hands. Second, with each act of violence, the tickle in his abdomen grew stronger, more persistent. Third, Abaddon had always been malevolent. It was a part of him as were his thoughts, his instincts, him motivations.

What remained unseen were any clues as to where he might be hiding now, in the present.

I was sickened and devastated by what I'd lived through in Abaddon's body, feeling like a prisoner trapped in an ongoing nightmare, unable to help Abaddon's victims and unable to restrain his actions. I was growing wearier with each passing experience when I came across the most devastating of all.

It left me stunned, my emotions in shreds, incapacitated, desolate. I never thought it was possible to know so much horror and grief at once.

When I was dropped in Abaddon's body again I expected to bear witness to another anonymous victim. But this one…this time…it was someone I knew.

Abaddon's limbs swung back and forth, I realized, recognizing immediately that he was walking. Trees surrounded him and a river moved off to the left side. It was a place of tranquility, one would come to reflect. But he wasn't alone. I learned this as he swiveled his head down and to his right where I found a girl, no more than seven, beside him. When she looked up, it caught me by surprise.

Her Indian features were distinct and familiar to me, even at that age.

It was Sarai, Abaddon's daughter.

I could see in her a way of cajoling that would carry over to her supernatural ability when she fell to earth and the intelligence burning behind her eyes.

They walked for only a short while, hand in hand, until the sound of another's voice could be heard, faintly at first and growing more distinct as they strolled towards it.

It was speaking in German, giving a commemoration, it seemed.

As Abaddon and Sarai came through the trees, I learned that I'd guessed correctly. A group had gathered around a mound of fresh dirt on a small overlook above the river below. At the head of the mound was a cross with a wreath abundant with flowers, blue and purple, hanging from the neck.

The man at the gravesite finished and Abaddon and Sarai watched from a distance while the group slowly dispersed, leaving only the speaker and another man.

With their backs to us their faces were obscured. Yet, the shape of one triggered something in me, and I nearly ran to him before remembering that I did not control the actions of the body I was in.

His voice low, the speaker placed a comforting hand on the other man's broad shoulder, and said, "She will stay with you in spirit now. You may not see her but she is here."

He then turned and followed the path of the others, leaving the despondent man alone at the graveside, unable to comfort him further.

The sadness I felt in watching this scene was overwhelming and yet I felt nothing but apathy, a dark void, from Abaddon.

Sarai made a movement to step forward but Abaddon's hand came down and stopped her.

Abaddon appeared to be waiting for something.

Then, his head rotated to find the path the others had taken was now vacant. Only then did he drop his arm.

By this point, however, the man in front of the grave had dropped to his knees, sobbing, crippled over in agony.

While my sorrow for him deepened, again I felt only emptiness from Abaddon. Only when the man's cloak slid to the ground did I sense a change in Abaddon.

The man was naked from the waist up, shirtless despite the frosty afternoon air. As his shoulders shook uncontrollably, something began to sprout from between his shoulder blades.

Instantly, I knew what they were but Abaddon, having never seen them before, was overcome with intrigue. His entire body seemed to come alive then, that sickening tickle in the bottom of his stomach rising up again. He was exhilarated, amazed, and he coveted what he saw.

The man's appendages unfolded and lay against his back's natural contours. Stark white and nearly the size of the man himself, they were glorious, breathtaking.

Several things happened at once then, so fast that I nearly lost track of them all.

First, Sarai spoke and broke the silence around us. It wasn't a statement so much as a demand. She lifted her small hand and pointed at the man. "Wings."

Her voice disrupted the despair of the man at the graveside and he rotated at his waist, looking behind him.

Second and at the very same time, Abaddon's hand came under the breast of his jacket where his fingers found a piece of cold metal. He tucked it underneath the sleeve of his arm, keeping it hidden from sight.

Third, the speaker returned, coming up the path, his overcoat removed and folded over his shoulder. Without having to be told, I knew this man had returned to offer the additional warmth to the man on his knees.

But none of this shocked me. What did was the face of the man in sorrow staring back at me.

His hair was gray now and his skin was defined by wrinkles and my heart opened at the sight of him.

"Eran," I whispered from inside Abaddon's body.

Then, without warning, Abaddon's hand slipped the metal piece from his sleeve, unfolded it, and launched it at the man who had returned.

The metal landed squarely in the man's chest, redness instantly spreading below the protruding metal piece. The man blinked but his eyes were empty, not staring at Abaddon but through him.

Eran ran to the man, his wings withdrawing by the time he'd reached him. Kneeling beside him, he scanned the body as he'd done mine on so many occasions since this scene took place, surveying the injury and the possibility of survival.

There was none, the man's last breath wheezing from him confirming it.

Abaddon started across the frozen ground, passing the grave marker on the way. As if the scene unfolding wasn't enough to unnerve me, I caught sight of the wooden cross as Abaddon passed it. While it meant nothing to Abaddon, at this point having never heard of the person they'd buried, it made me constrict.

Chiseled in the wood was a single word:

Magdalene

This had been my grave. Eran had been grieving for me. And Abaddon had intended to hurt him in the midst of his sorrow.

Rage swelled in me then and while I was cognizant of the fact I couldn't move on my own volition, I hoped that somehow my emotions would transcend time and bring Abaddon to his knees.

Despite my most unrelenting push for it, Abaddon continued his stroll to the side of the man he'd just killed, stopping to stare down at what he'd done.

"He…He startled me," Abaddon muttered. "It had been a reaction."

And it had been. Abaddon was just as shocked as the rest of us. He'd only wanted the wings, Eran's wings, and he'd been distracted in that endeavor.

But something moved in Abaddon then. A door had been opened. Whereas before, Abaddon had assisted in the killings, watching from afar, this time he participated, and the reaction I felt in his body, the exhilaration that ran through him, told me that he enjoyed it.

Abaddon bent down and took hold of the knife still protruding from the man's chest, pulling it out.

Then he spoke again, words that didn't make sense at first, not until his actions followed.

"But now that I've done it…" he muttered.

Still holding the knife, he stood up, moving his wrist so that the blade was elongated. Using his upward motion, Abaddon's arm moved under Eran's neck and slid across it, making certain the knife connected with the skin as he pulled it towards him.

I knew what had happened though I couldn't bring myself to believe it. My mind would not process the understanding of it. I refused to believe it.

But when Eran's chin lifted to follow the knife from his neck, it made visible the devastation it had left behind.

The cut opened and blood spilled from Eran, coursing down his chest and on to the man lying below him.

"No…No!" I screamed and my limbs began moving, throwing punches, kicking, hitting, attempting to inflict every bit of harm to Abaddon possible.

Of course, none of it was possible. I was reliving something that had already taken place, the very occurrence that Eran had been trying to warn me about.

Abaddon kicked Eran in the shoulder then, sending his body to the hard ground. From there, he knelt and began sawing at the apex of Eran's appendages, each slice causing me to weaken, sickening me.

The first appendage fell to the ground and Abaddon went to work on the second, hands bloodied, grunting with his efforts.

When the second one was severed, he leaned forward over Eran who was taking his final breath.

"Thank you. These will look perfect mounted on my wall."

Then Eran was gone. Killed by Abaddon's hands.

It was my greatest fear come true, one that I would have done absolutely anything to prevent. And I had watched it unfold in front of me, had felt the movements that brought Eran pain.

I opened my mouth and released the emotions that had been building up, tightening within me, clawing to come out.

The scream raged through my being, from every part of it, a roar of such magnitude it shook me to my core.

It continued on until I was no longer in Abaddon's body, restricted by his movements, his motives, his destruction.

Suddenly it was my chest caving in, my hands gripping the edge of the cover laying over me, my face contorting against the anxiety of what I'd experienced.

"Magdalene! Magdalene!"

The voice came through from a distance, growing louder and more urgent with each attempt to lure with my name.

"Magdalene! MAGDALENE!"

Arms surrounded me, holding me against a chest firm and strong. They held me there, until I had no breath left in me and my scream came to an end.

But it was Eran's fragrance that broke through the horror, his gentle earthy scent that brought me to awareness. As it were my very first breath, I drew him in, filling my lungs as deep as they would allow.

"I couldn't stop him…" my voice mumbled. "I couldn't…"

"It's all right, Magdalene…" he stated softly. "It's all right."

"I couldn't stop him…"

Then the weeping began and through the sobs I said the words again.

Eran pulled me away, his hands on my shoulders, dipping his head so that our eyes were level. "You couldn't have stopped him…You weren't there."

"I know but I…"

"If you had been there, I have no doubt you would have tried to stop him…and I would have fought you on it…and you would have ignored me and interfered…and I would have had to fight while keeping an eye on you…and then…"

Eran continued on, his charming English accent melodic to me, pacifying the turmoil inside me until my emotions had ebbed. Even if he were describing the frustration in keeping me from engaging in conflict, it helped.

In the end, I was again leaning against him, my tears streaking down the mass of muscles protruding from his chest and stomach. His hand ran gently up and down my arm, soothing away the tension that had built up since I was dropped inside Abaddon's body.

"You tried to warn me…to prepare me but I…I had no idea…"

He shushed me quietly. "I never expected you to listen…though I did try."

"I wish I had."

"You wouldn't be you if you'd listened." He laughed quietly, causing my head to roll with it.

"The worst part..." I swallowed, hating to admit defeat. "The worst part is that it was for nothing. I didn't find a single clue that we could use."

My jaw clenched together. "All for nothing."

"I wouldn't necessarily say that..."

This voice wasn't Eran's and came from across the room, near the door.

We weren't alone, we realized.

"She's fine, Gershom. You can go back to bed," said Eran, still holding me.

"No," I said pulling away slightly, though keeping my hands on Eran's forearm, wanting to remain close. "What do you mean, Gershom? You said it wasn't all for nothing but I didn't...I didn't find anything we could use."

He sighed and turned on the lights, bringing a groan from both Eran and me. Ignoring it, Gershom walked to a chair across the room and facing the foot of the bed. He sat down, bent forward, his elbows leaning on his knees and his hands clasped together in front of him.

"I'm sorry to intrude," he said, genuinely apologetic. "But I...I knew what Maggie had seen when I heard the scream."

"She doesn't need to relive it," Eran replied curtly.

"I'm fine," I insisted but when Eran tilted his head at me with a knowing lift of his eyebrows I corrected myself. "I will be fine. Go on, Gershom."

"Umm...Maybe I should explain it in the morning."

Eran and I both groaned at his suggestion and Gershom's hands flew up in defense. "Okay...okay..."

He collected his thoughts and then continued on gaining confidence as he spoke. "I know Abaddon better than anyone here. Maybe, if you tell me what you saw, I can identify a clue on where he is hiding. Just...something."

"No," Eran said with evident disgust of the idea.

"Just a second," I said. "Maybe Gershom has a point…"

"Recounting what you saw means remembering it," Eran warned.

"I know…" I said and repeated it when Eran gave me a doubtful face. "I know."

Before he could oppose further, I went on to describe what I'd seen of Abaddon's past. Gershom listened intently, nodding at times, his eyes narrowed in thought. Occasionally, my body would shudder at a specific memory, chilling me entirely when I reviewed Eran's death. When I finished, Gershom considered what I'd told him and then began to speak.

"At the time that Abaddon took the life of the pastor overseeing Maggie's memorial service and then took Eran's life immediately after, he wasn't aware of the repercussions of his actions. I know this because he told me. Only when Abaddon passed on some five years after did it become clear. He was met in the afterlife immediately after arriving and told of his new fate. Then, he was escorted to earth by those who later joined Eran's army. They dropped him unceremoniously in the cold of winter in the middle of nowhere. And that sealed your fate."

Eran's eyebrows furrowed together. "So those who weren't in my army at the time left him in the middle of nowhere and now he wants vengeance on Magdalene?"

Gershom sighed in frustration. "No…no. I don't think that's it exactly. I don't think this is about Maggie. I'm wondering…if his vengeance might be related to your death. It was your death that was the cause for his fall, Eran. Even though he is the one who committed the act, he blames you for the fall."

"Wait…" Eran shook his head, attempting to clear it. "Magdalene had nothing to do with my death or the fall."

Gershom appeared slightly exasperated so he considered how best to clarify his explanation. Then, he stared across the room not at me but at Eran. "I don't think Abaddon is after Maggie. He never has been. He's after you, Eran. You are his focus."

"Me?" Eran's head jolted back in confusion.

No one spoke. Our heads swiveled back and forth, staring at each other, unable to find the words racing through our minds.

"But his attempts have centered on Magdalene."

"Yes, and there's a good reason for it," Gershom said and then spoke with absolute clarity to ensure his message was clear. "Abaddon can't feel you."

Understanding lit up Eran's eyes. "But he can feel Magdalene."

"And where Maggie is, he knows he'll find you," Gershom summed it up.

"But…his plans have always involved trying to kill Magdalene," Eran challenged.

"Because he knows it would destroy you. He feels he has suffered the worst punishment imaginable for himself. He wants to deliver the same fate to you. Maggie's death would mean two things…Failure as a guardian and that failure would send Maggie to her eternal death. She would pay the ultimate price for your failure and you would live the rest of eternity living with that fact."

Stunned to silence, we simply stared back at Gershom, who waited for us to process what we'd just been told.

"All this time…centuries…and I thought…" Eran blinked back his amazement. "How could I have not known…"

"I wouldn't blame yourself," said Gershom. "Abaddon is conniving and inexplicable. I spent over two hundred years with him and he still baffles me. I wouldn't expect you to know much about him."

"Gershom? Can I have a moment alone with Magdalene?"

"Of course, I won't disturb you again. I'm sorry. I-I just thought…I'm glad we at least understand that much now."

"And we do appreciate it," Eran consoled.

"Yes, we do," I added, nodding vehemently, not wanting him to question what he'd just done. Because, in fact, he'd just given us a better understanding of who Abaddon was and why he acted the way he did.

Gershom left then but not before he returned to his typical sheepish nature, lobbing across the room and clumsily closing the door.

Eran sighed and took both my hands in his, holding them firmly and with such intensity I expected a shock to come through them.

"You are the most important-"

"I know, Eran. You don't have to tell me."

He opened his mouth to speak and no words came out.

"You have nothing to be ashamed of," I said, already understanding his worry.

"I am the reason you are in danger," he said, anger brewing beneath the surface.

In an effort to keep it from overflowing, I replied, "He is the reason I am in danger. You are the victim, Eran. He murdered you." I paused, remembering the image, the pain of watching it happen, and I shuddered against it.

Eran drew me to his arms, wrapping them around me, securing me to him. My own arms slipped around his waist as I tucked my head against his shoulder.

"I'll protect you," he reinforced, his breath rustling my hair before he tilted his chin and gently placed a kiss at the top of my head.

"It was somehow easier when I thought he was after just me. I didn't have to worry as much." Already my instinct was to protect Eran, an irony considering his defensive skills far surpassed mine.

I guess...now I know what you go through each day," I whispered against his skin, noticing how worried my voice sounded.

"The fear of knowing someone is intent on killing the one you love?" he asked, restating my thought.

"Yes, it's a potent emotion."

Eran sighed heavily. "Yes it is."

"Watching him...when he slid that knife...that knife across your throat..." I consciously pushed aside the nub growing in my throat. I will not cry, I told myself, repeating it once more before I spoke again. "It was the most devastating episode of my existence..."

Eran responded with a tightening of his arms around me.

"All those times you took my life, even in an effort to save me from final death...I never knew...what you'd gone through. I never understood the horror. But I do now..."

"I'm so sorry you do," he said, his voice chocked.

"I never want to see it again, Eran. In this body or any other." I paused then, determination rushing through me. "I'm going back in."

"To Abaddon?" Eran asked with a jolt. "No, Magdalene."

Before he could get farther down that path of thinking, I corrected him. "Not Abaddon's life. I reviewed a good portion of his and found nothing. But there may be a clue in one of his follower's past lives."

Eran quieted but remained tense nonetheless. "Sarai...Elam..."

"Achan..." I joined him in unison.

I allowed Eran to come to terms with this new plan before asking something that I desperately needed to know. "Before...Before I go in, I want to know...Did anyone else hurt you? Is Abaddon the only one?" I wasn't sure if I could handle reliving that pain again.

Eran's answer was somewhat relieving. "No, Magadalene. Of that group, only Abaddon took my life."

"Of that group…" I repeated in a mumble. The fact he'd distinguished the end of his lives at the hands of others in that way disturbed me. How much pain had Eran endured throughout his existence?

"Magdalene?" He drew my attention.

"Yes?" I answered softly.

"While the ends of my lives haven't been…pleasant, the rest of the time was extraordinary…because I've spent it with you."

That brought a smile to my face and I pressed myself closer to his chest, enjoying the rise and fall of his breaths. "Every second with you is a gift."

He didn't respond but I sensed him smiling.

Then, as an afterthought and in an effort to prepare me for what was to come, he added, "Please don't think watching the lives of Abaddon's followers will be any easier."

"Oh, I wouldn't fool myself in to thinking that. I've dealt with them enough to know."

"Yes, you have."

"I'm not worried so much about what I'll see as about finding what we need. What if we don't find a clue and Abaddon attacks again? What happens then? To the Alterums? To us?"

He shushed me quietly. "Let me worry about that. You focus on helping us locate Abaddon. I'll prepare the Alterums for what is coming."

"We just need to do it quickly," I urged softly.

"Yes," Eran agreed, hesitant. "Our time…" He heaved a deep sigh. "Our time is running out."

13. SARAI

Knowing our time was limited and that Abaddon could strike us any day, I tried every hour to fall back to sleep. But my last attempt hadn't ended well and my subconscious was consciously keeping me awake with images of what I'd seen the night before.

Brief recollections of the death and devastation Abaddon had caused flashed before my eyes and, despite the warmth of the room, I shivered. I even tried to read a few of the textbooks that Ezra had brought for me. It didn't help. Even during intermittent attempts to lie down and fall asleep again, the images would come back…clearer, more distinct. It was maddening.

One good thing did come out of my hours awake, though. I'd already selected the next Fallen One's scroll.

Sarai.

She had been close to her father and likely spent the most time with him. Therefore, she was the next most likely to provide some clue to his whereabouts now.

Throughout the day, Evelyn checked on me, inspecting my wound with a straight face and leaving me to wonder how well it was healing; my housemates who brought a breakfast of quail eggs and toast – which was surprisingly good; and Gershom.

By the time he visited, he already knew my plan, giving me the information I needed to relive Sarai's past.

Ever true to his word, Eran joined the Alterums in the courtyard and helped Ms. Beedinwigg reinvent the training process, developing schedules for morning and evening sparing and lunchtime tutorials by Gershom on what to expect from his past cohorts.

With Eran's assistance, it seemed as if everything came together, the pieces fell in place, and the Alterums began to learn rapidly how to defend against the Fallen Ones.

Later that evening, Eran brought the both of us a plate of food for dinner. Prepared by the cook on staff, the ingredients were decent and familiar.

"Lamb stew and biscuits," he announced placing the bowl in my hands.

"Thanks," I said.

Only the chewing and clanking of our spoons against the bowls could be heard for a few very long seconds. Then Eran's hand came across the bed, from the edge where he was sitting beside me, and laid on my knee.

When I looked up, his expression was filled with compassion. "Just remember…it isn't real. You are watching something that has already passed."

He knew me so well…picking up my nervousness about tonight's visit to Sarai's past life.

I nodded, thankful. "Right. It isn't real…"

"You-"

"I know," I cut him off before he could say the words. A clue to Abaddon's hiding place could be close. I couldn't stop now.

"How are the Alterum's doing?" I asked, trying to take both our minds off the subject dominating us.

Eran nodded, more to himself but pleased. "Christianson is strong and quick. Agile too. Philius…the short one who looks like a salamander...He's stealthy...Would be good with reconnaissance..." Eran went on then to describe those who stood out to him in one way or another, defined by either their talent or their personality. It was helpful, not only to get to know the men he was working with and who might one day save our lives, but because it also took my mind off tonight.

Still, when the food was gone and Eran had exhausted his evaluations, there was no avoiding it. As I laid my head down on Eran's chest, just as I'd done the night before, my eyes refused to close.

The window allowed the moon's light in and I could see the outline of Eran's body beneath me, stretching out towards the end of the bed. His legs were long, almost reaching to the point where his heels hung off the side. They were also muscular. Even through the covers keeping the cold off us, I could see their definition, the solid build of a fighter's body.

While I knew he couldn't come with me on this visit, I credit him for giving me the strength to dismiss my nerves. He didn't know it but the very fact that his tough, sturdy body was so close to mine gave me the comfort I needed to close my eyes and ward off the horrible images of Abaddon's life.

When I opened my eyes, I was back in the Hall of Records. Wasting no time, I found and pulled Sarai's scroll from the wall. It was under 'P' for Paris, France, where she'd last died as a human, before falling.

Sarai Rautenstrauch – Died Paris, France January 8, 1535

Sarai Rautenstrauch – Fallen Paris, France January 8, 1535

Sarai Rautenstrauch – Eternal Death Bavarian Alps February 10, 2011

Just like her father, she had lived only one lifetime on earth as a human, having fallen after the body she had existed in came to its end. And she did it the same day she died.

It was a choice of fate I could not understand.

Placing my finger over her name, I swiped and was instantly transported through the tunnel that was now so well-known to me.

When I landed in Sarai's body, I immediately felt different. Unlike Abaddon's body, which was stiff and restrained, hers was languid, flexible. It felt as if I could bend backwards and finish a marathon that way.

Sarai's back was arched, actually, but only a little. She was leaning seductively against the wall of a busy street corner, one hand at the side of her chin, playing with the edge of the hood she wore.

As her eyes scrutinized the street, or more precisely the men on the street, I was able to catch a good look at her surroundings.

From the signs mounted over the doors of various shops, I deduced that she was in France and, from the size of the streets and the number of the horse drawn carriages, that it was Paris.

It was the middle of the day and those around her were committed to their errands, all except the older male gender. They had noticed her, or the rather tight bodice she wore, and she knew it.

Exhilaration pumping through her, she pushed herself off the wall and ambled along the street, keeping an awareness of the men around her.

"Mademoiselle," one called out from behind her but she refused to turn.

"Mademoiselle," he said again, more urgently.

Finally, he reached her, stepping up alongside and bending forward to peer inside her hood. As he did, he stepped back, stunned.

He made a sound of surprise and then turned and headed off across the street.

It wasn't so much his reaction that astonished me but Sarai's. Her joy was instantly washed away when the man had gotten a look at her beneath the hood.

Curiosity gnawed at me then, wondering how anyone could react with such repulsion after seeing Sarai. Remembering her too clearly, I knew her beauty was awe-inspiring. This man, on the other hand, had clearly been repulsed.

Only a few storefronts down did I get my answer.

She swung her head to glance behind her, checking on whether any other admirers would approach, and then I saw it.

She was young, still a teenager, but something had happened since I last saw her. The left side of her face was coarse, her skin rising in ridges where it was once flat and soft to the touch.

Somehow, Sarai had been maimed.

The hood she wore now made sense to me. It concealed the one part of her body she was most embarrassed by while accentuating the parts that drew the most admiration.

I realized then how Sarai had come to discover her supernatural ability to overpower and seduce men…She had crafted it. Years of refining had given her the ability to manipulate them, fulfilling her in a sick and disturbing way the need to be desired.

Suddenly, I was pulled from Sarai's body and down the tunnel, abruptly dropping back to it later in her life.

The noise of the street was dulled now and the offensive smell of horse manure and rotting garbage was gone, replaced with the subtle aroma of roses.

A bouquet was arranged in a crystal vase directly in front of her, alongside delicately painted tea cups, still filled the rim and steaming.

I felt her emotions then. They were heightened and to my astonishment I found that she was nervous.

When she glanced up, it was across the table at three people in front of her, two of them I knew instantly.

Campion stood in the back of the room, hands clasped behind his back, his hair as stark white as ever. He seemed to want to blend in with the background, as Eran does when he's watching me in The Square. Recognizing him, I smiled instantly inside.

While he stood behind a couch, the other two people sat on it, facing us. One was a woman dressed in traditional clothing. Although she seemed out of place surrounded by a room of ornate décor, she appeared relaxed. Her name was Éléonore and she had trained with me as a messenger. Thinking back, remembering her, I knew that she was excellent with the lance and that she hadn't returned from this lifetime. I studied her face as quickly as Sarai's fleeting looks would allow, wanting to absorb every detail as this may be the last time I see her again. But Sarai paid them little attention.

It was the teenage boy next to her that held Sarai's interest the most.

He was tall and wiry with a nose long enough to arch downwards towards his chin, nearly touching it. The style of his clothes told me that he did not come from wealth. Yet, none of this mattered to Sarai.

She was giddy, her heart flipping in her chest each time their eyes connected. It nearly broke right through her chest when he grinned proudly at her.

I couldn't believe it was possible but I couldn't deny it either…Sarai was in love.

"And how is it the two of you came to know each other," asked a woman to Sarai's left. She spoke in perfect French, with an underlying accent.

When Sarai looked up towards the woman, I found that she was older with beauty that rivaled Sarai. Clearly, they were mother and daughter. However, unlike Sarai, who had definite Indian features, this woman's skin tone and her heritage were less distinct.

"In the market," said the boy eagerly, also in French. As an afterthought, he added,

"Isabelle…uh…Mademoiselle."

The woman made a sound that showed she didn't appreciate him or his lack of etiquette.

"And how long have you been courting my daughter?" she asked, her tone nearly a demand.

"I…We…" He paused to clear his throat, clearly intimidated by Sarai's mother but regained his composure and answered clearly, "Several months now, Mademoiselle."

"I see," said Sarai's mother, her lips pinched together by the end of her retort.

Inside Sarai, I felt her growing more desperate. She sensed she was losing this battle with her mother, who evidently deemed her too worthy for this boy's lowly station. Sarai, on the other hand, had never known adoration like this from a man, especially one who had seen her face.

The woman beside the boy spoke for the first time, her usual steady evaluation of Sarai's mother breaking briefly. She too spoke in French, directly to the point, and with a grace in her tone that made her sound almost as if she were singing them. "Arnaud was not born with wealth but instead with the ability to earn it. He is strong, intelligent, and willful, and he will care for Sarai-"

"She doesn't need caring for," Sarai's mother interrupted causing an abrupt and uncomfortable silence.

"We were sorry to hear of your unfortunate accident," said Éléonore.

"Thank you," Sarai said, speaking for the first time and in a nervous rush. "When the carriage toppled, it crushed my mother entirely. The doctor said she…she died but he was wrong. She's as strong as ever. Arnaud…" she heart skipped a beat as he spoke his name. "He was so comforting when it happened."

Ignoring the look Arnaud and Sarai shared, the woman brushed it off, "Yes, I fared well."

In response, Éléonore nodded knowingly.

That was when I picked up on it. Something was different about this conversation. It wasn't so much the fact that Sarai's mother obviously did not want Arnaud and Sarai to be together as it was the way Éléonore and Sarai's mother seemed to be dancing around some vague truth, one I couldn't discern yet.

As if Sarai's mother had heard enough of the conversation, she said, "Let me make this unquestionably clear…" She dipped her chin slightly to level her eyes at Éléonore. "Having met you, I will not allow your son to see my daughter again."

"Met her?" muttered Sarai, confused.

"You have no idea who you are dealing with, my dear," said Isabelle to her daughter. "Loathsome, vile creatures."

Unruffled, Éléonore replied simply, "I recall you being one of us at some point in the past."

"And then I became wise," Isabelle retorted.

"After your death, no doubt," reasoned Éléonore. "When you could have lived in harmony for the rest of eternity."

Isabelle leaned forward, seething. "I chose to fall."

"Fall?" asked Sarai, bewildered. "What are you talking about?"

Isabelle disregarded her, the conversation having blown up now to a full scale argument while Arnaud and Sarai watched helplessly. They had no idea who the others were sitting opposite them. Sarai didn't know Campion to be a guardian and Arnaud hadn't known Sarai's mother to be a Fallen One, or that they were arch enemies.

"Then that makes you more foolish than I originally suspected," said Éléonore, meeting Isabelle head on.

Suddenly Isabelle was on her feet, a dagger in hand.

Éléonore was standing suddenly too, a sword appearing at her sword.

But the two were separated, Campion coming between them so rapidly his movement had been a blur.

"We'll be leaving now," Campion said coolly.

"No…" came a voice from behind a side door often used for servants. It was a voice I recognized instantly, one that would stir nightmares in me if I were ever able to sleep.

Abaddon appeared, a sneer lifting his thin, tight cheeks.

"No, you won't be leaving." He said this nonchalantly as if he were suggesting they stay for another round of cards.

"Pleasure to see you again, Campion," he added cordially.

"I can't say the same to you. Sorry."

Abaddon gave him a tight grin, taking a place next to Isabelle, his wife. Now it was Abaddon, Isabelle, and Sarai standing on one side of the coffee table and Campion, Éléonore, and Arnaud on the other.

"I heard you had fallen," stated Éléonore.

Abaddon's arms flew out, causing everyone in the room to tense. "Now you see the rumors are true. Rumors have a way of being so, don't you think? True, I mean. Take this little meeting between our families. I thought it couldn't possibly be so that my daughter had fallen in love with the son of a messenger. I thought it laughable, ironic…to be a rumor. And yet here we see the truth. One that will need to be remedied."

The threat hung in the air like an unfinished sentence causing a tense moment to pass with no one saying a word. And then…simultaneously wings sprouted from everyone in the room – everyone but the humans, Sarai and Arnaud.

The room spiraled to mayhem. Abaddon reached across the table and took Campion's collar, lifting and tossing him against the wall. Éléonore and Isabelle's swords clashed, stepping around the table for a better angle at each other.

Somewhere in the midst of it, Arnaud grasped Sarai and hauled her to the corner of the room, blocking her from any errant strikes by either party. She held him tight, terrified. I could feel her heart pounding rapidly in her chest as she kept her face buried in Arnaud's shoulder.

Then he left her side.

Shaken beyond control, she watched as Arnaud picked up a dagger that had slid across the floor in the chaos. Holding it in his hand, he moved forward towards the fight.

"Arnaud?" Sarai called in disbelief.

If he heard, he didn't respond, continuing to enter the fight, looking for a way in.

It came but quicker than he expected.

In one fluid sequence of motions, Isabelle temporarily got the best of Éléonore, throwing her across the room, and Arnaud took her position, stepping up to face Isabelle. But he was untrained and facing the speed, accuracy, and rage of a Fallen One. The sword came across his chest, tearing through him just as Éléonore returned to the fight.

Sarai cowered in the corner, her eyes locked on the man she loved, a cacophony of deep emotions beginning to stir in her as she made her way to him on hands and knees. Yet, even as she reached him we both knew the truth. Arnaud was gone.

"It isn't real," I told myself. "It isn't real."

In nearly the same thought, without any pause, I continued, "Look for the clue...Look for the clue."

But I found none.

Éléonore, who sensed it too, acted with motherly instinct, taking a single swipe of her sword and severing Isabelle's head.

But Isabelle had seen the strike coming, plunging her sword through Éléonore, their final assaults happening at the very same moment.

Sarai, who sat watching in surreal puzzlement, suddenly found the emotions welling up in her and released a scream that resonated through the room.

The two people she loved the most in her life now lay dead only a few feet from each other.

The fear and confusion she felt brimming inside became steadily replaced then with rage, like a cup filling with water until it reached the edge of the glass and overflowed. At that point, she took the weapon Arnaud still held in his hand and charged Campion, racing directly towards the frenzied clash of swords.

From inside her body, I actually tried to stop her, contracting my muscles as if I could somehow revert time, halt her movements, and keep her from certain death.

But she continued onward, coming too close. The edge of the weapon, that particular blow that came across her throat was not intended for her. I knew this because it came from her father as he struck at Campion.

His hit was good and the two of them fell back together, Campion landing against the wall and Sarai collapsing on the couch.

The pain was severe but not as intense as the terror that overwhelmed her.

Abaddon was suddenly in her view, his hand in hers. Instinctually, I pulled away but Sarai did not move. This was her father and he was going to console her.

But it wasn't consolation he was after.

"Die, Sarai," he encouraged. "Die…and return here to me."

Her eyebrow curved inward. She was confused, just as I was.

"Die, fall, and you will renew. Your scars will be gone...You will have incredible command over others..."

While I was certain he meant power to inflict injury and destruction, Sarai, in her naivety must have understood his promise to mean command over men. The fear ebbed then as the light to the other side appeared, the tunnel forming.

As Abaddon's voice became an echo in her ears, promising unbelievable powers, Sarai did something that both astounded and infuriated me.

Unable to speak now, she gave Abaddon a single, weak nod, confirmation that she heard, understood, and would follow his request.

Then she entered the tunnel and I was instantly pulled back to the Hall of Records.

"No..." I muttered, my head in my hands. "No! No! No!"

Still repeating that word, I was snapped back to my body on earth, shaking against Eran's chest.

14. ELAM

"You're safe, Magdalene…You're safe."

Eran's tender English accent broke through to me, a welcome realization that my visit to Sarai's life had ended.

I drew in a deep, trembling breath, recovering.

"I know…Thank you," I said through my hands, which were still holding my face. The fact that my body was settled against Eran's told me so. Yet, as much as I knew what Eran said was true, I didn't have the motivation to come out yet.

Then I felt his fingers softly pry mine back and away from my eyes, carrying my hands to my lap where he wrapped his own around them. The heat of his skin permeated my fingertips, chilled from my experience reliving Sarai's past.

He gave me a second, watching me patiently.

"She was kind, Eran." It was all I could think to say by way of an explanation.

"Sarai?"

"Yes, she was innocent, Eran. As a human, she was innocent." I shook my head, still perplexed.

As Eran drew me closer, I told him, "Campion was there. He saw it happen."

He was silent and then he tilted his head back, coming to a realization. "Ah…" he muttered.

Lifting my chin to look at him, I found his eyes were now focused on the ceiling, recalling the details of the day.

"What?" I asked.

"So that is what the scroll showed you…Sarai's death."

When I nodded, he added, "Do you know her death was the reason Campion joined my legion?"

"It is?" I was instantly intrigued.

"Campion's ward was killed on his watch," Eran said. "By a Fallen One…sending her to eternal death."

"So Campion wanted to retaliate?"

"No…No, that's not in Campion…He wanted to ensure no one else would suffer the same fate."

That, I could understand. I'd been working towards that goal for the last several weeks.

"He was also there when Sarai returned to the afterlife," Eran continued. "He watched her fall and the resolve to return was evident in her, he said. Knowing she would join forces with her father, Abaddon, and cause destruction where they went, he did the only thing he could. He joined my legion."

"Why yours?"

"You don't think mine is good enough?" he teased.

"You know better," I retorted.

His grin faded and he explained, "Because mine was designed with a single purpose…To protect guardians and messengers. And he knew that Sarai would be interested in killing any messenger who crossed her path."

Despite already being aware of their motivations, I was slightly insulted. "I…You know I just don't understand why…"

"Because, Magdalene," he said patiently, "her mother and the only man who ever loved her were killed in a fight…a fight that involved a messenger and a guardian."

I drew in a breath, finally given clarity to the situation.

"Vengeance," I mumbled. "Sarai was after vengeance."

"Vengeance against messengers, against guardians, against men."

Unfortunately, remembering back, it was easy to recognize in Sarai.

"Eran, he took an innocent young girl and taught her to be a monster."

I shuddered again, understanding the depths Abaddon would go to secure what he wanted. He wanted an army of his own. He'd started it with Sarai and was continuing to build it to this day.

Having heard this all before and having gone through his own path of realization, he patiently brushed a strand of hair from my forehead, allowing time for me to absorb the reality of what he revealed.

"But she wasn't forced from the afterlife. She fell as an Alterum," I said, bewildered. "How did she end up that way?"

"Abaddon," he replied simply.

I nodded. "Abaddon," I repeated, though my voice was thicker with anger. "He sealed her fate, teaching her hatred and destruction, changing her from an Alterum to a Fallen One and ensuring her death would be eternal."

I scoffed with revulsion.

"Knowing this," Eran said, "can you think of any clues you might have picked up while watching through Sarai's eyes?"

I thought, hard. The conversation had not mentioned any particular location and the home in France had been too stuffy, too cold in its décor to have allowed for any possessions that might be deemed too personal, removing any possibility of giving me insight towards their tendencies as a family. In the end I had to release my pent up breath and admit defeat. "I-I can't…"

"You're observant, Magdalene. If you didn't see a clue, it's because one wasn't there."

"I'll try again," I said, curling up against Eran, intent on trying to fall asleep again.

"Oh no you don't," said Eran, lifting me up to an uncomfortable position.

I sighed irritably.

"It's almost sunrise. You can't go back to sleep."

Thinking about it, I replied, "No, I-I really think I can."

He laughed lightly, his chest quivering against my shoulder. "I mean that I won't be here when you wake. Ms. Beedinwigg and I have initiated early morning trainings."

I groaned.

"That is pretty much the same response we received from everyone else," he said, a little amused.

Shifting, he slipped out of bed and stood up.

The sun's light, already beginning to come through the window, cast shadows across his body, accentuating the contours of his muscles. I openly stared at him, taking in every detail before he could dress.

"Careful, Magdalene," he said, bending to pick his clothes from the chair. "You'll make me blush."

He said this with his signature smirk that literally took my breath away.

Then he took his time slipping his clothes on.

Whether intentional or not, the result was a strong urge to get out of bed and wrap my limbs around him. Regrettably, I couldn't do it. My wound was still recovering and my efforts would simply end with an escort back to bed and a scolding from Evelyn.

Instead, Eran left the room, returning a few minutes later with a tray of oatmeal and bacon and the confirmation that Felix had been purposefully led to believe he was needed far more in the courtyard for training than in the kitchen.

Eran kissed me lightly on the lips then, a considerable tease to me, and left the room to join the others already causing a ruckus in the courtyard below.

That was when the irritation began. I still hadn't found anything we could use to find Abaddon. Each passing day meant Abaddon grew more prepared, posing a greater threat than the day before.

For most of the morning, I studied my way through the stack of books Ezra left while trying to ignore the nagging irritation. But it was like trying to ignore a splinter stuck in your skin. To try and take my mind off it, I would occasionally step out of bed and cross the room to watch Eran tutor the Alterums.

I'd only seen Eran train once, having interrupted him during a sparring session, and it had ended quickly after. This time I was able to enjoy it, sitting on the windowsill, taking in the fluidity of his movements and the strength of his attacks. The beauty of him took my breath away.

He noticed I was watching during the afternoon on the third day, hesitating so that he was caught off guard. It was the only time I saw Eran struck. Laughing it off, he'd returned to practicing but every once in a while took fleeting looks to see if I was still there.

The truth was I wished I was down there with him, working on getting my body back to the level it needed to be. The Fallen Ones were preparing too and I needed to be at my peak when they returned.

Time, at that point, was my enemy.

Then, on my fifth return to bed, I found an exam in between two textbooks, clearly hidden there by Ezra. I scoffed but nonetheless took the pencil mischievously slipped in a book spine and began to scribble my answers.

I'm not sure when it happened but the next thing I knew my body was laying straight against a hard stone bench.

Bewildered, I sat up and looked around at the pocket of scrolls. That irritation stayed with me, even in a place of absolute peace and tranquility. That told me something, which was…I needed to address it.

I ignored the concern that Eran was not beside me back on earth, ready to comfort me when I returned and headed for the scroll that listed those who died last in Paris, France.

I could almost see the frown Eran would have when he found out.

Still, I pulled the scroll from its pocket and allowed it to unroll. As expected, it was very long, taking several minutes until it was fully open.

"Elam Philocrates."

As the scroll slid through my hand, fingers came in to view and wrapped around on my wrist.

"You don't want to do that," said a voice directly behind me.

Rotating at the waist, I found Dominick staring back at me, concerned. He withdrew his hand and, because we were floating, he flapped his wings, almost indistinguishably, and shifted to face me.

"Trust me…" Something in his tone made me question my impulse so I glanced down at the scroll and Elam's name, deciding for myself.

I knew what Dominick was warning me against. Elam's lives would not be easy to revisit. Still, I had been through others, including Abaddon's who was the most malevolent of them all.

Elam's lifetimes were listed as most others, I noticed, but when my scanning of them reached the end my head jolted back. Something I hadn't expected stood out to me.

"He's-He's still alive," I muttered to myself.

"He is," said Dominick plainly as if everyone knew but me.

"But he was in the cave...the prison...with Abaddon. He was involved in the fight, wasn't he? He couldn't have survived..." But I already began to question it. Thinking back, I hadn't sent him to eternal death. I would have noticed it.

Dominick smiled patiently. "Abaddon survived, didn't he?"

"Yes."

"Then what makes you think Elam didn't?"

I thought for a moment but had no answer and Dominick explained further.

"Elam is not only elusive, appearing when needed and disappearing when he is not, but he also is very difficult to kill."

That I knew.

"Then he's helping Abaddon..." I ventured.

Dominick nodded quietly in agreement.

"So I do need to visit his past lives." My resolution had returned.

"For what reason?" Dominick challenged, curiously resistant to the idea.

I didn't immediately respond, not wanting to say the words. Somehow voicing them would make them more real here and I wanted to retain some small measure of surreal ignorance in this place of tranquility.

"Maggie?" Dominick persisted and I went ahead to blurt the answer.

"Abaddon is building an army to attack us."

"Us?" Dominick asked, needing more information.

"The Alterums, Eran, me...everyone."

Dominick considered this news with amazing peace and self-assurance. He'd been through this before, or so he thought. To help him understand the potential impact, I

215

added, "I believe this is Abaddon's final attempt to take control."

"Of what?" Dominick's eyebrows furled, showing an ounce more concern.

"The world." I waited for that announcement to sink in before adding, "His plan is to dominate the other dimension entirely."

Dominick's head dropped in contemplation. It seemed to me that he was finally coming to a level of awareness that Eran and I had been at all along, but then I was proven wrong. Dominick knew more than he let on. I learned this when he said quietly, "It always has been."

He stared back with concern. "You expect this to be more than a battle," he stated, grasping the significance of what I was telling him.

I shook my head. "Dominick...I expect this to be the war."

I watched him as concern, of the same magnitude we'd been dealing with back on earth, crossed his face.

"So it is finally coming to pass..." he muttered.

"Yes...it is."

"He's using you, Maggie, as a reason to gather the Fallen Ones, to motivate them to becoming a single, unified force. But his goal is incongruous...it differs from theirs. While they will be bent on murdering you, he will be focused on total destruction of all Alterums, opening the way to dominating that dimension."

"How do you know that?" I asked, astounded now. "How do you know so much, Dominick? How do you know about Elam...about Abaddon? I don't understand..."

He reached out and laid his hand on my shoulder briefly. "You can believe what I am saying. Elam told me himself." His arm fell then and his eyes glazed over as memories returned to him. "When I participated in Eran's army, long ago, Elam was my focal point, my initiative. My mission was to remove him…entirely."

"Send him to eternal death, you mean."

"Yes, I was to locate and deliver him to a messenger for the final strike…and I came close. After finding Elam administering the Russian gulag, performing experiments on its inmates, I incapacitated him…or so I thought. He demonstrated his resilience somewhere over Germany, debilitating me instead. While restricted, he took his time with me, motivating me to remain alert with each slice by feeding me information on Abaddon's plan, the same plan I just mentioned to you." When he was finished, his expression showed no anger, no animosity, no fear. He had recovered from his ordeal, with only Elam's words leaving an impact…thankfully.

"That is all you will find in Elam's scroll, that and the substance of nightmares," he warned, tipping his head towards my hands that still held it.

My mind did not comprehend the warning, though. It was centered on one overwhelming fact. Elam confirmed that all Abaddon was waiting for was a single unifying reason.

"I gave him that reason, Dominick. The Fallen Ones are rallying because of my hunts, my executions of their kind."

I exhaled, the reality of the destruction I had caused, will cause, caving in my chest. It felt as if sand had filled my lungs but it was only me…the realization of the destruction I had created coming at me with full force.

With one last glimmer of hope, I challenged Dominick's assertion.

"But Dominick, how could Abaddon possibly think he would ever be able to destroy the Alterums completely? Once killed, they can just return to earth in whole again."

Dominick lifted his eyebrows, allowing me time to figure it out for myself. As it came to me, I sucked in a deep breath of air.

"Elsics…He's going to use the Elsics…"

Dominick nodded again, this time a sadness floating across his face.

That epiphany spurred something in me that I hadn't felt for some time, a deep sense of urgent drive.

"Dominick? Could you do me a favor?" I asked, trying to contain my emotions.

"Anything, Maggie."

"Could you alert the others here, specifically the rest of Eran's army? Tell them to get ready…We are going to need them."

15. ACHAN

I never did get the chance to visit Elam's past life. The nervousness created during my discussion with Dominick sent me back to earth, waking me from my nap, the memory of Dominick's message running through my mind.

…gathering the Fallen Ones…

…going to use the Elsics…

…dominating that dimension…

No, no. *This* dimension.

Eran came through the door of our room then, disturbing my line of thought.

Before he could close it, I was already sitting up.

"Eran, I need to train with you."

He halted in the middle of the room with a tray of food in his hands to stare back suspiciously. Then he verified just how well he knew me. "Did you fall asleep?"

My shoulders dropped. This was urgent, couldn't he see that? There was no time for questions.

"Help me. I need to get dressed," I said, already trying to stand.

"Oh…no you don't," he said, rushing to the edge of my bed and stopping me, which made me groan.

"Magdalene, do you see any Fallen Ones?" he asked, using his seductive sense of reason.

When I refused to answer, he did it for me. "No, you don't. Until you do, you will remain in recovery." He sighed in irritation, bending to sit on the bed next to me. "You did, didn't you? Picked out another scroll…"

"I didn't go through it though," I said allowing myself the credit. "Dominick stopped me."

Eran's face relaxed then. "Thank you, Dominick," he said out loud, his face slightly tilted to the sky, and then he turned to me. "This isn't healthy, Magdalene. You're…unraveled."

That was when it happened. I felt them coming and fought them back but in the end they won. Tears spilled over my lids and down to the cover.

"It's all my fault, Eran," I said through my weeping. "I brought this war on…I gave the Fallen Ones a rallying cry. All of you are in danger…again…because of me."

Eran remained still, no movement, no speaking, letting me release the guilt that had built up over so long. Then, when my body had relieved itself of the shudders and tears, I lifted my head.

He was gazing at me, his lips puckered in disapproval.

"First, you don't put us in danger. We put ourselves in danger. It's not your choice. Second, this is not my wife. She would not resort to self-pity when she is needed most. Now wipe off the tears and go find her…because I love her and I want her back."

Sniffling, I nodded. Then it was him who reached up and with a few soft brushes of his thumb my face was cleared of its streaks. Then he slipped his fingers below the rim of my jaw and drew me towards him until our lips met, brushing against one another, soothing my upset.

"He's going to use Elsics," I said in a whisper, unintentionally, my mind betraying me and reverting back to my conversation with Dominick.

That caused Eran to pull back. "Abaddon is going to use Elsics?"

"Yes, I don't know how or when but…but Dominick confirmed it."

"Then we can be certain that's accurate information." His expression was firm for only a few seconds and then relaxed. "I'll inform the others. We'll need to modify our training." I could see he was already contemplating it.

Elsics would pose a greater threat and a stronger defense. Knowing this, Eran was already formulating a plan. As he did, I watched him, taken by his focus, determination, and the spirit in his eyes.

"In the meantime," he said, his attention returning to me. "I see that you haven't finished your exam." It was his attempt to redirect my thoughts away from Fallen Ones.

He pointed to the piece of paper that had been so dull I'd fallen asleep while filling it out.

I groaned.

"Ezra wouldn't be too impressed to hear you right now," he cautioned.

"Then let her take the test."

He laughed at my retort and then leaned towards me, stopping just an inch away. "Welcome back, wife."

I smiled back, loving the sound of that name.

"No more dozing," he commanded then with a wag of his finger. "If you do, deliver messages. Give yourself a break from reviewing past lives. You need it, sweetheart."

There was something in his tone or removed from it actually that made me reconsider falling back asleep. As I watched him, I knew what it was. His lack of insistence told me that he was cautioning me but not enforcing it. He couldn't. He had no way of stopping me once I was back in the afterlife. Therefore, he was relying on my judgment, even though it hadn't proven to be so good lately. For this very reason alone, I silently promised to follow his advice, or more precisely, consider it.

"Don't forget your lunch," he motioned towards the tray he'd brought with him, which he had set next to me. "It'll help you get your strength back…even if it was prepared by Felix."

A quick glance validated it. The plate had three mounds, each of varying degrees of brown hues.

"What is this?" I asked.

Eran was at the door by then. "Mush." As I inspected them from afar, he added wistfully, "Don't worry, they're edible. He made me try them."

"I'm sorry," I called out.

"So was I," Eran replied as the door closed.

The remainder of the day was taken up with studying, visits by my housemates in the evening, and taking messages for Alterums before Eran advised them it was time for my rest. That night, after landing in the Hall of Records, I purposefully ignored the P's, or more precisely the scroll for Paris, France, and headed for the scrolls that would take me to the loved ones of those I was delivering messages to.

While there were quite a few messages, I was able to deliver them efficiently and by the end of my mental list of names I was back sitting in the Hall of Records, waiting for the morning to arrive.

The hall was resoundingly quiet with not a single soul there but me as I took a seat on my stone bench. After a few minutes I began to tap my feet, then I started to hum, and then my fingers began drumming my thighs.

Then I drew in a deep breath, filling my lungs with the cool, refreshing breeze that consistently floated through the hall. It calmed my agitation but only momentarily.

Before I knew it, I was up and my wings were out. They took me off the ground and across the hall, stopping directly next to the P's.

There I paused and evaluated my feelings. I was calm, rational, and aware. Still I had the burning desire to visit the past lives of the last of Abaddon's closest followers. I could handle this…

Pulling the scroll from its pocket, I spoke his name, "Achan Aemilius," and the scroll began to move.

It stopped at his name, the rows of his past lives lining up with the tip of my thumb. He had been to earth nine times, by far the most of any Abaddon follower.

I couldn't visit each one. There just wasn't enough time. I was at the end of my time here, instinct telling me that the sun was just about to rise back in the other dimension.

So, I narrowed my selection down to the last lifetime before eternal death, the one he'd lived after falling.

I swiped my finger across his name and found Achan striding through a long, dark, and twisting hallway carved of mortared stone. Torches lit the way, giving just enough light to see the rats that cowered at the sound of his approach. The air was musty with a layer of decomposition.

He was slight crouched, from the low ceiling as well as an attempt to project casual strength. He did this because he wasn't alone.

When the voice came from behind Achan, my recognition of it made my muscles from inside Achan's body tighten.

"You live this deep," said Abaddon in French. It was more of a statement, a speculation, than a question.

"It keeps me hidden from sight," replied Achan, also in French. A few steps farther and Achan added, "Burials are what bring people down here…and they don't stay long."

As he made his comment, his hand swung the torch he carried towards the opening of a room, one filled with bones.

The conversation between Achan and Abaddon was stiff, I noticed, which hinted at one thing. The scroll was showing me when they had first met.

They reached a stone portal, an entryway, with an inscription: Arrête! C'est ici l'empire de la Mort.

Without having to be told, I knew what it meant.

Halt! This is the Empire of Death.

Neither one of them halted.

Achan heaved open the thick, wooden door and entered another hallway, this one lined with intricately arranged bones.

"How many did you slay atop the Bastille?" Abaddon asked casually following behind.

Achan turned quickly and entered a room off the main hallway, one suspiciously void of bones. "Thirty…maybe forty. I don't count when they're not messengers."

For emphasis, Achan swung the bag of arrows from his shoulder and set it down, along with his bow, propping them against the wall near the door. He then unsheathed a dagger and approached a wooden altar, notched with rows of deeply carved lines. He took the blade and carved one more line and then stood back to observe his work.

"How many have you killed in total?" Abaddon asked from behind him.

"Messengers? Count them for yourself," he said, gesturing to the altar.

My breath caught as I realized what Achan was referring to…for every messenger he'd murdered, he'd made a notch in his altar. In the brief time before Achan turned from it, I counted fifteen notches, fifteen lines, fifteen messengers.

I suddenly felt sick.

Abaddon approached and bent forward for a closer look. "Fourteen messengers," he stated. "A fine job."

Achan swung around, smirking. "You've miscounted. There are fifteen lines there."

Abaddon shook his head. "The one you killed tonight doesn't count. She will return."

"Return?" Achan laughed. "My arrow found its mark."

"It did. They all did," agreed Abaddon. "But she didn't die by them."

Achan crossed his arms, testing him. "Then how did she die?"

Abaddon met his challenge head on. "By her guardian, Achan…the man beside her was her guardian."

Rage swelled in Achan then, causing his lip to curl back, and his fists to clench together, nails digging through his palms. Clearly, it wasn't often that he was duped.

Slowly, I began to piece together what they were referring to. Achan had been at the Bastille, killing the rebels, only to be pulled away to execute a messenger.

In my past life, I had witnessed the Bastille burn and I had seen Achan's arrows break through the glass of the estate where I'd lived, landing where they intended, in me.

I was the messenger they were discussing and Eran was the guardian who saved me.

Abaddon strolled from the altar with indifference towards it and across the room where Achan stood. "But I can make sure you get a second chance…" he promised.

Achan's emotions calmed, but only slightly. "How?"

"Join me…Join me and you will have your chance at Maggie again."

At the sound of my name, I flinched.

Achan assessed his options before answering and then I felt a smile spread across his face. "What must I offer in return?"

"When she returns, and she will, hunt her. Find her and you may take her life but do not touch her guardian."

225

"And why?"

"Her guardian is mine," Abaddon stated with a finality that sent shivers down my spine.

Achan extended his hand.

"A gentleman's pact," said Abaddon, taking Achan's hand only for a brief shake.

"Are you not a gentleman?" I felt Achan's eyebrows rise.

"I am," replied Abaddon insidiously. "The worst of their kind."

They each responded with laughter and almost as if a wall had been breached, their shoulders fell, their faces relaxed, and they welcomed each other as more than acquaintances.

"Just one more thing," said Abaddon. "I'm curious…What drives you to kill them? I've known others of our kind who would slay messengers when crossing their path but I haven't known one to hunt them."

"They can send me to death…eternally," Achan pointed out. "Thus, I get to them before they get to me."

Abaddon slowly nodded in concurrence. "That…is good enough for me…"

Now it was my lip that curled up, in disgust, but it didn't last long.

I was yanked from Achan's body and back to the other dimension.

When I opened my eyes, Eran was sitting in a chair next to the bed, watching me.

I blinked a few times, clearing the blur from my sight, and found him watching me, a slight frown turning his handsome face downward.

"You visited another scroll," he stated with frustration. Without waiting for confirmation, he asked, "Was it worth it?"

My answer would have reaffirmed in him that he was right in suggesting I take a break. I had come back with no clues, once again. So, I remained quiet.

Slipping my legs over the bed, I noticed it was dark outside the window.

"The sun hasn't come up yet," I commented, trying to take the conversation off me.

It didn't help.

"It rose," said Eran stiffly. "And it fell."

"It's night again?" I exclaimed.

"Yes," said Eran flatly.

"Huh…" I muttered. "I must…I guess my body really needed the rest."

Eran, who had been slouched in the chair, sat up. "Do you want to know how I knew you'd visited another life?"

"Not really," I said slowly and in all honesty.

"Because I waited for you to wake up…every minute of the twenty four hours you've been asleep."

"Oh, Eran, I'm sorry." And I truly was.

He stood and moved to the edge of the bed then. "Your body here was writhing while you visited the afterlife," he paused and corrected himself, "the scroll. Are you all right?"

"Yes, I think so." I lifted the shirt I wore and peeked down through the bandage covering my wound.

Eran drew in a deep breath and released it gradually, making me realize that he'd been holding his breath, anxiously waiting to ensure I was fine.

"I'm sorry," I said again, placing my hand on his.

With my health confirmed, he was back to himself again. I knew this when he grinned.

"You know…" he said, standing, "I would have to live in denial to believe you would listen to me."

We shared a laugh and then his gaze dropped to my waist.

"Your thrashing was fairly aggressive so I'm going to venture that you've healed well enough to make it to the dining hall. I'm told there are a few Alterums who want to make your acquaintance, ones who have been admirers from afar."

"Really? Who?"

"Oh…all of them," Eran replied casually, as if it wasn't meant to have any effect on me.

It did and I was left slightly unnerved.

Eran helped me dress then, taking extra care to veer his eyes when he felt it was prudent. It almost made me chuckle.

I learned, as we headed for the dining hall, that I had built up the energy and tolerance needed to get around without much help. So much that I was already considering training with Eran tomorrow by the time we reached the hall's door.

Interestingly, it was far different from the cafeteria at school. While nearly as large and filled with bodies that turned to stare at me when I passed through the door, the faces on those watching me now were with admiration.

"Mags," Felix shouted, haphazardly standing and tipping his chair in his rush to greet me.

Rufus growled at him as Felix's hip bumped the table and sloshed his milk. "She ain't runnin' in the other direction. What's the rush?"

If Felix heard him, he chose to ignore it, wrapping his arms around me.

"It's all right, Felix," I laughed. "I can do this on my own."

"Oh, I know it," he replied casually while leaving his hand on my elbow for support.

He guided me to the table, kicking the leg of Rufus's chair to get him to move. The problem was he had already moved.

"Ya'll knock it off if ya wanna keep that foot," Rufus threatened.

"Well," I said, leveling myself gently in a chair. "Sounds like everything's back to normal."

Ezra and Ms. Beedinwigg responded with a grin while Felix and Rufus continued to bicker. Ezra shushed them a moment later.

Eran, who'd left to gather a tray of food, returned and we set about eating. Tonight's menu consisted of chicken stew and dumplings so I knew Felix hadn't been let back in the kitchen for a full dinner service yet.

As we ate, the conversation changed topics often until landing on one that seemed to be on the top of everyone's mind. It was Eran who addressed it, though it was unintentional.

"Felix, how's your leg?" he asked.

"Fine…why?"

"I saw one of the Alterums you were working with today make contact…and it was a good one."

Rufus, who'd been quiet most of dinner, opened his mouth and released a barrage of guffaws at Felix.

Felix balked with a roll of his eyes but said nothing, returning to plate of food instead.

"They're looking better," Ezra commented.

"Much better," Ms. Beedinwigg agreed.

Then the table fell silent as the realization landed on us all at once.

The time had come to select the best ones to accompany our hunts.

"Are they ready?" I asked, wanting to be certain, requiring it, in fact.

Eran, Campion, Ms. Beedinwigg – the best fighters of the group – glanced at each other. One began to nod and then another until all came to a consensus.

"They're ready," Eran confirmed.

My eyes dropped to the table then, noticing a carving etched in the ancient wood table.

E + J forever

My thoughts turned then, away from those sitting beside me, and towards the person who had carved those initials. It reminded me of the carving Eran had made on the inside of my hut in the tranquility of the afterlife and I wondered if E…or J…whichever had left the carving felt the same passion as Eran and me.

It was my choice to determine who to ask to join our close knit team and I didn't take it lightly. In reality, I could be asking E or J to leave the other behind, put their life at risk for the sake of a greater good, and threaten the possibility of their love's longevity. It was an overwhelming request.

Should E or J be chosen and should they accept, he or she would not only be putting themselves in danger they could also put the rest of us in danger, given they'd only recently learned how to fight enemies armed with centuries of training.

A pair of warm, heavy hands on my shoulders jolted me from my thoughts then. Thinking it was Eran, I turned, cautiously so as not to reopen my wound, and smile up at him only to find it was Magnus standing behind me.

"I'd like you to meet a few of the more established in our crowd," he said, his voice just as hearty as the last time I'd heard it. I knew instantly that by established he meant more experienced and wiser.

Behind him was a line of men and women, some still in their teenage years. As they approached me, I noticed several things about them. They all moved with powerful, assured grace, a confidence that told me that they knew what was coming for them and wouldn't shy away from it. Looking in their eyes, I saw in each of them something that I hadn't expected…an audacity that told of a common belief that this was their world and they were going to protect it. Lastly, they were each quick witted, some going so far as to verbally spare with Rufus, knowing him from their time in an Irish orphanage. Their subtle jesting said they had seen a lot and that it wouldn't stop them from enjoying the life they'd come here to live.

After I thanked each of them for introducing themselves, Eran leaned towards me. "I believe you just met the additions to your team."

I blinked back at him, astounded. Watching the entourage weaving through the tables and back to their respective seats, I realized he was correct. I hadn't recognized it at the time but they were right for our team.

Grinning, I finished my dinner, feeling the assurance that only accompanies the finding of a perfect fit. When the plates had been cleared, Rufus introduced me to more of his friends from the orphanage, the same ones who'd been detained in the cells below the assembly room for having sided with Rufus. That didn't seem to matter to them, however. As Rufus took the time to point to each of his various tattoos and relate how the stocky Irish man or woman sitting in front of me came to conjure such an imprint, their faces were bright and amused. Many of them had endured difficult childhoods only to be met with challenging adulthoods but not a single one of them carried bitterness. They laughed from their bellies, clapping their hands heartily on the wooden table and threatening to leave a crack from its force.

Not to be outdone, Felix sought out his friends and introduced them as well. Being just as quirky as him, they had their own multi-colored hairstyles, unique way of dressing, and funny terms such as "that was double throw down stupid" and "I have no fight in that dogma". They were nomadic for the most part, travelers who had missed the call for assembly and only recently arrived. Still, they blended in well and gave as good a ribbing as they took from Rufus's friends.

Well after others had left the dining hall, Eran and I went back to our room where I curled against the side of him, cherishing his warmth, sleeping better for the first time since I could remember.

In the morning I awoke rested and with the feeling I was back to my normal level of strength. This was a good thing because something deep down, an intuition that had been finely honed for centuries, told me that tonight I was going to need it…

16. DISTRACTIONS

Eran recognized my discomfort right after I'd stepped out of bed.

"How's your side?" he asked. "Can I get you anything?"

I responded with a thankful smile but shook my head.

"You look...pale..." he concluded.

"It's not from the wound."

"Then what?" he persisted, circling the bed to sit next to me. The mattress dipped heavily from his solid body and mine inadvertently leaned towards him, causing our shoulders to rest against one another.

Neither of us moved, enjoying the contact.

Eran waited patiently for his answer, evaluating my face.

"I...I have a bad feeling, that's all."

His eyebrows lifted. "You have a bad feeling and you think that's all?" He was astounded. "Magdalene, when have any of your bad feelings been wrong?"

I gave him a momentary look accompanied with a shrug.

"It's been a while since you've had one so you may have forgotten but they've always been dead on accurate."

My face must have been blank from an expression because he continued.

"Luxembourg," he stated. "You had a bad feeling and that evening while taking messages, Fallen Ones invaded that home. France…we ignored your bad feeling only to encounter a slew of arriving Fallen Ones entering Paris to storm the Bastille. Pennsylvania…you had a bad feeling. Believing it to be the coming of the British we discounted it and found ourselves surrounded by our enemies the following day. Magdalene, I've since considered your bad feelings to be an extension of your radar." He paused, thinking. "I'll put my men on alert and double the number of them on sentry duty."

He was already on his feet, slipping a shirt over his head. It fell too quickly, teasing me with only a glimpse of his muscles and I immediately felt guilty. Here I was telling him the attack we'd been waiting for might happen sometime today and yet I was preoccupied with his physique.

"Is there something else wrong?" He stopped after noticing my expression.

"Oh, it's nothing…" I said sheepishly.

"Magdalene, it's not a good idea to hold anything back at this point."

Realizing he wasn't going to back down, I admitted, "I was…I was just disappointed that I didn't get a better look at your…at your body before you dressed."

Without hesitation, he grinned boastfully and when my gaze dropped to the floor he waited for me to look up again.

He was watching me keenly, his signature smirk having lifted his lips. "I'm glad to have that affect on you…"

Then he was gone, leaving me to dress while he prepared his men based on my premonition, one that was steadily becoming a nagging persistence.

I headed for the dining hall wondering whether I'd encounter Felix and Rufus's friends when I took a detour.

It was a sudden decision and not one consciously made. Something deeper down was driving me, an urgency to hold my sword again maybe. Recalling back, whenever this had happened in my previous lives, I'd allowed myself to go with the inspiration, to follow my subconscious and it had always ended in the same situation…with a sword in my hand. This time was no different, realizing that I had been heading for the weapons room.

Inside, the armament was nearly empty, with only a handful of weapons suspended on the walls and far more hooks hanging empty. Remembering the fact that every one of the Alterums in the dining hall had carried some sort of weapon, I understood why this room stood vacant and pillaged.

Still, one sword in particular was hard to ignore. It had been left untouched, cleaned until it shined even in the dim light.

My sword, the one that I carried with me in battle, had been left alone. Somehow I knew this was a sign of respect by the Alterums, again I was quietly humbled.

Taking it from the wall, I lifted it above my waist, resisting its weight and the slight ache it caused to my wound. I practiced a few techniques, realizing I was faster and more in control than I thought I'd be.

Smiling with relief, I strapped its sheath to my waist and slipped the sword in and then turned to leave.

Magnus leaned against the door, his arms crossed casually, his eyes dancing with laughter.

"Just couldn't help yourself?" he asked with his gruff voice.

I shrugged, snickering at myself. "It was calling to me."

"Mine does the same." He pushed himself off the doorframe and motioned me to follow him. As I did, he spoke and led me through the passageways towards the courtyard, "The blade you hold was used by Ignatius, a fellow comrade now comfortably retired to the afterlife. He is one of the best swordsmen I've known, different from the Alterums here and more like you."

"Oh?" I muttered, intrigued. "How so?"

"He doesn't take orders from anyone."

"Hmm…"

After a fleeting look at me, he grinned knowingly at me. "Didn't think I knew that much about ya, did you?"

Chuckling I admitted it with a quick, tilt of my head.

Magnus stopped suddenly and rotated at the waist with a quizzical look. "He'd be proud to know you carry his weapon."

"I'm proud to carry it, Magnus."

He nodded once, firm and in approval, and then opened the door to the courtyard.

There, amidst the clanging of swords and grunts from those in exertion, morning practice was being held. It stopped as we stepped through the door, all eyes watching me as I walked with Magnus towards Eran, who stood against the wall also watching me. His expression differed from the awe the Alterums held. Eran's was filled instead with a hesitant expectation.

"Figured you could use one more instructor…" Magnus offered to Eran as we reached him.

"I'm not sure I agree with you, Magnus," said Eran, surveying me.

"I'm ready," I reassured him.

I was certain of it. My instinct had led me to the weapons room, the same feeling that told me danger was coming very soon and that I would need to be ready for it.

"Rest if you need to, Magdalene. Don't push it," he suggested, already anticipating I wouldn't follow his advice. Still, he shouted to the rest of the Alterums, his voice booming through the yard with commanding presence, "Drills!"

They promptly returned to their training and I took up position as an instructor. The Alterums had advanced in their skills but they held back with me until I couldn't take enough of their timidity. After an abrupt assault on the largest of the Alterums, one that Magnus had introduced to me the night before named Christianson, he landed with a heavy thud against the back wall, stunned. After that eye-opening interaction with me, he fought hard and unrelenting. The rest followed suit and I was encouraged by the end of the day that they would no longer allow me the courtesy of sympathy.

Later that night, after dinner, I stood on the top of a turret overlooking the dark countryside surrounding the Alterum's fortress when Eran addressed it. He'd been momentarily relieving Campion from his sentry duty.

"They were soft with you," he noted.

"Not for long." I grinned.

He chuckled. "So you are feeling better?"

"Almost entirely. A little stiff sometimes when I move in the wrong direction, but overall I think I've healed quickly."

"You have," he agreed fervently. "I don't believe I have ever seen anyone heal at that speed, Alterum or human."

"Not even yourself?" I asked, tracing the remnants of a scar along his forearm. He trembled under my touch.

"No," he said, his voice quivering with the surge of excitement at my touch. "Not even myself."

I enjoyed hearing it and kept caressing.

"I think my body is trying to heal itself before…" I stopped myself.

"Before the Fallen Ones attack us again," Eran finished the statement for me.

"Yes," I said tightly, sorry for bringing it up. I removed my hand from Eran's arm to absentmindedly brush it across the rough edge of the turret's stone wall. "I-I want just one night for the Fallen Ones not to invade my thoughts."

I looked up at him. "Do you think that's selfish?"

His eyebrows curved upward. "Not at all. Magdalene, if anyone deserves a night of rest it's you."

"I just…" I sighed, for once allowing my frustration to show itself. "My intuition, the feeling that our enemies are planning something, hasn't ebbed and yet…here we are at the end of the day and we haven't seen a single one."

"You've been struggling with that unnerved feeling all day, haven't you?" he asked with a frown.

I lifted my lips in a half-smile, affirming it.

He lifted his arm over my head and slipped it around my shoulders, the weight of him soothing me instantly.

A scuffing of feet broke the solitude around us and we turned to find Campion coming over the wall. He stooped on the edge of the turret briefly assessing us. "Am I disturbing something?" he asked, tentative.

Eran shook his head, though I sensed that wasn't an entirely honest response. Campion must have felt it too because he was hesitant stepping down to the inside of the turret.

As Campion's wings retracted, he crossed his arms and raised his shoulders, both signs of awkward embarrassment. He wouldn't even raise his eyes to us.

Eran looked down at me, his eyes soft and searching. "Come with me?"

I felt my eyes brighten at his suggestion.

His appendages unfurled behind him and I responded with my own extending outward and readying for flight.

We nodded good night to Campion and lifted ourselves towards the inky sky, going so high that lights shining from within the fortress disappeared entirely. In the far distance, after a wide swath of blackness, London sprawled like a shining cluster of diamonds.

When we stopped to hover, the wind in our ears fell away and we were surrounded by silence. Only the intermittent flap of our wings, keeping us aloft, broke the silence. The air was still, with no hint of a breeze, and a chill surrounded us but it was welcoming.

"The last time you asked me to fly with you...you proposed," I said, insinuating.

He tilted his head back and released a hearty laugh before swinging around to face me. His hands reached for my hips to lie lightly against my waist, a touch that made my heart leap.

"Would you like me to propose again, Mrs. Talor?" he asked, genuinely interested.

Now it was me who laughed. "I imagine it was tough enough the first time. I wouldn't want you to suffer through it again."

"It was tough," he acknowledged. "But only because I wasn't sure of your answer."

"And that...that still amazes me. How could you not have known?"

He shrugged and I realized I was witnessing a rare moment when Eran was unsure of himself.

I reached up to place my hand against his cheek, something that caused him to inhale sharply, a surge of passion rushing through him. It was quick, but I noticed it.

"It will always be yes..." I whispered, lightly kissing his lips...

"I will always be yours..." I continued, kissing along his jaw line...

"And I will always be by your side..." I finished, kissing his neck.

Intending that to be all, thinking we would stay a few minutes longer, pass the time quietly holding hands, caressing each other with a brush of our fingers, until it was time to return, I couldn't have been more wrong.

A fleeting look, after drawing back, told me this with certainty.

I'd started something that had set off a chain of events inside him. His jaw was now clenched against the passion surging through him. His breath was lodged somewhere inside, stilled by the power of his reaction. His eyes were pulled shut as he battled to contain his emotions.

When they opened they were pleading, but not with me. He was begging himself for a reprieve, to allow himself to toss aside his idealized dream to create the perfect night of intimacy. Being that we'd only been together once before, I understood his persistence for it. But here, at this very moment, it paled in comparison to what we were feeling, to what we each wanted.

"Please…" I whispered my own longing showing.

It was all he needed.

He released a sigh of relief, taking my face in his hands. His lips were intense, soft, exploring as if he'd never experienced this part of me.

I arched my body against him and he moaned in favor of it. Arching deeper, pressing harder, my hands came up his hips, rippling over the contours of his muscles, lifting his shirt higher.

Then we both realized the same thing at once.

Our shirts couldn't get passed our appendages.

We pulled back, our mouths slack, drawing deep breaths.

"Retract your wings," I exhaled in a rush.

He did, rapidly, as I held him with one hand and pulled the shirt over his head with the other, letting it fall through the night sky below us.

His appendages snapped back then, keeping us aloft as mine sank back in.

Eran's arm returned to my waist with an iron grip as his hand slipped underneath my shirt. His fingers moved firm and gentle up my waist, lifting the edge of my shirt higher and then paused briefly as they reached the raised skin marking my injury.

At risk of losing him to his more conscious side, I kissed him, soft at first and with increasing intensity, releasing him only when his hand began to move again.

I knew my shirt was off when the cool air hit my body and my muscles contracted.

Eran felt my reaction and pulled away. His expression was alert and concerned. Instinctually, his eyes scanned the length of my body searching for the reason behind my quiver. Finding nothing, he moved to return to me when he realized exactly what he was evaluating. Pausing, he openly stared at me in the dim light of the moon.

I realized then it wasn't just the cold but the abrupt realization that I was in front of Eran with my shirt floating down towards the English countryside that had caused my reaction.

This was the moment he'd been waiting a century for, had patiently restrained himself for until it was the perfect time. It was a lot to live up to and I wasn't certain I could meet his expectations.

I'd never been with anyone but him. I'd never even kissed anyone but him. How could I deliver on something so perfectly defined in his imagination, his most pressing desire? I didn't want to fail in this. I couldn't.

He was still gazing at me as I was consciously aware that I might actually disappoint him.

Then he swallowed tightly and what he whispered next consoled me more than anything in the world could have.

"You're beautiful." The words seemed rushed, as if he too were suffering from jitters.

My inhibitions, so powerful just seconds ago, were thrown aside and when I pulled him to me the wanting smile he wore gave me confidence that there was no possible way I could let him down.

Our limbs wrapped around each other, fitting perfectly with the other's body. His hands, so large they nearly spanned the length of my back, pressed me to him, caressing me, exploring me. Slowly, with great awareness, his hips pulled back and gently slid forward...

17. INFILTRATION

My hands lay limp atop Eran's shoulders as my forehead rested against the curve of his neck. My legs, now dangling and exhausted, tapped him every now and then, although he didn't seem to notice.

I couldn't see his face but I'd heard the moan and I'd felt his body shutter just as my back had arched. I'd felt him just as certain as he'd felt me.

Now he hovered, drawing deep and slow breaths, gradually recovering. His arms, still wrapped around my waist, were loose but secure, unrelenting in their efforts to keep me close. His chest, resting against mine, expanded outward with each inhale. Our skin, damp from our exertion, peeled apart and reconnected in rhythm with each breath.

I felt his lips press down against my shoulder, a firm and long kiss, before he tilted his head up and whispered in my ear.

"You are perfect. I could stay here forever with you."

My appendages, which had seized helping Eran keep us aloft in my moment of ecstasy, were back to working again. I gave them a brief flap as a sign I agreed.

"I'm so sorry I couldn't wait..." His voice broke. "I just...you're just...it's been so challenging..." Finally, he gave up trying to explain, sighing, and rolling his eyes, feeling inadequate.

Slowly, a smile crept across my face. "You are always so controlled in your emotions...It was..." I paused, searching for the perfect words to explain what I felt over his spontaneous lovemaking. "It was intensely satisfying to see you lose them over me."

"It was?" he said, a teasing smile rising up to match mine. His arms tightened around me, moving me closer. "So what you are saying is you'd like to see it more often."

I laughed at the understatement, the truth being so clear to me that I was astounded it wasn't to him.

"Much more often," I confirmed.

"Hmmm," he mused playfully. "I'll put some thought to it."

I groaned. "Always a tease..."

He feigned offense. "How else am I supposed to keep you interested in me?"

"Oh, you don't need to worry about that," I reassured him.

He chuckled, his chest vibrating against mine.

"I think-"

My voice cut off at the first sign of them. The hair at the back of my neck began to twitch, slowly growing more irritated. Then the perspiration returned to my forehead and dampened my hands, this time for a different reason.

My eyes were now scanning the sky, searching.

Eran's hands were on my shoulders then, as he swiveled me cautiously back and forth, trying to gain my attention. "Magdalene?"

I tried to look over his shoulder and noticing it he glimpsed around but, after seeing nothing, returned to me.

My feeling had been correct, my mind screamed. That persistent irritation that something dire would be happening, the very feeling I was trying to annul with an evening flight with Eran, had finally proven itself to be correct.

"The Fallen Ones are here," I stated, my eyes locking on him, the overwhelmingly euphoric feeling I'd just experienced with Eran now being replaced with the unnerved alarm that our enemies were coming for us.

His lips pinched closed for a brief second. "Stay close to me."

Then we were falling, pointed directly towards the earth, the brisk air coursing passed us as we plummeted. Just before reaching the ground, we straightened our direction and flew just inches across the grass blades below us.

Eran found my shirt first, handing it to me in midflight. We found the rest of our clothes shortly after, scattered across a field just outside the fortress.

With clothes in hand we lifted ourselves upward a good distance and retracted our appendages just long enough to re-dress.

Our wings didn't extend again until we'd almost reached the earth, allowing gravity to do the job for us. Our appendages snapped out just before our feet touched the ground and only to break our fall.

Campion was the first to see us land. Given that it was uncommon to find two bodies dropping from the night sky, he knew something was wrong and was the first one at our side. His hand, already on his weapon's handle, was ready for Eran's orders.

"The Fallen Ones have arrived," Eran informed him. "Alert the rest and do it quietly."

Eran and I took up our swords where we'd left them earlier, leaned against the courtyard walls. He then took my arm and led me inside.

"Where are we going?" I asked, urgently.

Eran's pace didn't slow, even as he answered. "To find your recruits."

"My recruits?" I muttered, thoroughly confused.

We made it to the north side, where the Alterum bed chambers were built, and hurried to one section of corridors in particular.

"Stay here," he said, releasing my hand.

He then began a sprint down the hall, never pausing while slamming his fist on various selected doors. There was nothing identifying these doors from any of the others. No numbers, no differentiating marks. Yet, he clearly knew which ones interested him.

Then I realized what I was watching. Eran, an expert strategist, had taken the time to locate the rooms of each Alterum we had preselected to be on our team.

They'd been given no notice, had been given no option to decline, and yet as they each stepped out of their doors, they were attentive and ready.

They'd been trained well.

What impressed me more was that these peaceful beings that had never picked up a weapon in offense before had emerged in their full fighting gear, without ever having to be told to prepare for the worst.

As they emerged, one stark detail about their assemblage stood out.

Not a single Alterum looked the same.

Unlike a typical military in which troops were issued the same clothing and weaponry, this group of fighters had selected the clothes and weapons that best fit their abilities and style of fighting. They were their own unique army.

Eran gathered them together and explained hastily, "Fallen Ones are attacking. Do not engage them unless they engage you first. Your primary goal is to keep Magdalene safe."

The Alterums glanced down the hall in unison as I stood at the end of it feeling very much like a doll on display.

Refusing to be a helpless damsel in distress, I withdrew my sword, enjoying the grating sound of its metal edge sliding along its sheath. "You won't be alone."

Eran's gorgeous face lifted in a half-smile. "And keep her out of trouble."

With that, he ran back towards me, kissed me passionate but quick, and disappeared down the corridor towards the courtyard.

I looked back at the Alterums standing in a huddle in the middle of the hallway. They looked unsure of themselves now and I couldn't blame them. But they were the least of my troubles. Right now, we had our enemies to handle.

The hair on the back of my neck picked up again, intensifying, and without thought to it I spun around and ran in the direction opposite Eran. Only a few steps down the corridor I heard the Alterums racing up behind me.

None of them bothered to ask where we were going. It didn't seem to matter much to them. They had their order and were going to follow it no matter where it led them.

It led them, or really my radar led us, to the northwest side, where a short hallway jaunted off from the main one.

My radar flared again, my hair at the back of my neck standing taut and remaining straight to the tips now, and I knew Fallen Ones were close.

I'd never used my radar as a compass before, having never actually wanted to intentionally find Fallen Ones before a few weeks ago. At this very moment though, it was a technique, an ability which I appreciated.

I halted at the opening to the hallway with the Alterums so close behind me I could feel the breath of one brushing against my hair. It had been coming quickly, but slowing now and I knew he was trying to control his nerves.

Only two doors led to rooms off the hallway here. They were staggered so I stepped up to the first and waited.

The sensation on my neck didn't change.

Stepping up the second, I stopped again.

This time, my radar responded.

I gestured to the Alterums, signaling I would be going through the door.

A few promptly shook their heads in grave disagreement. I ignored them and opened the door.

There, inside the small room that served as storage, a Fallen One stood and another was coming in from a window above.

My weapon readied, I engaged the first and quickly ended its life. The second, realizing I was in the room, quickened his entry but by the time he reached the ground I was already waiting, standing over his partner's body.

This one was a more skilled fighter and harder to fall. The Alterums, by that point, had invaded the room and without much space in it to begin with the area rapidly became crowded. This didn't bode well for anyone, least of all the Fallen One.

Although I was the closest to him, I got in only a few abrupt maneuvers before an Alterum's weapon came around the side of me, a movement that didn't require a lunge because of our proximity.

The weapon, used mainly for battering, worked as it should and with another few swift snaps, the Fallen One collapsed against the wall and slid to the ground.

The Alterums immediately began placing hands on their colleagues, offering congratulations, but I couldn't do the same.

Even after delivering the final strike to the Fallen One, sending it to perpetual death, I knew our job wasn't finished.

Slipping through the group, I made it to the hallway and out to the main corridor, awaiting another reaction at the back of my neck, in essence, listening to my radar.

I was then racing down the corridor again towards the south side of the fortress, heavy footsteps behind telling me the Alterums were following.

The remainder of the fortress was awake now and scattering about in frenzy. All of them carried weapons but were finding no enemies to use them on.

This stood out as strange to me but I had no time to assess what was happening. I was following my compass to the next intruders.

We made it to an empty chamber just as three Fallen Ones breached the balcony. Two of them rubbed their arms as if they were trying to soothe away goose bumps but I knew that wasn't the reason for it. They were trying to calm the affects of their radar, one that had surely spiked in reaction to me being so near. The third one was forgoing his pain to focus on something else entirely, an initiative that actually made me pause.

He was crouched in front of the door, fingers moving rapidly around the dead bolt.

"He's picking the lock," I whispered to myself.

"He's what?" Christianson stood beside me, just as confused. "Why would he…?"

Fallen Ones were rarely delicate about their intrusions against Alterums, typically destroying everything in their path. These ones, however, were quiet and precise in their entry of the Alterum headquarters.

Again, I was stumped.

Then the door was opened and I had no time to ponder it. Weapons began clashing as quickly as they entered.

We met the small but volatile force head on and the Alterums, despite being significantly less prepared than their enemies, responded with amazing speed and accuracy.

The time in the courtyard was paying off.

Because of this, the fight was relatively brief. I finished off the maimed Fallen Ones and we moved on to the next intrusion.

Following my radar again, it ushered us below ground, to the assembly chamber where the door was slightly ajar. I pulled it open just enough to find a hole had been dug out from the ceiling near the far corner. From it, Fallen Ones were filtering into the room.

I saw them just as they saw me, our radar preventing any of us from a stealth advance. They immediately plunged towards the door, which I shoved open to face them.

The Alterums flooded in, immediately engaging the Fallen Ones. Weapons clashed, grunts resounded off the chamber walls, blood fell in streaks from the air.

As was their intention, they came at me, but the Alterums fought efficiently, stopping them and one by one rendering each incapacitated.

I flew to the head of the tunnel, waiting for the next onslaught as the room quieted. The remaining Alterums surrounded the opening, encircling it but remaining out of sight.

Only one sound could be heard from the tunnel then…

A pair of wings flapping hard towards us.

My weapon readied, I waited until it was at the opening and at the first sign of movement brought my sword down.

It was halted midway through the movement, coming to a stop against Christianson's own weapon. My eyes wide, I gave him a quick, furious look.

But he wasn't paying me any attention. He was looking at the one who'd just come through the tunnel.

"Colonel," he said firmly with a courteous nod and then casually moved away from the tunnel's opening.

It was not the kind of reaction I was expecting.

I'd already swiveled my head towards the intruder and found Eran smirking back at me.

"Magdalene," he said with a critical lift of his eyebrows. "Why am I not surprised to find you here?"

My anger had now been replaced with shame.

I opened my mouth to explain but realized there was no good reason for me to have engaged in the dangers of defense.

He sighed. "We'll talk later. Your work here isn't finished."

He dropped down to the writhing Fallen Ones scattering the floor at such a relaxed speed I was about to ask whether these were the last of our attackers.

Then I realized I already knew the answer. My radar was subsiding, almost entirely at this point because the only Fallen Ones remaining alive in our general area were here, a few feet away, and they were debilitated.

I went about sending them to their eternal death, mindful of my task but remaining intrigued at this new found realization. Eran watched over me, angry with me but diligent in his responsibilities.

When the last Fallen One was gone, an Alterum who was still the age of a teenager strode from the room with the confidence of an adult. And then something entirely unexpected took place.

From outside the assembly room, a rhythmic pounding began slowly at first and then it beat louder and stronger and faster. The walls began to shake and the floor started to vibrate, even the air pulsed with the intensity of it.

Only a handful of us were left in the assembly room but we collected at the door's opening, filling it entirely. Outside, lining the walls, stood the Alterums. Again they were bloodied from battle, their faces darkened from sweat and dirt. They had congregated like this once before – after the first attack – and had stood quietly in respectful tribute to us.

This time…they let their emotions free, banging hard against the walls, stomping their feet, and shouting when the thrill of it became too much to contain.

As we left the assembly room and walked through the line, Rufus clapped the hands of those we passed while Felix pumped his hand in the air. The rest of us walked on in quiet amazement.

Their reaction to overcoming the Fallen Ones had changed, metamorphosed from subdued respect to a vibrant, provocative display of glory.

Eran and I met eyes just once and I knew we were both thinking the very same thought…the Alterums had become warriors.

The emotion raged until we reached Ms. Barrett's office, where Eran had led us. They then dispersed with hollers to continue their celebration in the dining hall.

Inside the office, as the shouts died down outside, we took a position either seated or standing off to the side. Campion stayed at Eran's side as he moved towards the desk. Ezra sat in the sofa chair by the window with Rufus on one side and Felix tilted against the arm rest on the other. Evelyn stood at the door, stepping aside as Ms. Beedinwigg, Mr. Hamilton, and Alfred entered the room in a rush.

When they found us casually recovering, Ms. Beedinwigg looked directly at me. "I gather everyone here is fine."

I nodded confirmation and she took a seat beside Evelyn at the table in the middle of the room, only then allowing herself to breathe a sigh of relief.

As I stood beside the window, surveying the courtyard, one thing stood out to me. There were no dead bodies. I was shocked to find it empty.

"Where did the bodies go?" I mused under my breath, knowing well they couldn't have been cleaned up that quickly.

Eran was busy searching a row of maps folded over wooden bars next to Ms. Barrett's desk.

"Here," said Ms. Barrett. She crossed the room and pulled up a map to lay it on the table.

Eran surveyed it briefly. "How did you know this was what I was looking for?" he asked, both puzzled and impressed.

"It's what I'd be seeking," she answered plainly with a shrug before retreating back to the corner of her office.

I watched her only then realizing that she had completely given up her position of power, all in an effort to help save her fellow Alterums. It was a stunning demonstration of affection.

"What are you looking at?" asked Felix, elongating his neck towards the map so he didn't need to move any closer.

The oversized piece of paper that had yellowed slightly around the edges was now laid flat across the table. It was otherwise in near perfect condition.

Eran reviewed it quietly, his face tight in concentration.

I moved to stand over it, to see what Eran was assessing, and then Campion said the thing that I knew was on everyone's minds.

"They came from the air...across the ground...in varying numbers of groups..." muttered Campion.

"And they did it soundlessly," Ezra added.

"What was their strategy?" asked Ms. Beedinwigg, perplexed.

"Quiet infiltration," Felix offered.

"Rogue attackers?" suggested Evelyn.

Rufus shrugged. "Ehh, the blokes were just unprepared fer our might."

"They were looking for flaws." Eran surmised without bothering to look up.

"Yes." I sucked in a breath. "Abaddon sent groups of them with different instructions to breach our perimeter and of those who didn't return would tell him which ones were unsuccessful."

"But…I think we got them all," said Ms. Barrett almost inaudibly.

"We did," Eran stated with absolute certainty. "And that will answer his other question."

"How secure we really are," Ezra deduced.

"Exactly," said Eran. "And now that they know this about us, they'll formulate their final plan of attack."

Instantly, my muscles tightened in response to that assessment. "Then we need to strike first."

Eran sighed, his eyes still searching the map. "But where?"

I sought answers from the same piece of paper he was standing over. It was a map of the world, without detail to tell us of possible hideouts. Still, it clarified one thing: we knew too little about their hideout to deduce where to find it.

"Then we pick them apart, one by one," I stated, angry motivation surging through me. "We hunt them before they attack us."

Eran finally lifted his head to silently consider my implication. Finally, after considerable thought, he nodded in agreement.

"And we start tonight," I said, already heading for the dining hall.

There, I would find the Alterums who, without having to use words, had conveyed their willingness to battle Fallen Ones.

I only hoped their adrenaline still raged through them…and that they were ready for a few more fights.

18. PUZZLE

The nights that followed the Fallen One's latest invasion were demanding.

Waiting until nightfall, when we could be assured our flight out of the fortress and across the country would go unseen, was the greatest challenge to my patience. Although I understood it was necessary. One or two in daylight may escape notice but twenty of us in a cluster flying through the sky would be visible and precarious.

When the sun had sunk low enough to darken the horizon, we gathered in the courtyard, collectively discussed the night's raids and any known dangers associated with it – besides of course the inevitable encounter and slaughter of a Fallen One.

We eliminated three, sometimes four, a night, gradually becoming a stronger, more cohesive unit.

The Alterums, who had come so far in such a short period of time, stood more confident with each passing night, growing convinced that they were capable of defending themselves against their enemies, even within their enemy's domain. Gradually, they became comfortable enough in their own skin that banter became an inevitable part of the nightly routine.

Our team included Alterums from both Rufus and Felix's pasts, giving us a colorful spectrum of personalities. It wasn't rare to find one of them rousting another with a typical night starting with something similar to:

"You sure you can handle that bow and arrow?"

"I don't know. Why don't you run out a few yards and we'll test it out."

These were often followed by loud whoops and hollers until another series of playful insults were tossed around.

Eran would then collect their attention to leave, wings would snap out in unison and we'd take to the air, a layer of restlessness settling over us then. We would fly low over the channel towards Europe until we came across land, rising high then so that we were obscured from sight by clouds or distance. Then, either Gershom would locate a Fallen One or, if we were close enough to one, I would feel it. The raid would then begin, pausing intermittently until we found the next one, and ending just before the horizon began to brighten with the morning sun. We would then return and recover for the next night's raid.

It was Gershom who controlled the direction we took on these hunts, having the supernormal ability to track others better than anyone I'd ever known. In honesty, it was a source of frustration for me at times as I did my best to direct us. An ulterior motive drove me, one that I kept to myself until one night when we came across the residence of one particular Fallen One.

Then everything changed.

It was the last raid of the night with five enemies annihilated in just a few hours. Conversation was sparse as we flew over Austria, nursing the few wounds we'd suffered from the night's brawls.

Something odd stood out to me, weighing heavily on my subconscious, but I couldn't put it in to words. In fact, it was Eran who acknowledged it.

"Do you notice that we're encountering fewer Fallen Ones," he asked above the wind. "Every night we're finding one or two less than the night before."

I nodded vehemently then, asserting I'd recognized it too.

"Possibly we've executed the rest of those in this area," Campion suggested.

"No…" Eran shook his head. "We've continually pushed the boundary south each night."

"Maybe we've found a natural gap…where none of 'em live," Christianson called out from the far end of the flank.

"Could be," Eran said, speculative, but I knew from his expression that he didn't believe it.

Something was wrong. Fallen Ones typically scattered the earth, living in all geographies, every country, nearly every city. It was virtually unheard of to find a large area of few Fallen Ones, especially one with diminishing numbers.

As I watched Eran scan the cities far below, with a look of concerned concentration, I knew he was thinking the very same thing.

"How about we cross over Salzburg on our way back?" I proposed. "We haven't covered that ground yet."

"It's a little out of the way," noted Gershom.

"Not too far," I countered.

Eran peered at me suspicious as to why I was so insistent but he nonetheless agreed. "We're here. We might as well check it out."

As we redirected our line, I mentally plotted the position. Since we'd consistently started hunting, I wasn't simply following Gershom's lead or my radar. I was strategically singling out specific locations, marking them in my memory. I was in search of not just any site but one in particular.

If Eran ever figured out which site it was, he'd wholly disagree with me. In fact, he'd likely be infuriated.

Just as we came across the border of Salzburg my thoughts were disrupted.

The hair pricked along my neck, sending a spark through me.

"We have another one," I called out.

Gershom, who'd already picked up on it, nodded and pointed to a section of Salzburg where the lights of the city wound steeply around the Salzach River.

We slowed to a hover, each pondering our next move.

"We can't fly in," Gershom stated.

"Too risky," agreed Eran. "Looks like we're walking…"

He tipped towards the earth then and flew to the side of a hill, densely covered with trees. The rest of us followed, turning up our wings as he did once we met the treetops to course over them, just inches from their peaks. There were no lights below or around us, signaling that the area was void of homes and safe for us to land.

Eran chose a spot just on the edge of the forest, dipping down so that he dropped to the ground, turning up at the last second so his feet landed first. It was a powerful maneuver executed with grace that impressed on me once again how magnificent he moved.

Soon we were all beside him, although, unlike Eran, we landed with a simple drop to our feet.

The group strolled down the slight embankment and entered the street through a narrow alleyway, going unnoticed by the tenants of nearby apartment buildings.

Only a dog noticed, rushing around the corner of the building closest to us. Christianson leveled his arm at it, palm up, as if motioning for it to stop. It slowed to a sprint and finally a full halt before sitting back on its hind legs and watching us pass like a children's street crossing guard.

Openly admiring his ability, he took note of it and shrugged.

"One of the gifts I've retained," he replied flatly.

As we walked through the city my attention was equally split between the beauty of its scenery and the sensation of my radar.

The city, tucked alongside the Alps, seemed to intertwine with the rocks of nearby mountains. Roads wound up to grandiose castles while stone walls wove through the rock faces and disappeared around the mountainsides.

It was enchanting.

Still, the hair at the back of my neck reminded me why we were here, tweaking inconveniently as it told me which way to turn, unintentionally giving us a precise direction towards the Fallen One.

Gershom conferred with my assessment of my radar's compass, tweaking our path every now and then until we came across a tall, narrow building that I ascertained was actually a home.

It was void of personality with the exception of two rows of windows lining the front face, each one dark from within. It appeared to be empty, although I knew better. My radar was dancing chaotically right now, confirming we'd reached our destination. As if that weren't evidence enough, two bodies passed in front of the first floor window.

I knew Eran saw them too when he reached out an arm and protectively crossed it over my body.

When I tilted my head and lifted my eyebrows at him, he dropped it, whispering, "Sorry...habit."

He felt vindicated when I announced quietly in warning, "There's more than two in there."

"How-How many are there?" asked Gershom, pulling his flannel shirt tighter, and not because of the cooler weather typical of this region.

I judged the sensation on my neck for a moment. "Nearly twenty."

"You sound disappointed," Eran noted.

I laughed it off without confirming the truth. I was disappointed. The site I was seeking would have far more than twenty Fallen Ones.

Eran issued orders then, instructing groups of us to various sections of the building. I, of course, was in his group.

As the others sprang to life, running quickly to their posts, Eran turned to me, his left hand lifting to take my cheek.

"Twenty outnumbers us," he stated, looking up at me through his lashes, tantalizing me. "Will you do me the favor of staying here? I promise you can come in when we've contained the area."

"No," I replied flatly.

His shoulders fell in frustration, his hand falling shortly afterwards. His incentive had failed.

"I'm going in now," I informed him.

His head fell back and he released a quiet groan. "So stubborn…"

I strolled around him. "I could say the same about you, my love."

When I looked back for his reaction, he was fighting a grin. But, knowing it was an inappropriate time for it and that right now he needed to be focused, it fell quickly.

As I headed for the house, my senses magnified and I discerned two bodies were on the first floor, another ten were on the second floor, and the last one was moving up a flight of stairs, where I heard him stumble in his haste.

Every one of them was moving quickly. Doors were being yanked open, papers were being aggressively shuffled. It was as if they here trying to hide something…or find something.

We took the front entrance, walking straight up to the door. There, a small mailbox was mounted to the outside wall and on it was a nameplate. Chiseled in brass was the name Rautenstrauch, which left an impression on me. Maybe because it was vaguely familiar…

I wasn't certain. All I could identify with at the moment was the sudden, distinct feeling of guilt riding up. For the first time since I'd become a hunter of Fallen Ones I was about to enter someone's home, one who cherished it enough to post a name on the outside. He or she had likely furnished it, put thought towards where possessions were placed, had spent time here enjoying the comforts it gave. I was now about to enter it with ill intent and I felt no better than a common thief.

I blinked back the line of thoughts marching through my consciousness then.

What was I doing? I asked myself. This was the home of a vicious criminal, one that endangered anyone who crossed their path.

Then the door opened.

Those inside knew I had arrived…They had felt me.

Eran ducked in front of me just as the first of our enemies lunged out of the blackness within. He blocked it effortlessly as it was a scrawny one, the frail body slamming against the door jam.

My sword, already unsheathed, plunged through his chest. He groaned, sliding from the blade as I allowed it to follow the weight of his body to the ground.

I pulled my weapon up just as the second Fallen One came through the door. This one held two guns, one in each hand, and his trigger fingers were pumping in rapid succession.

Eran's appendages instantly folded around us, their layers of thick, impenetrable feathers forming a barrier of

261

safety. The cocoon only lasted a few seconds, Eran's intriguing eucalyptus- earthy aroma enveloping us, making me stronger.

When his wings withdrew, I was eager, ready.

My sword cut a swath through the air, taking both hands from the Fallen One. They tumbled through the air, fingers still wrapped around their gun's handles but no longer able to do any damage.

The Fallen One, swarthy skinned with a scar along one side of his neck, paused, his jaw falling open as he gaped at the stubs of his arms.

"You-You took my hands," he muttered with an accent blended by various cultures.

Judging from it, he'd been on earth a very long time with those hands. I could understand his discomfort.

"You won't need them any longer," I said, ironically attempting to comfort him.

"Your victims will appreciate the irony," Eran stated bluntly, apparently knowing this particular Fallen One. He confirmed it by using the name given to him. "Seaside Strangler."

He blinked back at Eran, surprised at the acknowledgement. Then, not to be outdone, he tucked his stumped arms to his chest, rotated at the waist, and launched a round kick at my head.

Eran was too fast for it, intercepting the leg and twisting it abnormally around the Fallen One's waist.

The result was a howl of pain as he collapsed to the ground, unable to hold himself up with only his one remaining limb.

As we stepped by him, I sent my sword through him, ushering him to eternal death.

The remaining Fallen Ones weren't a challenge, with the rest of our unit having met us inside by that point and dominating the small group left on the ground floor.

It was the Fallen Ones upstairs who fought with skillful vigor, nearly taking Christianson's head off. Eran stepped in on that collision and deflected the sledgehammer from its path. By the end of the bloodshed, we surveyed the damage, carefully stepping over the bodies and broken furniture.

"What were they doing here?" Eran asked, under his breath. "It makes no sense. Fallen Ones don't cluster like this."

"Burglarizing," I concluded.

"No...not stealing." He pointed to an opened safe in which money was still neatly stacked. It was untouched.

"I saw one looking at papers when we entered the room," mentioned Erick, one in our unit who typically didn't speak much but was diligent in his observing. "He was...inspecting it."

"Paper," Eran mumbled and then sighed in exasperation.

"We don't have much time," Campion cautioned.

"Right," said Eran. "The noise..."

From a distance, the wails of police sirens were already within earshot.

Then Eran stooped and picked something up. It had been lying beside the open hand of a Fallen One, having slid from his clutched fingers at death.

He unraveled and held it up for closer inspecting, drawing attention from all of us.

It was a painting, a kaleidoscope of colors and rendered with immaculate detail. The woman sat sternly in a chair facing the painter with taut lips that indicated she was attempting a smile. And I knew the face instantly.

"Isabelle..." I muttered.

Eran swung his head to face me. "You know her?"

"She's Sarai's mother...Abaddon's wife."

Then it hit me all at once, fitting together neatly like pieces of a puzzle. Memories that the scrolls had shown me of their past lives flashed before me. Isabelle in a parlor in Paris. Achan's underground home beneath the city of Paris. The listing of their lives on each one of their scrolls, all of them mentioning Paris.

I had been picking up clues all along. I just didn't know it.

"They're in Paris," I announced with absolute certainty.

Campion spun towards me, stunned. "How do you know?"

"They died there. All of Abaddon's followers. They're familiar with it."

"But Abaddon died here…in Salzburg," Philius pointed out.

"Right, and we are here but they aren't," said Eran in agreement with me. "That leaves Paris."

"But we've been through Paris," Christianson argued. "There were only three of them left there."

"Three of them left there in plain sight," I said.

Eran's head tilted towards me. "What are you getting at, Magdalene?"

"They're underground." As I made the statement, the rest of the room released a sigh of understanding.

"Of course…because…because they would want to remain unseen," said Philius.

I nodded.

"And they would be undetectable," added Gershom.

I nodded again.

Eran strolled towards the rest of us where we had collected in the middle of the room, his eyes blazing, his signature smirk rising up.

Finally, he cleared his throat and suggested, "I'd say it's time we paid him a visit…"

We glanced at each other to find the rest of us grinning, a unified sign of agreement.

With that, we left Abaddon's home to plan an attack on his hideout.

19. CAPTURED

We reached Ms. Barrett's office, which had become the unofficial discussion chamber, in record time. And even though it was late, our voices drowned each other out, everyone with a different opinion on what to do next.

"Full scale attack," suggest Christianson, who had grown fearless in the time I'd known him.

"A diversion. We need a diversion. Then we bombard them," said Philius, and I could see that he was already planning it out in his mind.

Several more suggestions were raised, all of them countering each other.

In the midst of it, my housemates, Ms. Beedinwigg, and Mr. Hamilton entered, each with blurry eyes but steadily growing alert. We had woken them, I figured, and they deserved to know why. I moved to Ezra's side where they grouped around me and I explained to them what we'd learned, their eyes widening as I told the story both from excitement and fear.

Eran waited for calmer heads to prevail before speaking up. He was bent over the map he'd been using to mark our previous hunts, attempting to find some pattern in their placement.

When the cacophony died down, he rotated his head to me with an incredulous expression. "They're in The Catacombs."

Those who were speaking immediately quieted.

"The Parisian catacombs…" Eran explained to those staring at him now with blank faces. "The cemeteries beneath Paris. When those not wealthy enough to pay for a church burial lost a loved one, often times they would be buried in central mass graves…"

"Below Paris…" I drew in a quick breath. "Yes, it's where Achan lived before he met Abaddon."

Eran's eyebrows lifted as he asked, "And how did you learn that, my dear?"

Knowing he already figured it was through my use of the scroll he'd specifically asked me not to use my only response was an aggravated sigh.

"The catacombs…Fantastic," Felix said with clear distain. "Diseased rats, the lingering stench of death, shadows of the dead creeping up the walls."

"Don't worry, Felix. You won't be going," said Eran, which conveyed to everyone that he'd already formulated a plan.

"The caverns and tunnels are complex so we'll want to take only a small group. We can't risk losing anyone and it'll make us visible with too large a group. Philius will need to go in first to perform reconnaissance…" Eran went on to finish every detail of his plan, finishing with, "Are there any questions?"

I was the first to speak. "I didn't hear what my role would be." Which was strange because I rarely missed those types of details.

As it turned out, I hadn't missed it.

"You will be staying here, preparing for an assault should we fail."

I blinked several times in disbelief, certain I'd heard him wrong. "Staying here?"

"Yes," he said, rolling up the map in order to avoid looking my way.

"But…No…"

Knowing this could blow up to a large scale argument, Eran strode across the room towards me. "We can't risk it. You are too important to-"

"Eran…I can't ask others to go in place of me. I created this war."

He shook his head, saddened. "No, you didn't. I did."

His meaning was evident. Abaddon had been punished because of the crime he'd committed against Eran. The only person not involved at the start of it was me.

Refusing to allow the argument to enflame, he explained to me in a way I could not misunderstand. "We need to enter undetected-"

"I'll be just as quiet," I retorted.

"It won't matter," he said calmly, taking hold of my shoulders, and attempting to direct my gaze towards him. "They will already know you are there."

The realization came at once, causing me to close my eyes against the truth. "My radar…They'll sense my radar."

"Yes," he said, gently, knowing how challenging this rejection was for me.

"I don't have a choice…" I mumbled.

Immediately, I was frightened for Eran, feeling somehow that if I weren't there with him than he wouldn't be safe. Yet, I knew what he said was true. My presence would put him in even greater danger.

"I suggest we get some sleep. We leave tomorrow night," he said without turning to face the others, keeping a watchful eye on me.

When the room had cleared, he pulled me to him, wrapping his arms around me as if sheltering me from any possible jeopardy.

"I'd like to spend the night with my wife," he whispered in my ear.

As much as it hurt to say it, I did. "You need your rest." I couldn't live with myself if I kept him up, sapping him of energy when he would need it more than ever before.

"Then lay with me."

From that point forward, time moved too quickly. And for the first time…ever…I did not sleep that night.

Unable to waste a second on something as inane as sleep, I spent the time awake, alert, and listening to the steady rhythm of Eran's breathing. My hand caressed his arms, feeling the texture of his skin and the strength of his muscles beneath them. I watched him at times in the dim light filtering through the window. His face was stunning even when obscured by shadows.

This man was my entire life. He gave me strength, rejuvenated me when I needed it, guided me to safety even as I fought him on it. He made me feel invincible.

As I lay there beside him, watching the steady rise and fall of his chest I knew one thing with absolute clarity…I couldn't imagine a life without him.

But that was just what I felt threatened by. Somehow, that nagging feeling had returned telling me to be prepared. In fact, it lingered there, just below the surface like a shark circling its prey, all the way through to morning.

When Eran woke, I still hadn't shaken the feeling and, of course, he noticed it instantly.

"You're worried," he said, point blank.

"Yes." Why deny it? It would be no use.

"Don't be," he said, rolling over to kiss me, briefly but with an intensity that pressed our lips together fully.

Then he was up and moving around the room. He stopped midway through dressing and pivoted towards me.

"You didn't get any sleep at all, did you?" he asked astounded, already knowing the answer.

I gave him a wavering smile.

Sighing, he approached me, kneeling so that he was at my eye level. "I'm going in quietly, surrounded by the best men I've ever had the fortune to work with. I'll be back before you know I'm gone."

I scoffed. "You know that's not possible."

"No, it's not," he agreed softly. "You'll know exactly when I leave and exactly when I return, won't you?"

"Down to the second."

His lips lifted in his signature smirk then. "It's actually somewhat nice to have such a devoted admirer."

"Admirer?" I gasped.

He chuckled, knowing his tease had gotten to me. "Wife...I meant devoted wife..."

"That's better."

"Good," he said, heaving himself to standing position. "Now up. You'll need breakfast if you're going to have enough energy for your chores today."

"Chores?" I inquired, dropping my feet to the floor, the chill of it jolting me awake.

"You're going to manage the final phase of our defenses today," Eran announced.

As it turned out, Eran did most of the finalizing, which was just fine with me. He knew where each weapon was best suited and how to position them so they worked most efficiently. By the end of the day, the fortress was firmly secure and Eran was ready for his night mission.

He and the group he'd selected, which was limited to just five Alterums, gathered in the courtyard at dusk. They had followed Eran's advice and now appeared rested, wide-eyed and energetic. Eran blended in effortlessly with them, a part of their pack but with the authority and respect of a leader, something that always captivated me.

I had to forcibly stop myself from running to him and throwing my arms around his neck, begging him to stay. He wouldn't and it would only put the others ill at ease. I wanted them, needed them just as they were…confidently equipped to handle whatever they might encounter.

Not wanting to distinguish this night from the others, he made no more acknowledgement towards me than he regularly did at the start of the night missions, other than a casual wink just before he sprang in to flight.

I quickly learned that while the night before had been the fastest of my existence, this night was the slowest, dragging on so much that seconds felt like hours.

Worse, that nagging feeling grew steadily worse with each tick of the clock.

I spent the entire night in the empty dining hall with Felix, Rufus, and Ezra, our voices echoing off the walls.

Their efforts to comfort me were welcomed but unsuccessful. Even when Felix set a tray of banana splits in front of us – without any mysterious, unknown, or unappetizing trimmings included – I still couldn't bring myself to smile.

I wasn't trying to be difficult. I wanted to settle back, kick up my feet, and feel as if this were just another ordinary evening back in New Orleans. But that nagging feeling just wouldn't allow it.

Then the feeling ended. Just like that. As if someone had snapped their fingers. And for a brief moment I felt absolute calm, a brief reprieve before what came next.

Just as Felix finished his last spoonful of ice cream, theatrically smacking his lips in appreciation, I felt it.

The awareness of it caused a violent inhale.

And I knew, somehow, that at that very same moment, as I drew in that breath Eran was exhaling his last.

Then every muscle in my body froze.

And my eyes refused to move, to blink, to see what I was looking at.

My heart beat harder, faster until it pounded in my head.

Suddenly, my legs straightened and I was standing, the chair I had been sitting in tossed backwards with such force it rolled against the table behind me.

"No," I snapped at no one in particular. "NO!"

Only vaguely I registered that my housemates were watching me, mouths ajar, stunned and partially terrified.

I drew in another breath and this one released with such fury it made them stand too. "NOOOOOOOOOOOO!"

The next thing I knew, my knees hit the ground, a loud thump resounding through my body but void of any pain.

Then my head was bowed and I was sobbing.

"Give her room," Ezra warned, her voice a wallow in my ears.

"Room?" Rufus roared. "She needs a shot."

"Quiet your voice," she demanded, perturbed. "Felix, some water, please."

A cup of water was forced in my hands but I felt it tilt, having no control over my limbs, and spill to the floor, my tears falling in, mixing with, the puddle it created.

Then I heard a growl of frustration. "Stand back," came the demand just as I felt myself go airborne, lifted by powerful hands that I processed as Rufus's.

The wind was then on my face, cold, bitter, unwelcoming, and Rufus's voice was thundering in my ear.

"Snap outta it!"

"This ain't helpin'!"

"Eran'd be sick seein' ya like this!"

I heard him but I didn't understand him. Nothing registered with me. I was in a hollow, impenetrable shell.

Then he was spinning and my limbs flapped like straw in the wind.

271

He ducked downward and soon something was splashing against my face, cutting through the wind like tacks against my skin. Below us in the darkness, something crashed and writhed and my eyes, in their hazy state, found we had made it to the shore and that it was ocean spray catching on my skin.

Still, it didn't help. Nothing did.

Sometime later, it ended and I was laid gently against a mattress as a cover was pulled over me.

There were whispers and footsteps and then silence. A period of time later, I couldn't be certain how long, snoring began from the vicinity of the chair by the window.

I lay there neither awake nor asleep as time passed until warmth began to spread across my face. I realized, ironically, that on any other day, in another lifetime, it would have been comforting. For me, it was just a sensation.

Not long after, whisperings began again, though this time I heard and understood them.

"She'll want to hear this…" Felix said.

"I'm not sure she's ready," replied Ezra.

"Then you kin deal with 'er wrath when she finds out the only survivor wanted to speak to 'er n' we didn't get 'er up."

As they bickered about whether to interrupt me, I sat up and put my feet on the floor. Then I was standing and heading for the door.

They had grown quiet when they noticed and now only their footsteps behind me told me they were following.

In the courtyard, two men were crouched, one lying against the other's arms, being held up because he didn't have the strength himself.

It was Christianson and he looked like I felt…Dead.

I knelt beside him, taking the edge of my shirt sleeve and wiping the caked blood from his eyes. He blinked then and I pulled away, noticing the bite marks across his body.

"Tomorrow…" his voice gurgled. "They're…coming."

"Of course they are," I whispered void of emotion. I sensed no fear, no rage, nothing at all.

For once, the Fallen Ones had no leverage over me.

As Christianson's last words faded away so did his life. He was already leaving his body when I took the dagger of the man holding him and shoved it through Christianson's heart.

There were no gasps of surprise, no words of explanation. They weren't needed. The bite marks told Christianson's story. An Elsic had been unleashed on him for one simple reason: It was the only way to ensure eternal death.

I had stopped Christianson but I couldn't stop Eran. The injustice sickened me.

It was how the rest had been killed, Eran included. I knew this with unquestionable certainty.

"Alert the others," I said barely above a murmur, sensing that these were Eran's words. He should be the one here speaking them, not me.

Despite who said them, the scuffing of feet told me that the message was being spread, announcing to the Alterums that their most dire threat was heading their way.

While fear, uncertainty clamored through the stronghold, I found my way back to my bedroom, my housemates again following quietly behind.

No sooner had I laid down when Ms. Barrett burst through the door.

"What are you doing?" she demanded and even with my eyes closing I knew the question was directed at me. "They. Are. Coming! Up! Get up!"

Maybe it was her choice of words or the ornery tone in her voice but a small battle began at the entrance before I sat up again.

"Let her in," I said and my housemates reluctantly stepped aside.

Ms. Barrett straightened the vest she wore and marched up to me. But only then did she actually see me.

I didn't think it was possible but some of that intense devotion she held for the Alterums was momentarily passed to me. Her eyes softened and her frown disappeared.

"What-What happened to you?"

"She lost the only man she ever loved," barked Felix, seething, ready to lunge at Ms. Barrett until Ezra and Rufus held him back.

I held up a limp hand, having no motivation to do more.

"They're in your hands now," I said to Ms. Barrett. "The Alterums are in your care."

Her jaw dropped in opposition. "But...But I can't. What...if I fail them?"

"You haven't yet."

"But we need you," she exhaled, lost.

"I'll be there," I said. "But you can't count on me. My focus won't be on coordinating the defense."

Her face twitched in confusion. "What will be your focus?"

As I lay back against the pillow, allowing my body to succumb to exhaustion, I released the one word raging through my mind with a tapering whisper...

"Revenge."

20. ERAN

I awoke in the Hall of Records with slightly more energy, but only because I anticipated what I was about to do.

Wasting no time, my wings sprouted and I lifted myself up through the warm breeze, heading for the P's.

Once again, I found myself standing before the pocket that held the scroll of Paris deaths. There, it sat undisturbed, as if it hadn't been touched since I had held it last, as if it were waiting for me.

Pulling it from the pocket, I didn't allow it to unravel entirely before I spoke. I had suddenly grown impatient.

"Eran Talor."

Instantly, the scroll slid through my fingers, settling on his name.

I reviewed the list even though a sharp pain ran through my stomach when I saw the most recent entry and its accompanying statement…eternal death.

My jaw clenched against the anger until I allowed it to settle. Focus, I told myself. Focus.

I gazed at that last entry a bit longer, knowing it was the reason I'd come. It would lead me to discover exactly what had happened to Eran.

Still, I couldn't bring myself to run my finger across it. I was drawn by the desire to see him again, to feel him again, one so strong I couldn't fight back.

Bringing my index finger to the paper, I locked on his first life in Germany and swiped it.

Dropping into Eran's body, I felt entirely different than I had seconds ago. His body was strong, powerful, fluid, as he walked through a field of knee-high grass. His boots squished through the spongy mud making up the countryside and his arms swung alongside his body with ease.

He was healthy…and alive. And it was a bittersweet taunt.

Maybe this wasn't such a good idea, I considered, suddenly wanting out. But there was no out.

Feelings, a mixture of them, rose up, becoming a maelstrom of emotions fighting with each other over the need to leave and the need to stay.

Then he lifted his head and swung it to the right, hearing the break of a stick in the distance. His eyes sought the source of it and then something came over him, a pause.

Time stopped then.

He froze in place, his breathing halting, his mind numbing, his eyes locked on the girl strolling through the field several yards away.

She was petite with long, curly, cocoa-colored hair, which she was drying in the morning sun.

I'd seen her before, reflected in my mirror at home.

The girl was me.

As he watched, a comfort washed over him, an unbreakable confidence, one that would mock anyone who tested it. Alongside this feeling was a longing, soft but powerful, and an awareness that if anything were to hurt this girl they would suffer excruciating pain.

It was then, as I watched him notice me for the first time, I discovered that Eran had been my guardian long before he was ever given the title.

I was whisked away then to land in his body at a later date. He was older now, feebler, less energy but still strong. His body was slightly hunched and his hands shook when they brushed the hair from my face.

He sat over me as I lay in bed, my breathing raspy.

Fighting against the nervous awareness that the end of my life was near, I watched him lean forward to place his mouth against my ear.

The words came but not without a struggle. He had to forcefully swallow twice before the lump in his throat would subside.

"I'll see you soon," he whispered, the lump in his throat rising again to jar the release of his sigh. He swallowed once more and said, "But it won't be soon enough."

He remained there, leaning forward, unable to bear moving away as I released my final breath. Teeth clenched, his lips quivering, he fought back the tears but they spilled over and streamed down his cheeks.

From deep inside, I felt a void begin to grow, an emptiness that sucked the vitality from him, a lost and hopeless despair that actually felt palpable, weighing him down.

He found my hand and held it firm and gentle as he spoke.

"I am in love with you, Magdalene. What I feel for you is timeless. And when I die, when this body releases me, I will find you and I will be your eternal protector."

Then I was shouting at him, my voice unheard as I had no control over his lips. Still, I yelled my warning anyways.

"Run! Refuse my funeral! Run!"

But it was of no use. Eran would attend my funeral and there Abaddon would kill him. It would solidify

Abaddon's fall from the afterlife, giving birth to a desire to take Eran's life, leading him to exactly where he had ended up now. A never-ending death.

Even as I was pulled back through the tunnel, I screamed for Eran to run, my voice given its freedom and echoing in my ears.

It continued until I was planted back in the Hall of Records, still holding Eran's scroll.

Unnerved, I took a trembling step back. I was headed for a collapse but I stayed upright. My breath was tight in my throat and my mind was spinning but still I managed to brush my finger over Eran's next life.

Back through the tunnel, I was transplanted in Eran's body again. This lifetime was spent in London, a place I recognized instantly.

He was in flight, fighting with his wings to move faster, a sense verging on panic overwhelming him. The wind whistled in his ears as his eyes frantically searched the empty streets below him.

His wings tilted slightly and he began his plunge towards the center of the city.

The sense of dread engulfed Eran then, causing him to strain his appendages, flapping harder with an even and concentrated focus.

The difference was that the emotion he felt didn't come from Eran. It came from somewhere outside his body, pulsating towards him, landing deep in his chest were it radiated like a harsh, constant light.

As he swooped down and through the side streets of London, that radar remained steady, drawing him in, directing him with each turn until he reached the street where its source stood.

He didn't stop, instead bracing his body for the impact to come.

Flashes of movement to his left and right told him that he wasn't alone. He didn't pause, not even when his body slammed against another as he emerged from the mouth of the alley and out to the street.

Suddenly, his body was an amazing display of movement, techniques to gain the upper hand on the being he was now fighting. Teeth, jagged and stained, lashed out at him but he deftly moved aside. Claws gripped for him but he caught its wrists and used that force against it.

Then, out of the corner of his eye, he caught sight of a girl. It was no surprise to him that she was there watching. He knew her and the sensation within him that had drawn him to her.

His awareness turned to frustration then, as he caught sight of her stepping closer, engaging in the fight.

After avoiding a fist coming at him, he drew in a breath and grunted, "Stay…back…Magdalene."

But she didn't listen and his irritation grew.

Instead, he sighed while noting that she'd torn the cloak from her shoulders and was entering the fight.

From inside his body, I watched, an awareness dawning on me…I had known for a while that Eran could feel my emotions as I could feel him. But it wasn't until that very moment that I understood Eran had his own type of radar, one directly tuned to me.

Then I was yanked back through the tunnel to once again stand in the Hall of Records.

I stood, quietly amazed, enjoying the solitude of the moment.

Eran continued to amaze me, even in death.

My lips trembled against the hint of a smile and then it was gone, replaced with an incredibly strong desire to hold him again just once.

It actually made the void in me widen.

In an effort to end the feeling of emptiness, I swiped my finger over his name in his next life, carrying me back to him during his life in France.

Sadness invaded that void momentarily when I recognized that this was the lifetime when Eran had finally admitted his love for me. A commanding, confident man who was so drawn in by our love that it had been one of only two times when I witnessed him behaving nervously, the other being in his next life while proposing to me. The memory of both almost made a smile surface.

The scroll, however, didn't show these. It took me to another part of his life, this one when he was younger.

Being only ten years old and with a memory that told him there were better things to wear, he squirmed against the insistent buttoning up of the shirt collar he was being forced to wear.

The man knelt in front of him, glowered, and said, "Stop fidgeting," in French.

Eran did, allowing the man to finish, before responding politely in French, "Thank you, Papa."

"Now…eat," his father commanded and Eran did.

I was shocked, having never seen Eran follow orders before. He always gave them.

He bent and took a piece of meat from a basket only to stroll to the chairs set out directly next to them. Another family was sitting beside them, and as he walked by the ladies he gave them each a tip of his hat, causing them to giggle and making it clear that Eran knew how to impress women at any age.

But when he reached the last and youngest one, he stopped.

She looked directly at him and oddly enough I knew it was me because I recalled this very moment.

He and I grew up together as family friends and on this particular occasion we were taking advantage of the warm weather to have an outing together.

But as we stared at each other, we knew something they didn't. Having come to earth as Alterums, we remembered each other.

He nodded towards the small space at the end of the bench, which I conceded to give up.

Then, as he slipped up beside me, only a brief moment passed before his hand slipped underneath mine to take hold.

This I could never forget because it was the first time, ever, Eran had touched me with evident interest, beyond compassion a guardian would feel for their ward. And it caused my stomach to burn with excitement.

I had never known it until now but his reaction was the exact opposite. Touching me soothed him, like a salve to an open wound, immediately calming him and putting everything around him in perspective. It made him feel powerful, like a lion calmly surveying his territory.

He turned his head ever so slightly then to peek from the corner of his eye at my reaction.

This, I couldn't forget either.

I was smiling.

Then, far too quickly, I was pulled from this life, through the tunnel, and dropped back to the Hall of Records, only taking a second to realize why.

I was running out of time. Daylight was approaching in the other dimension.

It's too fast, I thought. I haven't had enough. I haven't felt him enough...

Quickly, I swiped my finger across his next life, landing in his body again. This time he wore clothes that fit him, loose and rugged, breathable. As he strolled the street I noticed we were back in Pennsylvania. Thick green trees towering over dusty storefronts leading to a dirt avenue overrun by horses and carriages told me so.

He shifted something heavy lying across his right shoulder to a better position on just as he came across one store in particular and entered the darkly lit room. Inside the street sounds dulled but the smell of freshly cut lumber still hung in the air. At the back, stood a man leaning forward on a bar that ran the length of the room. He was trim with a beard that covered most of his face. Clear green eyes shined out from above, lucid, catching every movement Eran made.

Eran approached, his face lifting to a grin, telling me this man was familiar.

"I see you have them," said the man.

Eran nodded and dragged the weight off his shoulder to the bar in front of the man.

They were furs, I found as Eran placed a hand on them, the tips of the hair prickling his palm.

The man grinned and pulled money from a satchel, handing it to Eran.

"But I don't think that's what you really came for," suggested the man, which prompted a loud laugh from Eran.

"I was thinking you might have something else for me…" Eran ventured with a smile, which faded as the man withdrew a ring and placed it on the bar.

It was stunning, taking even Eran's breath away.

Cut on six sides and resting in a white gold setting, even in the dim light, it was spectacular.

Fighting to restrain a proud smile, he reached across the bar and clapped the man hardily on the shoulder.

"Thank you. It's perfect, Mr. Beedinwigg. Perfect."

I almost missed the name and then jolted inside when I did.

As Eran spun around he took a final glance at the man, in which I rapidly absorbed every detail I could.

Yes, he had the same mischievous grin as Ms. Beedinwigg.

I released a sigh from inside Eran, pondering the surreal reality of it. Ms. Beedinwigg's ancestor had sold Eran my engagement ring…

The familiar tug of the scroll pulled me back to the hall. There, I felt a sudden wave of panic, my internal timer telling me that my time was up.

Refusing to believe it, I moved my finger over the final entry next to Eran's name, the one with the words 'Eternal Death', and was rapidly sent through the tunnel.

When I stopped, the pain was excruciating. It was as if Eran's body had been lit on fire. He hadn't, however. I knew with sickening truth that it was the result of the Elsics.

They were feeding on him.

Through the blur of Eran's eyes, I found that Eran had been held captive underground, surrounded by piles of bones, and Elsics salivating for another piece of him.

Abaddon held them back, not with chains or leashes but with the gift he'd brought when he fell...He'd frozen their ability to move only to ensure Eran's punishment wouldn't end too abruptly.

Despite the hurt I felt pulsing through Eran, I lunged for Abaddon, wishing with every part of me that he would suffer the same fate.

Still, Eran's body remained in place, unchained and unleashed as well, but held against his will nonetheless. He kept his head high, unwilling to give Abaddon any satisfaction, the anger in him feeding the energy needed.

"So you see, Eran..." Abaddon said, curling up the side of his lip in disgust as he said Eran's name. "I've allowed your friend, the big one, to escape. Christianson, correct?" He paused not for a response but to draw in a languid, carefree breath. "You see he is going to be my messenger, informing your lover that we are coming, if he doesn't die before he gets there..."

Abaddon waltzed across the room, as much to taunt Eran as to enjoy himself. Reaching the wall where Eran was pinned, he twirled and allowed the blade he held to swing out, drawing across Eran's chest and spilling blood from a fresh wound.

The Elsics went in to frenzy, screaming, clawing for Eran, only to be restrained by Abaddon.

"They do like the smell of you…It's like a beacon telling them that human flesh is nearby, like a…radar, in fact. Speaking of radars, I have a special plan for you and your lover." His voice was joyfully mocking now as he slanted towards Eran to whisper. "I think you're going to hate it…" He giggled. "No Fallen One will ever touch her again…or, to be fair, at least they won't take her life. Now this may seem like a good thing on the surface but especially you would expect nothing from me but the worst so I won't play with your emotions. Instead, I'll tell you the really interesting part. I've made certain no one will touch her for one very specific, very significant reason…Do you know what that might be?"

Eran simply glared back, trying to contain the anger boiling in his belly.

"It's so she can't join you in eternal death…You will never see your precious Magdalene again. She will remain in this dimension, or the afterlife, but she will remain here…separated from you for eternity. So you see, she won't be dying by our hands at least. I've made certain of it."

The irony to Abaddon's message was that it was intended to antagonize Eran and yet it did the opposite. On that news, Eran went limp, relief enveloping him.

I didn't understand at first, certain that I would have had the same blank stare that Abaddon now held had I been in my own body. And then it dawned on me.

Keeping me out of eternal death wasn't a curse for Eran. It was a blessing. It meant I would forever be safe, never harmed by the Fallen Ones or Elsics.

It was exactly what Eran wished for the most.

Abaddon, however, couldn't understand. Every one of his actions was designed to please him, so much that while Eran had tried to keep me safe, Abaddon had delivered his own family to eternal deaths.

It was clear that none of this occurred to Abaddon as he suddenly released the Elsics from their hold and watched with a vengeful grin as they landed on Eran.

Flesh began tearing back, falling away as Eran held on to the scream building in his throat.

From inside, I felt every shake, every rip, every bite. And I wept.

It went on until the darkness began surrounding Eran, starting from the edges of the room and closing in. And just before it swallowed Eran entirely, he released the scream that had been building, an effort to cross space and time in one final attempt to warn me what was coming.

"MAGDALEEEEEEEEEEEEEEeeeeeee…"

It had reached me, I remembered, the jolt of it vibrating across land and water. I'd heard him by way of feeling him, our bond conveying his warning far greater than any other way could.

I watched then, terrified, helpless, as Eran became engulfed in total blackness.

21. THE SEIGE

I awoke with a start back in my bed at the stronghold, shaking uncontrollably. Without conscious effort, I fell to the floor, crawling towards the window, although it was for no reason in particular.

I believe I was simply trying to get away from the horror of what I'd just seen and felt, but I couldn't be sure.

My true love was dead and I had just watched him die. Where I went didn't matter.

Tears fell to the stone floor as I crawled across it, its ruts tearing at my skin, leaving behind a bloody trail.

I didn't care.

Nothing mattered at that moment but the crushing pain I felt in my chest.

"Pick 'er up!" a voice bellowed nervously.

Then hands were beneath me, lifting me. I was hauled against someone's shoulder, sobbing, unaware and without care as to who it was.

The shaking continued and the pained emptiness grew to reach every part of my body. I became immersed in it, leaving behind time, motivation, anything that might have gotten me moving on any given day.

I stayed that way, immobile, for a very long time…moving only when I felt the hair stand on the back of my neck.

It made me react like nothing else could.

Adrenaline suddenly surged through my body, driving my energy level back to and far beyond its normal level. My senses too heightened and with them everything came back in focus.

I found it was Ezra whose chest I leaned against without having to look. I recognized the beating of her heart, which had an extra beat to it. Rufus had left the room, probably unable to handle seeing me in pain. The big ones fall hardest. Felix, however, stood by the door, chewing nervously on his finger nails, taking short, impatient breaths.

Downstairs, I could hear footsteps moving casually through the hallways and the smell of rabbit stew starting to come to a boil in the kitchen.

Most of all, I could hear the wings approaching. Hundreds of them.

I pulled away from Ezra, who was pleasantly surprised to see my movement.

"We need to assemble the Alterums at the front of the stronghold." Her eyes widened as I continued. "He's almost here."

And judging from the pain at back of my neck, he'd brought every last one of the Fallen Ones with him.

From that point, the stronghold became organized chaos. Alterums took their positions, weapons readied and waiting without the typical rush for them.

The day before, while waiting for Eran to return from his final mission, Ms. Beedinwigg, Ms. Barrett, my housemates, and I had arranged the defense and given instructions to the Alterums on what to expect. After countless hours of training and the finishing efforts to secure us, the Alterums were as ready as they could be.

Interestingly, the pounding of their feet as they moved to their positions were different than during previous attacks. They were hurried but less heavy, less panicked. There were no grunts as they accidentally slammed in to each other in their haste either.

It was dawn again, I noted. Abaddon hadn't had the patience to wait the day.

As the wings grew louder and the hair at the back of my neck spiked farther, I slipped in my black leather combat suit and attached my weapons to it.

It felt odd, different. I hadn't worn it since I'd learned of Eran's death and now it seemed uncharacteristic of me.

More unnerving was the reason I'd had it made. When I had walked into the small Cuban accessories store advertising a seamstress in the front window, the question never occurred to me.

Was I really this person? Did I have the bloodlust in me that my enemies had? Did it make me any different from them?

As I stared at my reflection in the window, I knew the answer. Had I asked these same questions a few months ago the answer would have been absolutely not. But as I recalled the last months leading to this point, I realized that I had acted very much the same as my enemies. Hunting them as they had hunted us. But there was a distinct difference that comforted me as I looked at the warrior girl in the reflection and found a woman staring back.

I fought to protect others from harm. My enemies fought to inflict it.

That, was exactly what I was about to do.

The woman in the reflection tilted her mouth up in a side grin, cocky…like Eran's. There was a burning in her eyes that sent out a signal: Pick a fight…I dare you.

No, I was not like my enemies. I was a messenger on my way to send a powerful message that was long overdue.

Minutes later, I entered the courtyard, my appendages already out. Thumping them once, I sprang to the overlook at the front of the stronghold.

A space had been left for me. On one side stood my housemates. On the other…the Alterums who had once imprisoned me. Those motivations gone, they now watched me closely for guidance.

I scanned them, their faces, their stances, and found that the Alterums had transformed. Their expressions were expectant, alert. Their postures were ready. Their attitudes were unshakeable, challenging. In the short time we had been here, they had become warriors.

Someone, my guess would be Ms. Barrett, had stitched bands for each of their arms, a swirl of blue on white fabric. It was the only unifying element and it made them stand a bit straighter.

Then, just as the first rays of sun streamed over the horizon, the hair at the back of my neck, the same ones that had been pulling angrily for my attention for so long whenever an enemy was nearby, stopped. There was no more prickle, no strain, no yank or twitch. They were silent.

It may have alarmed me…before Eran died. Now I noted it with remote complacency, knowing that I could only discern this as a sign of finality.

Even my radar knew I wouldn't survive this battle.

The land stretching from the edges of the stronghold out over the countryside was undulating, rolling hills of deep green. They were in stark contrast to what was currently coming over the tops of them.

Along the horizon slowly but with unity the Fallen Ones emerged, lining up in rows to appear dark and foreboding, a mass of dark colors other than their prominent grey wings. Those on the ground walked shoulder to shoulder, not a sliver of light between them, while those in the air nearly touched the tips of the wings next to them as they flew in.

Spilling over the hillside and down towards the Alterum stronghold, they approached as an organized horde, weapons in hand, roars of fervor rising from places within their ranks.

A slice through the middle of their collective army showed a line of inky black creatures swaying in unison, their mouths opened and screeching, revealing long, jagged teeth. The Elsics. The Fallen Ones greatest weapon. A fatal injury by any one of them resulted in eternal death. They, I knew, would be strategically used against us at the most opportune time.

Then the horde stopped, halting as one, as if a finger had been snapped.

Unmoving, unhurried, they watched us, observing their enemies from afar.

We had aligned the Alterums across the front and top of the stronghold, also shoulder to shoulder. It was meant to be imposing and may have been…had it not been for the overwhelming number of Fallen Ones now standing before us.

Outnumbered, ran through my mind but I pushed it back.

Surveying them, I recognized quite a few, but only one drew my attention.

Elam stood out front.

He hadn't changed much since I'd last seen him in the hallway of my school back in New Orleans. In fact, the only variation was that his artificial likability was gone, a hard, aged expression in its place. One hand held a spear and the other clutched a satchel, which I knew was filled with mysterious concoctions designed to maim and render us ineffective.

I, however, was going to make sure that didn't happen.

Taking a dagger from my suit in each hand, I bent forward and stabbed them in both of my legs, cutting downward, tearing the leather from my thighs until I saw blood beginning to seep from the wounds.

Gasps around me told me that others had seen. I disregarded them.

I knew from Eran's scroll that not one of our enemies would kill me, an incontestable command given by Abaddon.

Now I was going to test that theory.

Elsics became riled at the smell of blood. If my blood didn't cause them to go mad, at least it would distract and upset them, allowing the Alterums an advantage.

Ms. Barrett, who stood next to me, waited to see what I would do. She knew from our brief discussion the night before that I didn't intend to fight alongside the Alterums. I had an alternate plan. Now I'd made her feel that much more uneasy.

Placing a hand on her shoulder, I tried to subdue it. "Don't worry," I said. "I know what I'm doing."

Then, with the same conviction, I turned to my housemates. If I didn't forewarn them of what I was about to do they would follow me and make themselves vulnerable. And it was something I couldn't allow.

"I'm going to incite the Elsics…aggravate them until they are thoughtlessly reacting. It should buy you some time."

"No," Ezra demanded, reaching out to seize my arm.

The smile I gave her rose slowly. "They won't kill me. I can walk right through them and they won't touch me."

And they wouldn't. Just a simple touch of me would draw them in to a frenzy they couldn't control. It would inevitably result in my death…against Abaddon's wishes. They would then need to answer to him. And that was not an appealing prospect. They knew it and I knew it.

"How can you be so sure?" demanded Felix.

"Abaddon gave an order."

Hesitantly, Ezra released her arm. Her lips pinched, nervous and in disapproval, she nodded concurrence.

Wasting no more time, I sprang through the air, over the stronghold's wall, and towards the army assembled to murder those I love.

Despite all who surrounded me, at that very second, it was a very lonely sky.

The Elsics were already stirring at the smell of my blood and when I flew over them, just outside arm's length, a few bold ones took swipes at me.

My flight path wasn't unintentional as I circled the throng. I kept my eyes moving, searching. Somewhere in the midst of them was Abaddon...

The Elsics were screaming in agony now, my scent causing them physical pain. They broke rank, with a few heaving through the Fallen Ones in front and to the sides of them. This happened twice before anarchy broke loose.

Suddenly, the Fallen Ones rushed the stronghold. A mixture of grey and black wings sprang up to descend on the Alterums, becoming a blend of limbs, weapons, and bloodshed.

Only one person remained still.

Abaddon.

He stood at the back, his hands calmly folded together in front of him, as if he had been expecting the chaos.

I turned and aimed directly for him, almost oblivious to the wind shrieking in my ears.

My body never quite landed as I met Abaddon. I swooped across him, my wings carrying me in a half-circle, with just enough range to connect my fist with his face.

His head snapped back but those long, thin hands remained in place.

Then I was pummeling him, my fists hitting his face with such speed they were a blur to me. The contact felt good, Abaddon's aged skin giving way, caving in as my blows impacted him.

I released on him the fury that only a person who has lost a loved one at the hands of another can unleash. He took my time from me and Eran, stealing it away forever, and in return I gave him pain.

The flailing continued on immeasurably, all while Abaddon kept his hands clasped before him.

Only when my body was yanked back, arms coming around me and pulling me away, did I understand why.

Abaddon was smiling.

He wore the expression of someone who knew he'd just gotten the best of another.

My appendages were now being crushed between me and Abaddon's savior, but I still couldn't see who it was.

Then came Elam's voice, calmly maniacal. "Pleasure to see you again, Maggie."

That was when I went still.

If anyone was going to disobey Abaddon's command and kill me it was Elam, and I certainly didn't want to give him the impression I would resist.

"That's better," he said when I'd settled down but kept his arms around me.

Abaddon approached me, oblivious to the bodies hurling through the air around us; his coy smile conveying his thoughts before his voice. "I won…"

"You have won nothing, Abaddon. So you sent a guardian to an infinite death. But I'm still here…And so long as I am, anyone you kill will simply get an escort to the afterlife, where they have the choice to turn around and come again to this dimension. You will never dominate it." I grinned, taunting. "No, Abaddon…Try as you will to spin it, the fact is, you lose."

He wasn't the least bit concerned as he leaned in, his hands remaining together at his hips. "Dear Maggie…How

293

can they get an escort when their guide is under my control?"

For proof of his threat, Elam released me and my body spun against my will towards the battlefield. Using the same ability on me as he had on Eran, I was frozen in place, unable to move, to enter the carnage before us and defend my friends being slaughtered.

One by one, they fell as I struggled against Abaddon's iron grip. I had seen war before but not like this. What I was witnessing now was a massacre, with Fallen Ones pinning down Alterums for the Elsics' feedings while simultaneously sending Alterums to their final death. The screams of horror and pain were not coming from our enemies but they blended with the ferocious screeches of the Elsics and the shouts of excitement from the Fallen Ones until the sound filled the air.

Across the field, the blue and white arm bands were now soaked with blood. Alterum blood. Streams of red flowed through the grass to pool at the bottom of the hills. Limbs and pieces of flesh scattered the ground.

We were losing this battle.

"We need help," I whispered, unnerved by the sound of fear in my voice.

Then, as I spoke the words, as if they had been heard, the sky filled with bright, white lights. Moving with amazing speed in zigzag fashion, they descended on the battlefield.

Dominick had arrived, and he'd brought Eran's army.

A collision of such magnitude followed, it resounded with a boom of its own across the countryside.

The battle tipped then, and Fallen Ones fell at a faster rate. Hope grew in me that this would not be the end of us.

But then I saw the balance of power shift, Fallen Ones doubling, tripling up on the Alterums, and my heart sank inside my chest.

"Watch…" Abaddon's voice whispered in my ear. "Learn…This is how it is done, Maggie. How it has been for centuries. How it will always be. What you don't seem to understand, is that I'm not seeking to dominate this dimension…I already do."

The only motion I was allowed while under Abaddon's control was breathing, and right now I was seething.

Only then did I realize there was one power I did have not in Abaddon's grasp.

Breath.

I let the rest of it from my lungs, concentrating on pressing them back towards my spine until they were completely deflated.

Elam noticed what I was doing first. As I collapsed, he turned swiftly towards me. But I never got the chance to see what he was about to do.

I was already in the Hall of Records. The hall was silent around me, as I had always found it. The agonizing screams from the battle gone with only the hall's constant breeze reaching my ears. Still, they echoed in my mind as if I were there.

Rather than dying bodies surrounding me, it was scrolls. The metallic smell of blood was gone too. Fresh air filled my lungs now.

The ploy had worked. I'd fainted, in effect, putting me to sleep. Now all I had to do was wait.

Wait…I told myself. Wait just long enough for Abaddon to release his hold on me.

Wait…

Telling an impatient person to wait while her friends were being slaughtered was the greatest challenge of my existence. But it was the only way to free myself from Abaddon.

I hesitated as long as was physically possible and then I lay back down on the bench, closing my eyes.

Focusing on breathing steadily and relaxing every muscle I had worked.

When I awoke, my face was in the dirt, my body curled as if it had been kicked. The ache at the back, between my shoulder blades made me think this had happened.

Cautiously, I opened my eyes and found Abaddon alone, standing in front of me, surveying the harm he was causing.

Taking incredible care not to make a sound, I stood and pulled a blade from my suit. Only two steps…only two…

One…

Two…

Abaddon turned then, once again wrapping his grasp around me. I became frozen, my legs in a lunge, my hips twisted for increased power, my arm extended with my blade at the end of it. Although, I could no longer see it.

It had disappeared, planted now in Abaddon's chest.

Oddly, with Abaddon's ability to restrict my movements, I couldn't withdraw it even if I'd wanted.

"You weren't quick enough," I told him, releasing a sigh, feeling some measure of reward from it.

But he chuckled. "Oh…yes, I was…"

A disconcerting feeling came over me as he tipped his head downward. Following his eyes, I found Abaddon's blade had been imbedded in me.

"Neither of us wins," he chocked, his lips still twisted up.

I knew this to be true as the searing pain radiated from the fatal wound, along every limb, across every part of my skin, absorbed by every muscle, through ever molecule of my body.

Then my legs collapsed and I knew Abaddon was dying too.

He'd released me.

Each of us fell to the dirt, holding the weapons we'd both implanted in each other, gasping for one last breath of air, searching for some miracle to stop what had begun.

As the battle raged on, a living, palpable darkness began to consume me. Starting from the edges of my sight, just as Eran had encountered, it quickly and steadily drew in, tightening, solidifying, harnessing me.

The dirt gave way next, disappearing all together so that there was nothing to stand on, nothing to support me, to give me bearings.

I plummeted then. Not a single thing touched me, no hands, no wind, nothing. But I was spinning, head over heels, downward.

22. FOR ALL ETERNITY

There was no sound, not a single whisper, and entirely no light to illuminate my way.

The only thing that registered with me was the stench. It was potent, sickening, and it smelled like death.

Just as I recognized it, my body hit the ground. Hard. Knocking the air from my lungs. Because of it, I didn't notice what I had landed on for several seconds. Only when I was able to draw a breath, fighting the tearing pain caused by inhaling after the blow, did I realized the surface of death was cold and jagged.

Cautiously, I bent my legs up and heaved myself to a standing position. From the second I stood, the cold permeated my feet, reaching through the souls of the boots I still wore, along my legs and into my torso. Huddling against it, I looked around.

My eyes adjusted slightly and I found that I'd fallen in to a catacomb of tunnels, a rock column with countless branches opening from the center, spanning the circumference from the top, where I'd fallen, to the bottom, where I now stood.

"Eran," I called, though it came out a whisper.

After clearing my throat, I tried it again. "Eran?"

I waited then but my only response was silence.

Now I felt a little foolish. Of course, I was alone…

Consciously I expanded my wings, flapping them once for a test. They not only worked, they were stronger than I'd expected.

Pumping them rigidly against the dense air, I felt my feet lift the ground and the warmth return to them.

Trying my best to keep myself steady, I flew up towards the tunnel openings.

"Eran?" I shouted. "Gershom? Christianson? Magnus?"

I called out every name of those I knew were here and heard nothing in return.

And then I flew farther and called them again.

Nothing.

I pushed myself higher, peering inside another row of tunnels, calling again.

Then I felt him. And I couldn't stop myself from drawing a sudden, astounded breath.

The feeling was faint but recognizable. Our bond…the one that allowed us to feel each other's emotions worked even here, in the most desolate, loathsome place in existence.

Then I acknowledged exactly what I was sensing and unconsciously murmured his name in agony. "Eran…"

He was nearby all right but he was sad, hopeless, distraught. And it was bittersweet. I'd found him but he was not Eran.

I used it, as radar, seeking him out through the tunnels. It intensified the closer I came to him and at times I had to stop, lean against the wall, and contain my own emotions reacting to his. It hit me the hardest when I found the chamber where Eran sat.

The tunnel I was using to find him ended abruptly, at the mouth of an enormous cavern. And there at the bottom sat thousands of Alterums, messengers, newly imprisoned and veterans to this place, huddled together but without talking. Their heads bowed, their knees against their chests, their appendages wrapped around them as if they could protect them from the grief of eternal death.

The enormity of what I was witnessing took my breath away, caving in my chest, refusing me air.

Still, I shoved aside my reaction and flew downward, circling, until I found Eran.

He was hunched in the same position, and at the first sight of it a pain surfaced in my heart, latching on and burrowing in.

"Eran," I said, as I hovered over him. There was no place to land except on others, which I would not do.

When he didn't respond, I said it again more urgently. "Eran!"

That was when I heard it. He was moaning, a lifeless, distant whimper. And almost unnoticeably rolling his body from side to side.

"No," I said. "No! NO!" I was screaming it now, enraged, refusing to believe this was my husband, my love, my rock when things became challenging, my guide when I needed direction, my savior when I needed help.

Incensed, I flew hard and fast towards the ceiling.

Having very little concept of what I was doing, I flew harder, faster. If I didn't make it, if the rock above me remained firmly in place, at the very least it would make me feel better to ram something, hard.

My appendages moved with amazing power, increasing my speed until the rock walls around me became a blur. Whereas I hadn't heard wind on my fall downward, my force skyward was creating it now. The sound of a freight train roared in my ears.

Closer...

I was almost there...

I straightened my arms and clasped my hands together, forming a latched ball of curled fingers.

Then I met the ceiling, the hard rock cave that kept my friends and loved ones held against their will, deep in oppression, giving way.

I never felt the jagged edges touch my skin. There was no impact. No tremendous pressure holding me back.

There, on the other side, I found sunlight, trees, grass, and a thunderous battle below me. Against the horizon stood the Alterum stronghold and I was stunned to learning I had breached the barrier meant to restrict me and my fellow inmates to this dimension.

Glancing down, I found that the ground was untouched.

This was when it dawned on me. My supernatural talent I'd brought with me to earth wasn't simply the ability to visit the afterlife. That had never been it. Every messenger came with this ability. What distinguished me from the others was something I couldn't have uncovered had I not been killed by Abaddon.

While attempting to send me to a place of death, he had ended up giving me life, awareness, knowledge.

Because of my death by his hands, because I was sent to eternal death, I now knew I could break through any dimension I chose.

The air was fresh, weightless in comparison to the everlasting death chamber I'd emerged from. As I sucked it in deeply, enjoying the clean feel of it, I knew I would need it for what I was about to do.

I turned and went back down.

Soaring downward, the rock face rushing by me once again in a blur, I reached Eran in seconds.

I didn't bother talking to him, telling him of my plan. He wouldn't hear me anyways.

Picking him up was a challenge, his body a dead weight in my arms. I drew him close to my chest and latched my arms around him, as I ascended.

The closer we came to the opening, the warmer he began to feel, the chill of the ground finally leaving his body.

At the opening, his head, which had been lolling to and fro, lifted and his eyes opened. A few seconds later, he spoke. His voice was groggy but adorned with its striking English accent.

"Magdalene?"

"It's me, Eran."

With that he heaved a sigh unlike any I'd ever heard. It was tantamount to taking one's first breath, to the firm realization that life had begun again.

When we reached the sunlight, he moaned, as if he'd never experienced anything so magnificent.

"How...How did you find me?" he asked his voice clearer now. He was coming to.

"I felt you."

"From above?"

"From below. Abaddon took my life."

"You...You..." He couldn't seem to find the words.

"I went through eternal death," I confirmed.

"Went through?"

"Survived it."

I saw Eran's forehead furl in confusion.

"I can breach dimensions, Eran."

His jaw fell open and he let out a stunned chuckle which quickly grew to a deep, exuberant, bellowing laugh.

While I didn't join him, I knew what he was experiencing. Triumph. My ability would allow us to bring back the other messengers, who could escort those dying on the battlefield to the afterlife, where they could fall again.

First, however, I needed to release them.

My plan had been to find a safe place where Eran could recover but we were rising over the battle now and he had an alternate plan.

"The battle…" he said, referring to the conflict below us. "Get me down there."

"Eran," I said in warning.

"Magdalene." His reply was calm. "I'm needed."

Surveying the battle again, I knew what he said was true. While the Alterums were resisting our enemies, they were slowly being killed one by one.

"I'm not letting you go without a weapon," I stated.

Then I felt a hand on my hip, which took me by surprise, and I released a gasp because of it.

Eran snickered. "Even fresh from death, I can still excite you. Nice to know…"

Holding in a laugh, I replied, "Good to see you're back."

Our humor faded as we reached the outskirts of the battle and it was gone completely by the time Eran rotated his head towards me, giving me a firm kiss. It was as wonderful as it could be considering that I was releasing him to a battle in which our enemies' strength came in four against one now. Eran would be badly outnumbered.

The moment he landed, three Fallen Ones were on him and the sword he'd taken from my hip was flying through the air.

That very scene motivated me. While I could help in the return of those souls held captive in the death chambers below, those here, in this dimension, fighting so hard in battle would suffer immeasurable pain before reaching that dark place of death.

I soared back through the breach I'd made and down towards the Alterums. Only a small shaft of light gleamed through the ceiling, directly from the hole I'd created, which made me realize something midway down.

There was no rock surrounding us, no true tunnels or caves or caverns. This dimension was a fabrication. Nothing I saw was actually palpable. It only held its prisoners through the emotional destruction it leached in to their consciousness the feeling of helplessness, immobilizing, eternal confinement.

It was the reason I hadn't heard, felt, or seen anything on my descent here.

The light straining in came from the other side, through the breach I'd created.

Glancing down at the number of Alterums below and back up at the breach, I knew something needed to be done.

We needed a bigger hole.

Pumping my wings harder and faster than I'd ever done before, I pummeled through the fabricated boundary that kept earth separate from the chambers of death below.

By the time I was done, light beamed through the cavern, warming it, illuminating it. And from high above, I saw a spectacle that took my breath away.

The bodies below, the hollow shells of Alterums, were stirring.

Soaring downward, closing the distance between us, I found their heads lifting, their wings shaking out and stretching. Then they began to stand and look around, helping those beside them to a standing position also.

Before I knew it, they were ascending, strong and powerful pumps of their wings lifting them off the ground and towards the light.

Hundreds of them, filtered upward, through the breach I'd created and back to the other dimension. I watched this sight, taken by such beauty in the depths of the darkest place in existence.

And then every last one of them was gone.

Knowing there were more, I made a search of the remaining tunnels, repeating this process where I found huddles of Alterums, avoiding those places where I found Fallen Ones, until I'd exhausted my search.

Then I returned to the other dimension, leaving as I found Alterums dying in the battle entering. I stayed just long enough to confirm my suspicions. Only when the Alterums landed on the cold, jagged rock below and sprang from the surface, towards the light, through the breach I'd created, and back to the other side did I leave.

The Alterums, messengers included, were now free.

Coming through to the other side, I didn't hesitate, entering the fray and working my way inwards, killing off our enemies as I met them.

Doubt no longer weighed me down. I now knew who I was, what I was, and understood the power I held.

None of our enemies could hurt me. They never could. I was invincible, not only able to return from eternal death but capable of escorting those imprisoned there to freedom.

Abaddon had already lost his soul, and as I carved my way through the mass, meeting Eran in the middle, I realized something else.

Abaddon had also lost his war.

In the end, as the battle came to a close and the last of our enemies were being given their final rites at the end of messengers' swords, Eran and I found ourselves surrounded.

From the billows of dust came the Alterums, the messengers, everyone of them familiar to me. Wiping dirt, sweat, tears, and blood from their faces, they made a circle around us, watching us for our next move.

Eran, knowing this, took my hand and lifted us off the ground. Rotating from above, we surveyed the thousands of Alterums who had become warriors, who had gathered, learned to fight, to defend themselves, and saved each other in the process. These were the victors, not us.

For them, he raised his free arm in the air, his fingers rolling in to a clenched fist as a sign of power and unity. And they responded. Raising their fists in the air in silence.

Then, from somewhere in the crowd, a shout echoed over their heads, followed by another and another, until our ears rang with their elation. Their energy they emitted was palpable, bringing goose bumps to my skin.

When Eran and I returned to the ground, we found ourselves surrounded by a single group of them in particular.

The messengers had gathered together and emerged. The very ones who had fallen at the hands of our enemies and had lived imprisoned in eternal death for centuries.

Two of them stepped forward, their faces so starkly familiar I froze in place. Their smiles, so welcoming, so endearing, I struggled to think straight.

These were the faces of my parents, the very same ones who had escorted me to earth on each occasion.

"Maggie," said my mother, taking me in her arms. "We have a lot to catch up on."

I shook against her with laughter. "I'd say so…"

As my father embraced me, he had a different message. "Thank you…from all of us."

I knew what he meant. He was appreciative of me releasing them from the gloom they'd endured for so long. But I couldn't take the credit.

"Thank the Alterums. Without them, none of us would be here." And this was true. Because they had united, we had survived.

He nodded, a gleam of undeterred admiration still in his eyes.

Overhearing a sob, I turned to find Ezra and my mother embracing too, recalling they'd been friends long before I was born in to this lifetime.

But a quick glance around told me that the reunion wasn't limited to them. Around us, friends were reuniting after being apart for hundreds of years, arms thrown over the shoulders of others, laughter echoing through the air.

"Well, its over," Felix clapped Eran on the shoulder. "It's finally over…"

"I prefer to think of it as just the beginning," Ezra called from over my mother's shoulder, breaking their conversation just long enough to, once again, counsel us to be positive.

That may have been the case for them but it was not for me.

I had one final trip to make.

My appendages flapped, lifting me skyward, but I moved across the ground with less urgency now.

This was an excursion for confirmation.

As I dropped through the hole I'd created and back down the chamber of death, I noticed it was empty now, and I smiled.

That smile, and the elation behind it, stayed in place until I passed through the tunnels and came across the chamber I was trying to find.

There, at the bottom of it, were thousands of Fallen Ones, all in the same hunched position, arms wrapped around their curled legs, wings enclosing them against the pain they were enduring.

Descending towards them, I searched for two faces in particular, coming across them at the same time.

Abaddon and Elam were side by side, moaning in pain, though it was evident neither one knew the other was there. Each cowered in the same position as the rest, their heads tilted down, their expressions showing only dread.

I watched them, neither of them aware of my presence. And I understood without having to be told that they, and all the other Fallen Ones and Elsics in this cavern, in all other caverns in this desolate place, would never move from their spot. They would remain in place, cowering in fear…forever.

Now, the battle was over and my life could begin.

23. THE BEGINNING

New Orleans had never looked so beautiful.

As we flew in just before dawn, I couldn't stop the lump that grew in my throat.

"Are you all right," Eran called out next to me, sensing my swell of emotions.

I nodded, not trusting myself that I wouldn't break in to tears if I spoke, struggling against them until we reached the back door to our house.

Inside, it actually felt like it was welcoming us. The rooms were as we'd left them, mine being the exception. Apparently, Ms. Barrett and her guards hadn't bothered to put anything back in place when they went in search of the book of dossiers. But it really didn't matter in the whole scheme of things.

My mother and father had followed us back and were given the spare bedroom next to Rufus. Felix made a quip about Rufus's snoring rattling the walls which started a fight between the two. My parents took it in stride, proving they would fit in nicely here for as long as they chose to stay.

We'd left London a few days following the final battle, staying until the Alterums had dissolved their celebrations. And as they scattered back to the lives they'd left to join the fight, forever changed but retaining their wise confidence, the rest of us thought we should follow their lead.

A few days after our return, we all sat at the kitchen table in the small house we called home, Ms. Beedinwigg, Mr. Hamilton, and Alfred included. And we discussed what our future would hold, coming to the realization there were a few loose ends we needed to clear up and a day later I was headed back to the school where I was certain I was no longer accepted.

The Academy of the Immaculate Heart looked oddly the same. I wondered, with the Fallen Ones and Elsics gone and our lives free to be lived out as we wished, whether it might appear larger, or smaller. But no, the U-shaped brick building was still old; the ivy still draped over the face of it; and the grassy quad was still speckled with benches and shady, towering trees.

While the surface of it had remained unaltered, there was something new about the school.

It's owner.

When Eran and I arrived, we did as we always had, on my beloved, rumbling Harley Davidson motorcycle. Directly behind us rolled in Ms. Beedinwigg's Knight XV SUV. We parked next to each other and met at the head of the quad.

"Ready?" Ms. Beedinwigg asked, directing her question at the only person who really mattered in this case, Mr. Hamilton.

It wasn't imperative that Eran and I were here for what was about to go down, but we sure wanted to be.

School was already in session and from the looks of the parking lot, there were no absences. None but us. Of course, we probably were no longer considered truant.

Eran and I were likely marked with "Suspended" on our records while Ms. Beedinwigg had been unceremoniously terminated, considering we hadn't set foot here in several weeks and we'd left without so much as a note.

Still, we marched through the doors and entered the main hall, each with our own confident stride.

I'd never seen Mr. Hamilton on school grounds before but he was leading the way and doing a fine job. Clearly, he'd researched his latest investment and memorized the layout of the building because he knew the route to Mr. Warden's office. In fact, he didn't even pause in front of our principal's office door before heading in.

The office was quiet so we caused a bit of a stir coming through unannounced.

Ms. Saggy Arms, or Mr. Warden's secretary, stood immediately, a frown already on her stiff face before we'd even entered. It remained there when she spoke to us.

"Do you have an appointment?" she demanded.

"No," replied Mr. Hamilton flatly, without bothering to address her with his attention. He was already heading around her desk, towards The Warden's door.

Touché for Mr. Hamilton.

She tried to stop him, block his path, but she was too slow and Mr. Hamilton was already at the door before she could get her legs freely around her chair.

Glaring, she watched the rest of us march by her as well. '

"Mr. Warden…Mr. Warden!" she yelled in warning.

He was standing by the time Mr. Hamilton entered.

"What is the meaning of this?" he barked. Then he caught sight of me and snarled, "Why am I not surprised?"

Without missing a beat, he then saw Ms. Beedinwigg and launched in to a tirade. "You have no right to be here. None of you do. You, Ms. Beedinwigg, have been fired." He smiled maliciously when making this announcement and then continued on, sneering when using our names.

"And you two, Eran and Maggie, are no longer students at this school. And you, sir, are trespassing."

He reached down and picked up his cell phone.

"I'm calling security. They'll be escorting you off the premises shortly." As he declared this with unwavering confidence, Mr. Hamilton withdrew an envelope from inside his jacket.

"Before you make that phone call, you'll want to see this…" suggested Mr. Hamilton. He wasn't snide about it, coy, or snobbish. It was a matter-of-fact statement, one that must have broken through The Warden's self-absorbed importance because he took the envelope from Mr. Hamilton with a yank.

Opening the envelope, he pulled out the documents inside…and then we waited.

The office was so silent a fly buzzing in the corner sounded like a freight train.

The Warden's face twitched as his eyes scanned the first page. It fell entirely on the third.

"What…You can't…" he stuttered. "No…"

"Yes," stated Mr. Hamilton. "I now own this school and I'll be making a few changes today. The first is starting with you."

By this point, we could hear that someone had answered on the other end. But, unbeknownst to Mr. Warden, the school's security company which he was now calling had already been introduced to its new owner.

In fact, they were waiting for his call.

Still in shock, Mr. Warden didn't fight Mr. Hamilton as the phone was taken from his hand.

Mr. Hamilton placed it to his ear and said, "Roy, you may come in now. Mr. Warden is prepared to be escorted from school grounds."

At that, The Warden's jaw fell.

Ms. Saggy Arms was standing in the doorway, listening, but she made her presence known with a gasp.

311

Mr. Hamilton turned to her. "You'll want to collect your personal items, too."

The overbearing woman of a minute ago had swiftly turned frail, drained of her venom. Still, she managed to return to her desk and begin shuffling through her drawers.

"But…she's fired…" muttered The Warden, pointing at Ms. Beedinwigg. "And…and those two are expelled."

"Not anymore," replied Mr. Hamilton coolly. "Maggie and Eran will resume classes without a mark on their records and Ms. Beedinwigg…well, Ms. Beedinwigg? Would you like to try out The Warden's chair?"

The Warden didn't miss a beat, sucking in a harsh breath at the very hint that Ms. Beedinwigg would be commandeering his position. He exhaled it only after she replied, confirming the new arrangement.

"I believe I'll wait for the new office furniture to arrive."

With that, The Warden literally caved in. His shoulders hunched forward, nearly coming together. His head dipped down so that his chin rested on chest. There was no resistance whatsoever when Roy and his men came to escort The Warden away.

Eran, who had been quietly watching all this from the back of the room, stepped forward to shake Mr. Hamilton's hand.

With unquestionable sincerity, his English accent delivered the words the rest of us would soon follow with.

"Thank you."

"You are welcome. But expect no easy path. I know Ms. Beedinwigg to be a hard teacher."

I scoffed. That was the pinnacle of all understatements.

Ms. Beedinwigg followed with a reassurance to that statement. "Rest up. When you start again on Monday, two days from now, you won't have much free time. Take advantage of it now."

"Two days..." I murmured. "What will we do with them?"

Eran looked down at me and with his glorious signature smirk said, "I have a few ideas in mind..."

He refused to tell me, insisting that I be patient, which for me was equivalent to telling water not to move. I did learn of it but first I had to endure Felix's celebration dinner of salamander steak frites, pickled fruit tart, and blackened seaweed fresh from the Gulf as well as separate sleeping arrangements – making it clear that Ezra was back to her antagonizing maternal role. Of course, I vowed to test those limits she set but first I'd give her a break. She deserved it.

To Eran's credit, he came up with another solution, a less antagonistic one. I just wasn't aware of it until the next morning...

EPILOGUE

Before I even opened my eyes, I knew something was different. First, I heard an owl hooting and there were none of those in New Orleans proper. Second, the bed sheets enveloping me were made of silk. I didn't own silk, at all. Third, a warm, muscular body was lying next to me, covering every inch of my back and legs.

"Good morning, Mrs. Talor," Eran's charming accent whispered in my ear, tickling my skin with his soft breath.

I groaned and purposefully stretched so that I could more fluidly roll towards him. The silk drifted across my skin with the delicate touch of a cloud.

My eyes snapped open then. "I'm...I'm not wearing any clothes."

Eran grinned mischievously. "You are a deep sleeper."

I was. In fact, so much so that I was now undressed and lying in a different bed which was located somewhere outside the city limits of where I'd been the night before.

I sat up, pulling the sheets to my chest because I didn't trust them to remain against my skin.

To our left was an expansive kitchen with bay windows overlooking a forest of towering pine trees and the latest model appliances. To our far right was a vast great room with windows that presented the evergreen forest beyond as if it were a painting. It was decorated with a high beam ceiling, a state-of-the-art entertainment system, plush leather couches and chairs, and bookcases that ran the length of one wall from floor to ceiling. Directly next to this room was a bathroom that, while had only a narrow door, boasted a stunning marble sink, enormous claw-footed bathtub, and what appeared to be a walk-in closet already filled with clothes.

None of this looked familiar.

"Did we break in to someone's home?" I asked, wide-eyed.

Eran tossed his head back and laughed vigorously, shaking the king-sized bed. "Take a closer look," he suggested when he was able to draw a breath.

My eyes surveyed the room again realizing I hadn't noticed the fireplace. It was one I recognized instantly. How could I not? It was nearly the only thing left from the night Eran and I first made love.

I inhaled quickly. "This…is our cabin."

Eran was still grinning when he said, "Well, a portion of it anyways. I took out a wall here, a window there."

"But when? When did you have the time?"

He shrugged. "I didn't. Before we even left for London, a crew came in and remodeled. One that Mr. Hamilton suggested. The same ones who turned their basement in to a training room." He ducked his head coyly. "I've been planning this for a while."

I could see that. In fact, I was speechless, which didn't happen often.

"The refrigerator is stocked, the boat is docked for fishing, and…well, we have two days to decide which we'll tackle first."

I bit my lip, trying to compose myself, a challenge considering the butterflies batting around in my stomach.

"Of course," Eran went on. "There's always the other option…"

"Which is?" I asked.

"The one in which we stay right here, in this bed, leaving only when our bodies have exhausted themselves."

The butterflies batted harder.

He smirked. "I think you like that one the best…"

I giggled. It was impossible to keep any feelings hidden from him.

He reached out and placed his hand against my face, cupping my cheek. "That was my choice too," he whispered softly.

When he kissed me it was slow, patient, tender. He drew me in.

Then his lips parted and he said, "I love you, Magdalene."

In response, my own lips lifted in a smile. "I love you, Eran."

We drew breaths at the same time, our chests pressing against each other, our bodies warming with anticipation.

Then we spoke the words together. "For all eternity, my love."

Which started right about then.

The End

ABOUT THE AUTHOR

∞

LAURY FALTER graduated with a Bachelor's degree from Pepperdine University and a Master's degree from Michigan State University. She lives with her husband and two stray dogs in Las Vegas. Her website is www.lauryfalter.com.

Made in the USA
Charleston, SC
06 September 2012